The Stri

A Change in Tune

Ashley Rescot

Rescot Creative Publishing
Springfield, Illinois

The Strings of Sisterhood: A Change in Tune

ISBN 978-1-7366044-5-8   paperback
ISBN 978-1-7366044-4-1   eBook
ISBN 978-1-7366044-6-5   audiobook
© 2021 Ashley Rescot

This is a work of fiction. Names, characters, businesses, events and incidents are the products of the author's imagination. Any resemblance to actual persons, living or deceased, or actual events is purely coincidental.

Scripture quotations marked (NIV) are taken from the Holy Bible, New International Version®, NIV®. Copyright © 1973, 1978, 1984, 2011 by Biblica, Inc.™ Used by permission of Zondervan. All rights reserved worldwide. www.zondervan.com The "NIV" and "New International Version" are trademarks registered in the United States Patent and Trademark Office by Biblica, Inc.™

Scripture quotations marked (KJV) taken from the Holy Bible, King James Version, 1611. Public Domain.

Cover & Interior Design:
Robert Rescot

Library of Congress Control Number: 9781736604458
Rescot, Ashley
The Strings of Sisterhood: A Change in Tune / Ashley Rescot 1st ed.

First Edition

Praise for
A Change in Tune

Ashley Rescot created a colorful universe inhabited by endearing characters that all musicians can identify with. Her descriptive abilities bring us fully into the story, allowing us to experience the characters' emotions. This enticing story of the Pearson sisters is a fun adventure in the life of blooming young musicians. I wish that book had been around when I was a young violinist, going through similar emotions!

-Dr. Renée-Paule Gauthier

Violinist, host for the *Mind Over Finger* podcast, and director of the *Music Mastery Experience,* https://www.mindoverfinger.com

A Change in Tune immerses you in a world of auditions, rehearsals, and a relatable story about coming into one's own as a musician and embracing your own dreams vs those imposed on you from the outside. I would have loved this book as a teen studying the violin and viola, and found it engrossing and enjoyable as a music educator too. Ashley Rescot brings to life great characters grappling with real-life issues and weaves in stories of family, faith, and interpersonal relationships that many will be able to relate to.

-Christine E. Goodner

Violinist, music educator, author of *Beyond the Music Lesson: Habits of Successful Suzuki Families* and *Positive Practice: 5 Steps to Helping Your Child Develop a Love of Music,* and host of the *Time to Practice* podcast, https://suzukitriangle.com/

The composition of a satisfying musical score demands properly placed notes in order to create a pleasant and oft enjoyed tune. Similarly, in A Change in Tune, Ashley Rescot capitalizes on multiple artistic talents to offer listeners and readers a lyrical, well-paced, and entertaining story that showcases a broad cast of sympathetic and relatable characters. As an accomplished musician, Ashley knows the tension and pressure this world brings and writes and speaks from a place of authenticity.

-Mary A. Felkins

Author of inspirational books, including *Call to Love* and *What the Morning Brings*, https://www.maryfelkins.com/

Step into the world of a musical family, with all of the accompanying pressures, delights, and challenging decisions in Ashley Rescot's vivid new release, A Change in Tune. *Whether music is your world or you, like me, aren't a musician, you'll find yourself caught up in Victoria's story, rooting   for her through her victories and failures as she navigates her role as the oldest sister, discovers love, and determines her place in the musical community. A seasoned musician, member of a large family, and woman of faith, Ashley taps into her vast experience and bright imagination to create relatable, realistic characters in an enjoyable story that takes an honest look at mental health. I have hope for an entire series featuring each of the unique Pearson sisters!*

-Heather Wood

Historical author of *Until We All Find Home* and *Until We All Run Free*, http://www.heatherwoodauthor.epizy.com/

Resources

To enhance your reading of this book, the author has assembled additional supporting resources, including:

- audio playlists to share the music referenced in the book,
- music book club: "Fiction Fridays" on social media to connect with other fans,
- Questions for Reflection for educators or book clubs (also found at the end of this book),
- French glossary (also found at the end of this book), and
- an opportunity to connect directly with the author.

All of these resources and more can be found on the author's website at: www.rescotcreative.com (or scan the QR code below).

Preface

As a lifelong violinist, one of my greatest gifts was growing up in a musical family. My mother, a singer and violinist herself, taught my four sisters and me to play violin from an early age. Some of my fondest memories revolve around us performing together with our grandmother, aunts, and cousins.

It is important for me to note that, although my own four sisters were the inspiration for the Pearson girls, the characters are fictional and not direct parallels of any of us individually. (They're also more dramatic than I'd like to think we were at their ages.) Instead, I see aspects of myself represented in each of the Pearson sisters throughout different phases of my life.

However, the collective love the girls show for each other (eventually) *is* representative of our own musical sisterhood. Growing up, my sisters and I always considered ourselves the modern *Little Women*. In writing this series, I hope that readers can experience the joy we share with each other by virtually becoming part of our musical family!

If you enjoy this collection, I would greatly appreciate if you could leave a review on Goodreads or Amazon. This helps others discover the series and allows me to continue writing music fiction

Acknowledgments

With this publication of my first novel, I want to acknowledge many of the people who have encouraged me in my own creative journey.

To my husband, Robert, for giving me a real-life romance, for his tireless support of my music and writing, and for helping me every step of the way in navigating my role as an author. Thanks for sharing your hidden talents as a stellar cover and interior book designer.

To my two children for supporting me in all my artistic endeavors and being the biggest fans of my characters.

To my mother, Allison, who first taught me to play the violin and then how to teach.

To my father and grandparents, who came to countless recitals and have read all of my books.

To my dear sisters, aunts, uncles, and cousins, who have served as fabulous beta readers and proof-readers to help my stories shine.

To my parents-in-law, for loving and supporting me in my career like a daughter.

To my wonderful editors, Leslie L. McKee, fellow musician and writer, and Lindsey P. Brackett, contemporary fiction author, for their dedication to the craft and encouraging words.

To the cover models, my sisters Christy DeWillis and Brittany Merritt, for their willingness to help bring my book's vision to life, as well as Brahm George as the romantic lead. Thanks to stylist Erica Hobson for helping with hair and wardrobe at Echo Chic Salon. Thank you Susan Rohe for sharing your beautiful cello Bella with us.

To my music teachers, including my aunts, piano teachers, voice instructors, and college professors, without whom I wouldn't be the musician and writer I am today.

To my students and their families, for being a joy to teach.

To my critique partners in ACFW, for their expertise and support in helping these stories come to life.

To my fellow writers and coach Kent Sanders in The Daily Writer Community, for their accountability and encouragement in all aspects of the writing career.

To my Creator, the One who gives people the gift of creativity, as we were fashioned in His image.

I could not have accomplished this without all of your support!

Dedicated to my husband and four sisters—my best friends.

Chapter 1

Victoria Pearson clutched the neck of her violin as musicians filed onto the stage of Belton University's concert hall. Habit urged her to follow suit, but her new position as first chair kept her backstage—alone. Nervous anticipation quickened her pulse. A cacophony of flute trills and trumpet blasts bombarded her ears as the members of the orchestra warmed up. She smoothed the wrinkles in her black dress. This time, everything must be perfect.

She ran her free hand through her brunette bob. The softness of her hair, like silk, soothed her shaking fingers. A glance at the elegant shape of her instrument made her giggle. Jerry Chang, the first-chair cellist, had compared her physique to the violin—tan from the sun and similar in shape with its hourglass curves.

The conductor gestured with his baton-free hand for her to proceed.

A thrill of excitement shivered down her spine. She'd worked her entire college career to become first chair—concertmaster of the orchestra. Now, her senior year, she'd achieved her goal at last. Hopefully she could keep her position after the next round of auditions. Pride pulsed through her veins, followed by a wave of performance anxiety. She needed to lead the violin section with perfect precision to bolster her chances of acceptance to Johann Conservatory of Music for graduate school in New York.

She drew in a deep breath as she stepped from behind the heavy black curtain onto the luminescent stage. The light's glare forced her to blink. She strode next to the conductor's podium, then bowed to the audience. The intense light continued to blind her.

Her heart pounded like a kettledrum. After a quick swivel to face the orchestra, she pointed a finger at the oboist to play the tuning notes. When his note pierced the air, Victoria nestled the violin in its accustomed place on her left shoulder, ready to tune the four strings. Her

1

bow glided across the A, then the adjacent D. The low G peg had slipped, so she tightened it before tuning the high E string.

After the tuning subsided, she took her seat in the semicircle of elite musicians who surrounded the conductor's podium. Jerry, sitting opposite her, gave a quick thumbs up. Warmth spread to her cheeks. Was it the lights? Or something more?

"You've got this," he mouthed.

"Thanks," she mouthed back. Her knotted muscles began to unwind. He often had this effect on her. In contrast to her nerves, he always possessed a relaxed air at concerts. Handsome in his tux, black hair combed back, he resembled a younger version of the renowned cellist Yo-Yo Ma. Victoria met the dark eyes that sparkled behind large-rimmed glasses.

As a round of applause greeted her ears, she turned to see the conductor. He extended his hand, and she reciprocated his firm grip. The curtain drew back again, and Victoria's teacher emerged, violin in hand. Professor Chang's navy gown swept the stage floor in a regal fashion as she took her place as soloist next to the maestro. Victoria's gaze moved forward again to Jerry, who fiddled with his cufflinks, unmoved by his mother's dramatic entrance.

The pressure of leading her section as her teacher played Tchaikovsky's formidable *Violin Concerto in D Major* weighed on Victoria like a grand piano. One wrong entrance, and her career would be over. Her breathing accelerated. Professor Chang demanded perfection.

As the conductor raised his baton, Victoria nodded to bring in her section for the opening. Her breathing slowed in response to the music. Images of the peaceful, Midwestern plains surrounding this college town floated through her mind—waves of verdant cornstalks and colorful sunsets over fields of golden wheat. Perhaps Tchaikovsky had imagined a similar Russian landscape when he wrote the piece?

The conductor pointed his baton in her direction, and she snapped back to awareness. Time for the violins to take the theme.

Her pulse raced. Although she'd enjoyed Professor Chang's rendition, the opportunity to play the theme herself sent goose bumps down her arms. The melody welled up within her chest, and the music transported her to her childhood. In her mind, she ran through wheat fields with her four younger sisters on Gigi and Papa's farm, free from the demands which now hung heavy on her at the music school.

Focus, Victoria. All too soon, her bucolic visions faded as Professor Chang retrieved the melody, and Victoria enjoyed a few moments of respite. If only she could play with such ease. Maybe after her studies at the conservatory...

She straightened. Three measures until her next entrance. She placed her violin in position. Two. One. With a slight lift of her instrument, she swept her bow across the strings.

At the opening of the second movement, a new, haunting theme filled the concert hall. A chill stole through her body. Unlike the previous movement, the ethereal lethargy of the second created a hollow ache in her chest. If she were an artist like her sister Adrienne, she'd paint this movement gray. Professor Chang's instrument cried as though it concealed a tragic secret expressible through music alone.

As her teacher turned to face the orchestra at the close of the movement, something glistened on her cheek. Sweat ... or a tear?

The bombastic third movement jolted Victoria back to attention. Like a marathon runner nearing the finish line, Victoria's fingers sprinted over the fingerboard. This time, undeniable beads of sweat dripped down Professor Chang's face. Jerry, in contrast to his mother, flicked his bow back and forth with ease. How did he make it look effortless?

As the musicians neared the end, Victoria inched closer to the edge of her seat. Her heart drummed once more to keep up with her flying fingers. The bow sawed over the strings, and adrenaline flooded her as she joined Professor Chang in the final chord. Perfection.

A sense of euphoria enveloped Victoria as she and Jerry made their way backstage to the rehearsal room. "Jerry, your mom's rendition of Tchaikovsky... I have no words! Absolutely gorgeous. The first movement is beastly to play as the soloist of course, but the theme is pure beauty."

Jerry opened his case and tucked the cello away. "I'm starving. Want to get something to eat?"

Victoria stared at him. " Did you hear a word I said?"

"Of course." He loosened his bow and swept a cloth over the strings to wipe off the dusty rosin. "You were rambling about Mom. She plays with emotion or something."

"Yes, the minor theme was absolutely gut-wrenching."

"I suppose." Jerry organized the music in his folder.

"Are you even listening?"

"I am. I don't gush over her like you do."

"Well, I enjoy her performances. What's wrong with that?"

He closed his case with a snap. "You didn't have to grow up with her."

Victoria pursed her lips. "As you well know, I grew up in a musical family, too. I know what it's like to have a musician for a mother."

He blew a wisp of black hair out of his eyes. "Yes, but your mom is, well, more like a real mom."

"What's that supposed to mean?"

"She's just—"

"Victoria!" The all-too-familiar voice pierced the air.

A lone sunflower in a desolate field, her sister's bright appearance contrasted with the other musicians still dressed in black.

A moan escaped Victoria's lips. "Adrienne."

"I'm exhausted." The thump of Adrienne's viola case assaulted Victoria's ears as it hit the floor.

Victoria arched an eyebrow. "Didn't you enjoy the Tchaikovsky Violin Concerto, arguably the greatest violin piece ever written?"

Adrienne sighed. "Why couldn't we play a work for a lesser-known instrument?" She lowered her short frame into a chair near Victoria's case.

"Like the viola?" Victoria folded her arms across her chest.

"Yes, for example." Adrienne fluffed her blonde pixie haircut. "It's more original than the violin."

Victoria frowned. "Composers have always written popular works for violin."

Crossing her legs, Adrienne's ankle boot began to bounce up and down. "Well, I prefer original to popular." Her foot, which bobbed with extreme vigor, kicked over Victoria's violin case. "Oops." Her tone belied her apology. Why couldn't Victoria's twenty-year-old sister stop acting like a teenager?

Victoria slid her case closer to Jerry, away from Adrienne. "Is that why you're wearing a yellow sweater when you should be in all black— to be original?"

Adrienne's ski-jump nose rose several inches into the air. "There's no rule against changing attire after the concert. I need a little color in my life. Even if you don't."

"The quality of the music should speak for itself, not the clothes you wear," Victoria's eyes scanned her sister's ensemble. "But maybe viola players need something to compensate—"

Jerry coughed. "I hate to miss a good viola joke, but I've heard them about a thousand times, and I need food. Are you girls coming or not?"

"Yes." Victoria straightened her shoulders. "We need to discuss what to play for the service on Sunday." As the first violinist of their string ensemble, the responsibility of the music selection fell to her.

Adrienne popped up. "Let's go to Café Chocolat. I'm dying for coffee."

"Sounds good to me." Jerry opened the door, and the two exited the room. Victoria heaved a sigh. Her eyes lowered to her black dress. Perhaps she should have brought a change of clothes. Would Jerry have noticed? No time for such considerations now. She snatched her case and yanked open the door.

As Victoria stepped into the hallway, a light shone from the dressing room backstage, door ajar. Who would still be there at this hour? Muffled crying disturbed the otherwise peaceful corridor. Curious, Victoria peered inside the room. A woman in a navy gown hunched in front of a large mirror, a small rectangular piece of paper clasped in her hand. Her whole body shook as sobs overtook her. Professor Chang.

Chapter 2

Jerry Chang maneuvered his bulky cello case through the café door and propped it open for the Pearson girls to enter. He couldn't leave it in the car or the wood might crack from the heat.

A delicious aroma of roasted coffee and rich chocolate filled his nose. Man, he loved this place. Cozy and eccentric, its gourmet food appealed to French-pastry-loving patrons by day, and its vintage style and live music attracted students by night.

A tall, wavy-haired guy sang while he strummed a guitar on the wooden stage. His baritone and animated facial expressions commanded the attention of several giggling girls. Of course. They always fell for guitarists. Why couldn't someone notice the cellists every once in a while? At least the guy's voice was natural, sincere, and, to Jerry's relief, in tune.

He scoured the café for an open table. A young couple with their arms wrapped around each other had already commandeered the lumpy brown couch, and the patio table housed two girls with noses buried deep in biology textbooks. Probably what he should be studying right now. Ugh.

A wooden sign on the wall read, "Life's too short to sleep. Drink more coffee." The barista, Victoria and Adrienne's sixteen-year-old middle sister Marie, flashed a smile. Her dirty blonde hair was pulled back in a ponytail, and her bright blue eyes sparkled.

"I'll take a latte and an éclair." Adrienne pointed at the cream-filled pastry. "Jerry, do you want anything?"

"Just plain coffee and a ham and Brie sandwich." Too much chocolate caramel mocha-whatever-it-was-called was sugar overkill.

The hair on his arm prickled when Victoria brushed against him as she stepped up to the counter. A little too close for his own good.

Marie wiped her hands on her jeans and reached for the jar stuffed with tea bags. "Raspberry peach tea?"

"You know me too well." Victoria grinned. "I'll take a macaroon, too."

Adrienne lifted her chin. "It's a *macaron,* not a *macaroon.*"

Victoria rubbed her forehead. "Just because you speak French doesn't mean we all want a lesson. Marie knew what I meant."

Those two girls. If only they'd lay off each other.

"What flavor?" Marie pointed to the multicolored pastries. Smart way to dissolve an argument—with food. "The caramel apple is to die for."

"Perfect." Victoria said. "And a chocolate mint truffle to go."

Jerry dipped his head in the direction of an orange couch in the corner. "Let's grab that seat before it's taken."

"Great." When Victoria sat next to him, her intoxicating scent of roses and vanilla filled the air. His face grew warm. The café certainly was crowded.

Her chestnut eyes bore into his. "I wanted to ask you something. As we were leaving the concert hall…"

Concentrate on her face, you idiot.

"I saw your mom crying in the dressing room. Any idea what was wrong?"

Not another story about Mom. Why'd Victoria always bring her up in conversation? Didn't they have better things to talk about?

He sighed. "It was probably about the song. She's nostalgic about that piece, is all. Tchaikovsky can really take it out of you."

Wrinkles creased her forehead. " I don't think that was it. She held something in her hand, maybe an old picture."

"Hmmm." A lump formed in the back of his throat. He could take a wild guess who it was, but he didn't feel like going into all that tonight. "Not sure. But on a different note, I heard Mr. Vatchev has a big announcement for tomorrow."

She raised her eyebrows. "About what?"

Mr. Vatchev, the conductor of the Belton Symphony, also taught Jerry's favorite class, History of Symphonic Literature. Any announcement from him always piqued his interest.

"I don't know yet." But he let slip during cello sectionals that something was up."

"Do you think it has anything to do with the Fall Concert?" Victoria's pretty eyes sparkled with anticipation.

Jerry met her gaze and grinned. "I guess we'll find out tomorrow."

"Scoot over a bit, Victoria, will you?" Adrienne squished between them and plopped her case in front. She craned her neck. "I wanted a spot closer to the musician."

Of course she did. Only a year-and-a-half younger than Victoria, Adrienne knew how to catch a guy's attention.

"You're not the only one." Victoria nodded at the group of girls who huddled around the stage.

Jerry peeled off his tux jacket and loosened his bow tie. It wasn't too bad, sitting on a couch with two girls. Except they were checking out another guy.

Marie arrived with a wooden tray full of steaming liquid and handed each of them their drinks.

Victoria grabbed her arm. "Can you sit with us for a second? We need to decide what our string quartet should play at church Sunday."

After a quick glance at her fellow barista who was assisting the next customer, Marie took a seat on Adrienne's case. "Make it quick. I'm on the clock."

"Careful with that!" Adrienne jerked the viola out from under her, and Marie tumbled to the floor.

Jerry couldn't resist a smirk.

"Watch it," Marie exclaimed as she popped to her feet. "Where am I supposed to sit?"

Adrienne clutched her instrument. "Not on my case. You'll break it. Don't you know how expensive this is?"

"Yeah, firewood isn't cheap these days." Victoria sneered.

Adrienne scowled.

"So, Victoria, what songs did you have in mind?" Marie asked as she stole a sip of Victoria's tea.

"I was thinking of Handel's *Water Music*."

Marie shook her head. "I don't have time to learn something new.

"I guess we could just play Pachelbel's 'Canon in D.'" Victoria took a bite of the macaron, then handed it to Jerry.

As he popped a piece into his mouth, a delicious blend of apple and caramel danced on his tongue.

Adrienne crossed her legs. "Too cliché."

Victoria turned to Marie and Jerry. "What do you think?"

Marie took several more sips of tea. "I don't mind playing second fiddle, since we already know it. I've got too much on my plate right now to practice a lot, anyway."

"What about you, Jerry?" Victoria retrieved her half-empty drink from Marie.

Not exactly the most interesting song for the cello. "I mean, the bass lines are repetitive—"

"See, Jerry agrees with me!" Adrienne raised her cup in triumph.

Jerry took a bite of his sandwich. How could he stay on Victoria's good side? "I just prefer songs from the Romantic era." Of course, his preference had nothing to do with the modern definition of romance. But he'd always held a soft spot for nineteenth-century music, an era of emotion and passion. More powerful than the formulaic music of the previous eras and a lot more interesting for the cello.

Victoria straightened her shoulders. "Since we only have tomorrow to prepare, I think we need to stick with the Pachelbel."

Adrienne rolled her eyes. "I can play it in my sleep."

Marie swiped Adrienne's coffee. "It's fine with me." She took a sip, then set the cup back down. "I'd better get to work." She strode over to the counter.

"Gigi also wants us to play the hymn 'Chief of Sinners Though I Be.'" Victoria drained her cup.

Gigi, the girls' maternal grandmother, had been their church organist for as long as Jerry could remember.

Adrienne groaned. "Why does she always pick songs about sin? Traditional hymns bore me to tears."

Victoria clanked her teacup on the table. "I can't change the lyrics, and I don't think they're depressing. We all have to confront the sin in our lives."

"Ugh, you sound like Gigi." Adrienne wiped chocolate icing from her pristine nails.

Jerry took a sip of coffee. Time to diffuse the situation. "Victoria, why don't you write a new arrangement to spice it up? You're a great composer."

She paused a moment. Her facial features softened. He'd managed to chip away a fragment of her tough exterior. "Okay, I'll give it a shot, if Gigi doesn't mind."

Adrienne set down her éclair and looked straight at Victoria. "Don't tell her."

Victoria winced. "I hate secrets."

Adrienne arched an eyebrow. *"Really?"*

Victoria's face turned as red as the macaron. What secrets was she hiding, anyway?

The music stopped, and Jerry turned his head in time to see the blond guitarist approaching their couch. His stomach muscles tightened. Here to steal the girls.

"I take it all y'all are musicians?" The guy pointed to their instruments, his voice thick with a Texan drawl.

Adrienne flashed him a radiant smile. "Yes, we played a concert earlier tonight."

He grinned back, revealing beautiful white teeth. "My name's Matt. Do any of y'all fiddle?"

Victoria rolled her eyes. "I play violin."

Good. At least she didn't seem too enamored with the suave guitarist.

Batting her long eyelashes, Adrienne placed her hand on Matt's arm. "I can fiddle."

Matt's muscular biceps flexed as he stroked his stubbled chin. "You wanna join me for my next song?"

"You mean improvise?" Adrienne's face fell.

"Sure." He waved a large hand in the air. "It's easy. Just follow my lead."

Adrienne's eyes darted between the guitarist and her instrument, a look of uncertainty on her face.

"What about you?" Matt turned to Jerry. "What do you play?"

Jerry jolted back, surprised the guy had taken any interest in him. He tapped his large case. "Cello."

"Can you knock out a decent bass line?" Matt asked.

"Sure." Jerry shrugged.

Matt clapped him on the back. "Then why don't you join us, too?"

"Couldn't hurt to try." Jerry peeled himself off the couch to follow the guitarist. Maybe he'd score a couple extra cool points playing with the guy.

The trio climbed onto the stage, instruments in hand. Matt's voice boomed into the microphone. "Ladies and gents, a couple of guests will join me for my next song. On the fiddle, we have…" He handed the mic to Adrienne.

She cleared her throat. "Adrienne Pearson."

Jerry winced. Viola, not fiddle.

"And on bass…" He held the mic to Jerry.

Cello, not bass. But he could play the part. Imitate the double bass players he'd watched in jazz combos. He leaned forward. "Jerry Chang."

When Matt began to croon, Jerry plucked the strings of his cello with his forefinger. Maybe try a slap bass move. As he clapped his instrument in rhythm, the pulse of the music breathed new life into him, a sense of freedom. Although he'd never played the tune before, it turned out easy to pick up. Basic harmonic progression.

His gaze moved to Victoria, who smiled and waved. Too bad she wanted to move to New York for graduate school next year. And he'd be off to medical school wherever he could get in. His heart plummeted. Four more years of grueling education, not to mention residency after that. But Mom and Dad insisted it was the best path.

"Music's not a good career for you," his mom had lectured. "We music professors get paid horribly. Be a radiologist like your father. You'll make good money."

If that's what she believed, why had she insisted he practice three hours every day growing up, just to rip music away from him?

Besides, he didn't mind living here in a Midwestern college town nearly as much as Mom did. She considered anything less than a sprawling metropolis beneath her dignity.

At the sudden key change, his mind returned to the music at hand. He glanced at Adrienne, who'd barely played a note. After a few bars of complete silence on her part, she'd resorted to an open D string drone. Not much of a fiddler. Her eyes were as wide as whole notes.

All of a sudden, a flurry of commotion caught his eye. Marie had bolted from her post as barista, dashed to Victoria, and grabbed the violin case. She pulled out her sister's violin, situated the shoulder pad, then climbed onstage next to him. Never knew what to expect from the Pearson sisters. This should be interesting.

Chapter 3

Victoria's mouth fell open. What was Marie thinking?

Marie tightened the bow. All eyes followed her, including Matt's, whose widened in disbelief. She drew her bow over the strings and played a series of double stops in a long—short—short pattern. A simple rhythm, one of the first Victoria had learned as a child, but it matched the style of the song. Marie had spent the past two summers at a fiddle camp in Texas. It must've paid off. Her jeans and T-shirt blended well with Matt's denim and flannel attire. The crowd began to clap along to the tune. Even Victoria's foot tapped to the beat.

When the song ended, Matt's loud voice bellowed into the mic. "Who knew our barista tonight was a fiddler? Let's give it up for..." He held up the mic to Marie.

A shy smile spread across her face. "Marie Pearson."

The audience cheered. Marie gave a slight nod. So modest. Everyone beamed except Adrienne, who crept offstage with an envious glance at Marie. Victoria took her last sip of tea and stood to congratulate the musicians. But when she turned around, she found herself nose to nose with Adrienne, a furious expression on her face.

Victoria stepped back.

"Why did you let Marie borrow your violin?" The vein in Adrienne's forehead throbbed. This couldn't be good.

Victoria shrugged. "I didn't have much choice. Marie grabbed it and left. What was I supposed to do?"

"Take it back."

Hands fisted at her sides, Victoria took a deep breath to control her temper. Why did her sister care what she did with her instrument?

"Marie's a good player. I don't mind if she borrows it. Besides, it's not like it's a Stradivarius or anything." If only she could get a better instrument before graduate school.

"You wanted me to make a fool of myself. Marie totally showed me up with her fiddling in front of the new guy." Adrienne stomped off.

After she disappeared from view, Victoria released her breath. Adrienne was probably still bitter about the time Victoria made her play the viola part from memory in front of the entire orchestra. What a disaster. Adrienne had sat, frozen, unable to produce a note. In the end, the second chair violist took her place for the rest of the rehearsal.

Marie approached, the violin cradled under her arm.

"Great job." Victoria patted her back.

"It was nothing." Marie bent down to return the violin to the safety of its case, careful as always. She paused, bow midair. "Adrienne's upset."

The muscles in Victoria's jaw clenched. "Don't worry about her. She's jealous."

Marie tucked the bow into the case and turned the latch to click it in place. "I was trying to help her."

"I know. And you were wonderful. Quite the fiddler."

A sigh escaped Marie's lips. "Adrienne threatened that she might not play at church with us Sunday."

Wringing her hands, Victoria groaned. How could they perform a string quartet with only three people?

"In that case, I'd better go home and write the new hymn arrangement. Maybe Adrienne will change her mind if I give her something interesting to play."

"I hope so." Marie returned to the counter.

As Victoria drove home, sounds of Tchaikovsky and fiddle music fused together in her mind. What an odd juxtaposition: the classical masterpiece and the folksy ballad. The first expressed a depth of genius she could only hope to master one day. But the simplicity of the other struck a chord she couldn't ignore.

On autopilot, Victoria turned onto her street where the double-story Pearson home rose into view. A smile spread across her face at the sight of the jovial scarecrow standing sentinel over the white brick house. The windows were down in her red coupe so she could enjoy the night breeze. As she pulled into the circle driveway, she breathed in the fragrant scent of roses. A festive fall wreath made of orange and gold leaves graced the door. How she loved this time of year. Her mother always decorated for the four seasons, but Victoria favored fall with its crunching leaves and vibrant-colored foliage.

She'd missed the comfort of home those first two years of college living in dingy dorm rooms. Junior year, most of the upperclassmen lived off campus anyway, so she'd moved back home to save money toward graduate school. Thank goodness she'd received a full ride for undergraduate with a music scholarship. Every penny counted if she wanted to live in New York next year.

As the living room clock struck eleven, she snuck inside—best to keep quiet. She tiptoed up the winding staircase to the second-floor landing, where darkness reigned in three of the four bedrooms. A small ray of light shone under Victoria's bedroom door. She hadn't forgotten to turn it off before she left, had she? Only one person would be awake at the house at this hour.

The door creaked open, and Victoria spotted Louisa, her fourteen-year-old sister, snuggled up in the four-poster bed, book in hand. Her brunette hair hung long over her fleece nightgown.

Victoria walked to the bed. "Louisa, why are you awake?"

Louisa set her book down. "Stella wanted to sleep, but I wasn't tired."

A laugh escaped Victoria's lips. "Stella's only twelve, and she needs her sleep. So, do you."

Louisa's green eyes sparkled. "I couldn't stop reading. Not in the middle of the story."

The pillow-like comforter called to her, so Victoria flopped next to her sister. "Understandable."

"How was the concert?" Louisa wiggled her feet under the sea of shimmering crimson.

"The Tchaikovsky was amazing. Professor Chang's interpretation blew me away."

"She's a fabulous musician. But I don't understand how she can play a solo in front of all those people." Louisa shuddered.

"I'm sure you get used to it over the years. New York-trained musicians develop a thick skin."

Louisa's face fell. "You'll be just like Professor Chang when you go to New York."

Victoria reached out to stroke Louisa's long hair. The silky strands slid through her fingers like butter. "I promise I won't forget about you. See?" Victoria pulled the chocolate box from her pocket. "I remembered."

As Louisa closed her eyes, she inhaled. "It smells delicious. Like mint."

"Your favorite."

"Who else went to Café Chocolat with you?" She bit into the truffle.

"Adrienne and Jerry." Victoria wished she'd bought an extra piece of chocolate for herself.

Louisa looked up. "Marie was working?"

"Yes. We discussed what to play at church on Sunday. Adrienne thinks I should write an arrangement for the hymn. Otherwise it's *too boring*." Victoria folded her arms, still irritated at her sister's obstinacy.

Louisa sat upright. "Yes, you should. I love your arrangements. Remember when you used to make up songs for me when I was little?"

Victoria couldn't resist a smile. "Yes. What were they about? A frog? A lizard?"

"A little turtle." Louisa placed her hands on top of each other and wiggled her thumbs like the tiny reptile.

"How could I forget?" Victoria laughed. "But you're the lyricist, not me."

Louisa pulled her knees to her chest, hugging the comforter like a security blanket. "I don't know about that."

"I'm afraid this hymn arrangement won't live up to your expectations." Victoria lowered her eyes. "I don't have much time. I wish Adrienne weren't so difficult. Now she's upset because Marie upstaged her in front of her latest crush."

"What?"

Victoria recounted the fiddling incident.

Louisa finished her chocolate. "I'm sure it'll blow over. Adrienne's just..."—she paused in search of the right word—"artistic. Don't take it to heart."

Annoyance surged through Victoria's veins again at the recollection. "She's jealous. She didn't want her little sister to upstage her."

"Can you blame her?" Louisa's eyes met hers.

Victoria paused. She didn't like to be upstaged by her younger sisters either. But this was different. Wasn't it?

"Besides, she's challenging you to write something new. Don't you want to be creative?" Louisa's eyes bore into hers. She possessed a wisdom that far surpassed her years.

"Well, when you put it that way..." Victoria pulled her in close. "But you need sleep."

Louisa snuggled into Victoria's arms. "Can I stay with you tonight?"

"Yes." Victoria kissed the top of her head, grateful for the company. These moments wouldn't last forever. Could she bear to leave Louisa behind? Victoria had always been her babysitter when Mom played concerts or Dad got called back to the hospital for surgeries. If she left, Adrienne would watch out for Stella, and Marie could fend for herself. But what if Louisa needed her and Victoria wasn't there to help?

Chapter 4

The sun beat down on Jerry and warmed him from the outside in as he crossed the campus. The golden-domed building named for Dr. James Belton, founder of the University, loomed in front of him. A regal statue of the university patriarch stood erect in front of the hall. According to tradition, all seniors were supposed to pose with him for a graduation photo. Of course, as a professor's kid, he'd already posed with the guy about a hundred times. Were other universities this quirky, or was it just Belton?

Since he'd received a full tuition waiver due to his mom serving on the faculty, he hadn't applied anywhere else. He might have preferred a conservatory dedicated solely to the study of music, but his parents had insisted he receive a liberal arts education so he could be Pre-Med.

The redbrick building he and Victoria had christened "the castle" caught his eye. His pace slackened as he tarried to admire the four interconnected towers. The building housed the humanities where he'd taken several of his general education classes—English, foreign language, history, and religion. When had he lost the luxury to study a variety of subjects? Those days had passed so gradually he hadn't noticed his freedom slip away. Now science classes filled every aspect of his life, other than the few remaining music classes. He must've been crazy, deciding to double major in biology and music, considering they didn't overlap at all. But he couldn't bring himself to give up the cello. Not yet.

He glanced at his watch, which read fifteen till nine—ample time to peek inside for old times' sake. He pushed through the door to the outside courtyard, enclosed by the four towers. A fragrant floral scent greeted him as he entered "the secret garden." Green vines crept up the brick walls. Flowerbeds full of geraniums and daisies surrounded the walkway beside his favorite stone bench, which sat empty. He filled its void and placed his backpack at his side. His eyes closed, he breathed in the fresh air.

"I thought I might find you here."

Jerry's eyes flew open to reveal Victoria's face leaning over his. She slid next to him, and the heat from her body warmed his arm.

She brushed a stray hair from her face. "Sometimes it's nice to get away from it all."

He nodded. "Definitely."

A sweet sigh escaped her lips. "I hope I can find a place like this at the conservatory next year."

Jerry's insides twisted into a knot. "From what Mom's told me about Johann, you'll need it."

Concern clouded her eyes. "What's that supposed to mean?"

He traced a music note in the dirt with his foot, avoiding her gaze. "It's intense."

"You don't think I can handle it?"

"I'm sure *you* can, but some people … can't. Didn't." He swallowed.

"What are you talking about?"

He looked at her again. Gazed into those dark, chestnut eyes. Should he tell her? Or was she better off not knowing. His mouth opened to speak, but the bells in the tower chimed to announce the hour.

"Oh no, it's already nine," Victoria gasped. "We're late."

The two of them snatched their book bags and sprinted for the adjacent music building.

"Johann Sebastian Bach, the greatest composer of the Baroque era, spent his entire life dedicated to the musical craft." Mr. Vatchev's thick accent reminded Victoria of the Russian masters—Stravinsky and Tchaikovsky. "Although subject to the whims of his patrons, the German composer's love for his art never subsided."

What dedication. Victoria's eyes fixed on the picture of Bach displayed on the screen at the front of the classroom.

Jerry nudged her. "When do you think he'll make the announcement?"

"No idea." She glanced at Adrienne, who had cozied up next to the hipster on her right, Franklin Curtis. The hair on Victoria's arm prickled just looking at him in his fedora and skinny jeans. Her stand-partner since freshman year, the two had battled for the leading position of their section in the formidable orchestra auditions every year. Victoria would win, then Franklin, then Victoria, then Franklin.

Franklin flashed her a smile. She gritted her teeth. Their insufferable competition had continued for years, but this year, their senior year, she had to come out on top. She raised her chin. No one would take away her prized position as concertmaster.

Mr. Vatchev tapped his baton on the board. Victoria jolted to attention. This second picture of Bach featured him surrounded by at least a dozen children. What a nightmare to have so many kids! She could barely stand living with seven people running around her house. Especially since Adrienne moved back home this year. Ugh.

"The versatile composer maintained his prolific compositions in spite of his many duties as church organist, the demands of patrons, and a busy home life." The teacher paused to catch his breath.

Hmm. Apparently Bach didn't enjoy the peaceful, distraction-free life she'd envisioned. No, he served his large family and his church, just like she did. Perhaps constant interruptions had frustrated him, too. Or was he more patient? Maybe he didn't lash out so often, the way she did.

"On a different note," the maestro said with bravado, "I have an announcement."

Victoria sat upright. Finally.

Mr. Vatchev cleared his throat. "This year, Belton University will host the senior division of the Concerto Competition for the Midwestern Association of Music Schools."

A low buzz swept through the class.

The professor rapped on the podium. "Those who would like to participate must prepare their entire concerto for the audition in April. The winner will receive the opportunity to perform their solo with the orchestra at our final concert in May."

Victoria drew in a deep breath. She had always dreamed of performing a solo with the orchestra, like Professor Chang.

"Due to the generosity of several of our prominent donors, the winner will also receive a $20,000 scholarship to attend graduate school in music, as well as an optional Graduate Teaching position to accompany Belton's new Master of Music program, which we plan to launch next year." Mr. Vatchev pointed to the information on the screen.

Was this a dream? Victoria had finally found a way to fund her own graduate school conservatory education. She wouldn't have to borrow the money from Mom and Dad. But would she have time to prepare a whole multi-movement concerto along with all of the conservatory audition music requirements she already had to practice? And could the scholarship be used for Johann Conservatory? She had no interest in staying at Belton for a Master's Degree and serving as a teaching assistant. She'd never have the patience for *that*. Better ask Professor Chang for details at her next lesson.

"Please sign up no later than our Fall Concert, October 31st, so that I know how many students will participate." The professor turned off the computer. "Class dismissed."

Victoria frowned. If she'd known this sooner, she could have practiced the concerto all summer in addition to the audition music. Her heartbeat quickened. So much to consider, and very little time.

Victoria struggled to rein in her thoughts as she drove home from class. The image of herself as the soloist in front of thousands of people played through her mind on repeat. This was the chance of a lifetime— the culmination of her hard work. Her foot pressed the pedal, and the car accelerated to keep pace with her racing thoughts.

On one hand, performing as the soloist had been her dream since childhood. Six-year-old Victoria had held her mother's hand in the beautiful orchestra hall as a younger Professor Chang played a vibrant concerto—Victoria couldn't recall which one. The stunning shimmer of her red gown, the emotive slow section, the invigorating finale—all of these had planted a seed of desire deep inside little Victoria that someday she hoped would come to fruition.

Was that day fast approaching? Tension crept down her neck, and she cocked her head to each side to release it. She wasn't ready. She needed to focus on her graduate school audition material. Those dreadful quadruple-stop chords in the Bach *Partita* ate up all her practice time.

And oh, she'd almost forgotten, she'd promised to write that hymn arrangement for church this weekend. How on earth did Bach ever manage to get anything done, with all his performance, composing, church, and family obligations?

When she entered the living room, she set down her backpack next to the baby grand piano and rummaged for a sheet of staff paper and a pencil. Best to cross at least one thing off her lengthy to-do list.

She situated herself on the piano bench and stared at the instrument. The cold ivory keys offered little inspiration. Her eyes drifted to the periwinkle curtains draped over the bay window, then to the wooden bookshelf stuffed with music scores. Each shelf bore a label— Soprano Arias, Piano Sonatas, Beginner's Piano, etc. Her mother's extensive collection filled the six-foot shelf from top to bottom. No wonder Belton had invited Mom to become an adjunct faculty member a few years ago. Now she served as the primary accompanist, as well as a voice and piano teacher.

The blank staff paper on the piano mocked Victoria. Writer's block. This hymn arrangement proved to be more difficult than she'd expected, especially now that she had more important issues to consider, like the concerto competition.

She reached for the well-worn family hymnal to sing and play "Chief of Sinners." As she had never considered vocals her forte, she cringed at the sound of her own voice. The necessity to sing and play at the same time heightened the level of difficulty, and her fingers struggled to reach the cumbersome chords on the piano.

"Do you need some help?" The familiar voice spoke behind her. Victoria turned to see her mother in a light pink sundress tailored at the waist, golden blonde hair hanging loosely over her shoulders. Her warm eyes twinkled at Victoria.

"Yes." Victoria sighed. "I need to write a quartet arrangement for this hymn, but…" She gestured at the blank page.

Mom placed a hand on her shoulder. "I'll play the piano, and you grab your violin." Victoria stood, and Mom took her place at the instrument. She ran her hands over the keys in a swift scale and situated her feet on the pedals.

A few notes of introduction gave Victoria the cue she needed for the opening. The melody soared from her instrument like a prayer rising to heaven—simple yet subtle. Her muscles unwound as she settled into the verse, her fingers dancing on the familiar fingerboard. What a contrast to Victoria's awkwardness at the piano.

After the first verse, Mom stopped. "This time I'll sing the melody, and you improvise."

Improvise. Like Adrienne and Marie the other night? Victoria's stomach tightened. She closed her eyes and took a deep breath. Mom's sweet, silvery voice filled the room, inviting Victoria to join her. This time, the notes didn't come from the page but from somewhere deep within. The music led her as if by divine inspiration. She gave in to her muse and let the instrument be her voice.

At the conclusion, Victoria opened her eyes to see Mom looking at her. "Beautiful. You should play it just like that tomorrow."

"I hope I can remember what I did. I need to transcribe it before I forget."

Mom rose to her feet. "I'll leave you to it."

Lightheaded with the exhilaration of the previous run-through, excitement pulsed through Victoria's veins as she grabbed the staff paper. But as she reached for the pencil, her inspiration faded. What had she played first? A quarter note? An eighth note? She played the opening line again. *Eighth note.* She rushed to copy it on paper before it faded away again.

"*Et voilà.*" Adrienne's voice pierced the room.

No, she couldn't lose her train of thought now. But Victoria's eyes drifted from the page to Adrienne, who stood in the entryway, accompanied by their youngest sister.

"What do you think of my dance costume?" Twelve-year-old Stella twirled around in a white-bodiced leotard with pink sequins, a fluffy tutu, and ballet slippers. Her bright blonde hair was pinned back in a thick bun. "Adrienne sewed the finishing touches for me."

Victoria put down her pencil. "Stunning."

Stella danced on tiptoe to the piano and spread her tutu over the bench.

"What are you doing?" Victoria frowned.

"I need to practice piano before my piano concert tonight." Stella stretched out her palms in front of her.

Blood rushed to Victoria's face as she clutched her sheet music. "But I'm working on the hymn arrangement for tomorrow."

Adrienne strode to an easel next to one of the plush armchairs. "Can't you finish it in your room?" Her eyes scanned the painting in front of her. "You don't need the piano."

Victoria glared at both of them and scooped up the violin and writing supplies. The idea of moving away from this madhouse to New York was becoming more appealing by the minute. She trudged upstairs and slumped into the wooden chair at her mahogany desk. By now, the staff held lifeless notes on a page instead of the inspirational descant she'd played earlier. Perhaps she could refresh her memory. She placed the bow on the strings.

"Joyful, joyful, we adore thee…" Stella's captivating soprano rang through the house, accompanied by a piano part that sounded anything but joyful. Pulse racing, Victoria pounded her desk with her fist. She couldn't get anything done in this crazy house. Maybe next year she'd finally enjoy some peace and quiet away from her family.

Victoria poked her head out of the bedroom door, which opened onto the landing overlooking the living room.

By now, Mom stood hunched over the piano. "I don't think that was quite right, Stella dear. Try again."

The same clunky chords accosted Victoria's ears. She cringed and strode to the banister. "Still not right, Stella," she yelled. How had her mother put up with beginner piano students for so many years? This was driving her crazy. She'd never make a good music teacher. That's why she was moving to New York—to be a performer. And to get away from here.

A couple of hours later, Victoria breathed a sigh of relief. She'd finished transcribing the hymn. Time for a run-through. She picked up her violin to play the opening verse. The words rang in her head.

"Chief of sinners though I be, Jesus shed his blood for me ... As the branch is to the vine, I am his and he is mine."

As the descant of the second verse returned to her fingers, an urge to pray welled up inside her.

Dear God, I'm not gifted with words, but help me to have patience with my sisters.

At the close she lowered the violin to her side, eyes shut for a moment as the notes died away.

"Magnifique." Victoria opened her eyes to find Adrienne next to her, hands clasped to her chest. When had she come in?

Victoria smiled. "I'm glad you liked it."

"It was perfect. That's exactly how I envisioned my part."

Confused, Victoria took a step away from her. "Your part?"

"Well, yes. As the first violinist, won't you play the melody, and I'll play the ornamental part?"

Victoria's brow furrowed. In the excitement of composing she'd forgotten Adrienne wanted the new part. Victoria held up her violin. "The highest instrument plays the descant."

Adrienne shrugged. "That part wasn't very high. It fits within the viola's range."

Victoria snatched her manuscript and brushed past her sister, heart pounding. She needed some air—a chance to breathe. Adrienne wanted to play the beautiful descant, her creation, and the rest of the quartet would probably have to play from the hymnal. It wasn't fair.

Jerry clambered with his cello up the three flights of stairs to his parents' apartment. Why he'd agreed to still live with them during college was beyond even his own comprehension. "It's only temporary," Mom had insisted. "Your father and I will be moving back to New York as soon as we secure jobs there. Then you can have this whole place to yourself. Maybe you could rent out a couple of rooms to your friends to make extra money. No need to stay in those filthy dorms."

She'd said that at the beginning of his freshman year. Now, three years later, he was a senior in college still living with his parents. Not exactly a chick-magnet.

He turned the knob to the front door and walked inside. Red and gold curtains hung at the windows, while antique figurines— most of them from his grandmother, whom he visited in China every other summer—adorned the bookshelves. On the off years, she came to the States to visit them.

"I wish you could move to the US, Mama," his mother had urged when Grandma left at the beginning of August. "You would love New York. I'm so glad you sent me there to study music."

"No, Li quin." Grandma said. "I must return to China. It's where I was born, and you and Margaret." Her eyes clouded. "I have no desire to visit New York."

Jerry didn't blame her. He didn't want to go there, either. Why did that city hold such sway over his mother, especially after what happened? And now she'd convinced Victoria of its charms, too. His heart sank. He'd lost his chance to date her. She was bound for the conservatory, and he for medical school. Maybe with the new scholarship position at Belton, he could convince his parents to change their minds and allow him to pursue music instead.

"Jerry, good, you're home," his mother called from the kitchen. "I need you to finish making the dinner."

He entered the kitchen where everything had been remodeled over the past year. They'd spent too many nights eating carryout on the couch, since it took forever to install the appliances. Unlike Grandma, Mom had never developed an interest in cooking.

"I have a concert in Chicago next week, and I must start practicing." She stirred the chicken on the stove. "I'm playing the Sibelius Concerto, and you know how difficult that is."

Yes, she was always practicing while Dad was at the hospital, leaving him to cook and clean while studying to keep up with his double major.

"Okay." He pulled an onion from the fridge, diced it, and threw it into the wok. The scent of spices, chicken, and vegetables filled the air like an aromatic symphony. He took a deep breath. "Mom, Mr. Vatchev mentioned the concerto competition to us in class today. I thought I might audition."

She stopped stirring the chicken and held up the spoon. "Jerry Chang, you don't have time to prepare for a concerto competition. You'll be visiting medical schools in the spring, and you can't let your grades slip. The ones on the east coast won't accept students from a liberal arts Midwestern university unless you're at the top of your class. You must stay focused." She handed him the spoon. "Now finish up here. Dad has to work late again, but save food for him." She bustled out of the room.

He sighed. So much for a smooth conversation.

Chapter 5

Sunday morning, the clock at the back of the church showed five till eight. Victoria sat poised on the church stage, instrument in hand, ready for the first service. The early morning sun streamed through the stained glass windows and warmed her fingers. The ornate nineteenth-century interior reminded her of an elaborate wedding cake.

She inhaled to take in the splendor of the morning. She loved the feeling of accomplishment she gained from rising early. Marie, on the other hand, slouched in the chair next to her, violin resting on the leg of her black jumpsuit. "It's too early to be awake on a weekend," she moaned.

Adrienne nodded as she stifled a yawn. "I don't understand who'd want to be awake at this hour."

Jerry shrugged and leaned back in the chair across from Victoria. In contrast to his concert tux, this morning he wore dark slacks and a black button-down shirt. She didn't mind the informal change, although his hair kept falling over his glasses in a distracting manner.

She glanced at the clock again. Three minutes to the hour—time to start the prelude. Her pulse quickened, and, raising her violin, she nodded at the others to follow suit. She had selected an easy piece from their gig books, which the quartet had played numerous times.

A dissonant sound rent the air in the opening bar. Victoria cringed. She glanced at the others and drew a sharp intake of breath. Adrienne had stopped playing and fumbled with the pages of her book. "Wrong song," she mouthed.

This is what happened when they didn't have enough time to prepare. They'd just have to continue without her.

"Measure eight," Marie whispered a few seconds later. Adrienne nodded and re-entered, this time with a pleasing harmony. Victoria let out her breath. Thank goodness some of the congregation members would have arrived late and missed the opening.

After the prelude, the pastor gave several announcements. Victoria's eyes scanned the bulletin. The next song, "Chief of Sinners," was set to follow the Bible readings. Butterflies danced in her stomach. What would the congregation think of her arrangement? Some of the members could be quite opinionated.

Adrienne sighed, viola clasped to her chest. "I love this Scripture passage."

"What?" Victoria's intense concentration on the performance had prevented her from paying attention while her father was reciting the New Testament reading. As one of the senior elders and an avid scholar, Dr. Pearson frequently volunteered to help with Bible studies at the church.

"The love chapter." Adrienne smiled. "1 Corinthians 13, my favorite."

Dad stood at the podium in his suit and tie, his kind voice resonating throughout the room. He had the brain of a surgeon and the heart of a saint.

[4] Love is patient, love is kind. It does not envy, it does not boast, it is not proud. [5] It does not dishonor others, it is not self-seeking, it is not easily angered, it keeps no record of wrongs. (NIV)

One time Dad had suggested she substitute her name in place of love. "Victoria is patient. Victoria is kind. She does not envy…" A twinge of guilt pricked her conscience. A tall order to live up to, but she did her best.

She glanced at Marie, who slumped lower in the chair next to her, eyes closed. Victoria nudged her shoulder.

"What?" Startled, Marie looked around in a confused daze.

"We're at church," Victoria whispered. "Try to look like you're paying attention."

She eyed Jerry, whose fingers ran over the neck of the cello in a mindless manner. He must've been practicing the music in his head. What dedication.

Adrienne, on the other hand, sat in rapt attention, hanging on Dad's every word.

She probably didn't even have her music opened to the right page. Victoria craned her neck to get a better look at Adrienne's stand. Sure enough, it still displayed the previous song.

Victoria poked Adrienne with her bow. "Get ready," she mouthed. "It's almost time for the hymn."

Instruments in position, the four of them drew their bows across the strings in perfect rhythm. For one glorious verse, they came together in perfect harmony.

At the opening of verse two, Adrienne straightened her posture on the chair like a queen perched on her throne. She played her part, Victoria's arrangement, with such bravado that the viola sang with emotion in its rich alto voice. To her chagrin, the low register lent itself well to the part, rivaling the soprano of the violin.

As the verse drew to a close, a look of intense satisfaction spread across Adrienne's face. She glanced at Victoria. Their eyes met, but Victoria couldn't muster a smile.

###

"Excellent job." Isabelle Carter, a lifelong family friend, clasped ivory hands over her heart. "The viola took my breath away. I could feel the sinner's prayer rising to heaven."

A smile radiated across Adrienne's face. "I'm so glad you enjoyed it, Mrs. Carter."

Victoria pursed her lips. Why did her sister get all the credit?

Jerry shook his head at her in a "just blow it off" sort of way.

Eddie Carter, the quintessential tall, dark, and handsome boy, flashed an impish smile. His milk chocolate skin stood in stark contrast to his mother's ivory complexion. Three years Victoria's junior, he took to heart his role as the brother the Pearson sisters never had.

"I was particularly enamored with the second violin part," he said with a nod to Marie. "The way you held those long notes showed a mastery of skill beyond my wildest expectations."

Marie rolled her eyes. "Eddie, you know full well I didn't do much of anything."

"To the contrary." His eyes sparkled, lighting up his smooth, brown face. "You kept from falling off your chair while you slept during the sermon—quite a feat."

Marie frowned. "Was it that obvious?"

"Just to me." He straightened his quirky aeronautical-themed tie. "And to the rest of the congregation. If it weren't for Victoria's persistent nudges and pokes, I'm not sure any of you would have made it through the service."

Jerry chuckled.

Heat rushed to Victoria's face. Sometimes Eddie took his brotherly role too far. "I was *trying* to make sure everyone stayed on top of their parts."

Jerry placed a warm hand on Victoria's rigid arm and pulled her away. "Sorry Eddie, but we've got to pack up the instruments. I'll see you tomorrow."

Eddie nodded. "Catch you guys later." He sauntered to the back of the church.

"Victoria, don't let him get to you," Jerry said. "He was only teasing."

With a quick tug she removed the violin shoulder pad and tucked it away. "I know. He's never serious. At least not about music. Only airplanes and engineering."

Jerry twisted the screw that loosened the hair on his bow. "He's a good performer."

"Really?" Victoria frowned. "Every time we rehearse a program with him, he messes around and distracts Adrienne and Marie. He doesn't have the focus needed to be good."

"Then you don't know him very well."

Victoria arched an eyebrow. "And you do?"

Jerry wiped the rosin dust from under the cello strings. "Better than you."

How was that possible? Did he know something about Eddie that she didn't? He was practically her brother, after all.

Chapter 6

"Play it again." Professor Chang's staccato voice interrupted Victoria mid-song.

The knot in her right shoulder tightened, so she cocked her neck to the left. Her private lesson ran over the allotted hour, but the Bach "Chaconne" required extra time. When would she have the chance to ask her teacher about the concerto competition? Streaks of sweat soaked her palms as she held them in position, then drew her bow for the opening bars.

"Stop." Professor Chang leaned backward against the office chair. "Your quadruple stops are still out of tune. How many times do I have to tell you?"

That was because playing four notes at the same time on the instrument was virtually impossible, especially with her sticky fingers. The previous four movements of Bach's *Partita No. 2*, while difficult, had been attainable. But this one was a different story. Victoria struggled to wrap her brain, and fingers, around the piece. No wonder it held its place as a pinnacle of the violin repertoire.

Professor Chang rose from her desk and removed her own violin from its case. "When you play Bach, it must sound effortless. Your listeners want to focus on the melody, not the chordal accompaniment."

Then why didn't Bach write a piano accompaniment, instead of forcing the violinist to play four notes simultaneously? She wasn't a church organist.

"Let me show you." Professor Chang tossed her raven black hair behind her shoulders and settled her instrument under her chin. At her powerful opening, Victoria stepped backward. The highest notes of the chords soared over the lower ones like a flag over a battlefield. So they *were* possible to play. Maybe Victoria just lacked the technical prowess. The students at Johann Conservatory probably mastered quadruple stops with ease.

35

"Now you try." Professor Chang moved next to the piano to give Victoria enough room to extend her bow.

Victoria took a deep breath, then recommenced. The fingers in her left hand cramped as she stretched them across the four strings. She winced.

"Stop." Professor Chang nudged Victoria to the side. "Take a break. We don't want to see you in pain. I'll play it again while you rest."

"Thanks." As Victoria set her instrument in its case, the authoritative sound of her professor's Italian violin filled the room.

If only she possessed her tone. Maybe if Victoria owned a better instrument. She eyed her professor's antique violin, then glanced at her own. Light brown with an orange tint, her parents had given her the twentieth-century American-made violin for her thirteenth birthday.

"You're a teenager now," her mom had exclaimed. "It's time you had a full-sized instrument of your own."

At the time, Victoria had jumped at the chance to play a new instrument. In contrast to the cheap, smaller violins she'd played before, hers was phenomenal. But now, next to Professor Chang's powerful seventeenth-century Stradivarius, the wood faded with age, hers sounded like a mouse's attempt to roar with a lion.

Victoria frowned. She should be grateful—appreciative. Mom and Dad had given her the instrument as a gift. She glanced at Professor Chang's case. It's soft, velvet green interior featured several pictures across the back. As the "Chaconne" continued to ring in her ears, Victoria moved closer to examine the photos. In one, a small boy in large-rimmed glasses clutched a cello, a huge grin spread across his face. The corners of Victoria's own mouth turned up at the sight of little Jerry. How old was he at that time—maybe seven or eight? Even at that age, the natural way he commanded the cello gave him the air of a master.

In an adjacent photo, two violinists in matching red, sparkling dresses played together. The one on the left must have been Professor Chang. But the other? Victoria squinted. The woman resembled a younger version of her teacher—perhaps a sister or cousin? Probably the latter, since Jerry had never mentioned an aunt before.

Silence stole over the room like an icy frost.

"What are you doing?" Professor Chang's voice pierced the air.

"I… I…" Victoria backed away. "I was looking at your pictures. Is that you in the red dress?" She pointed to the older of the two women.

"Yes." Professor Chang's voice sliced like a knife.

"And who is she?" Victoria indicated the younger girl on the right.

Professor Chang slammed the case shut. "Never mind. I thought you were listening to the "Chaconne," not examining my personal affairs." Fire flashed in her dark eyes. "You have a lot of work to do if you want to attend Johann next year, and I can't have you distracted during lessons. If you want a letter of recommendation, you'd better focus all of your attention on practice."

"But what about—"

Her nostrils flared. "My next student should be here."

Professor Chang swung the door wide. That weasel, Franklin Curtis, stood outside with a larger than usual smirk on his face. No doubt he'd heard the exchange. Just what she needed after the disastrous lesson. Victoria packed up her violin and rushed out of the arctic studio.

Franklin sauntered inside. "I've brought the Khachaturian *Violin Concerto* with me today. My favorite. It'll be perfect for the competition."

Victoria's heart sank. The Khachaturian, one of the hardest violin concertos ever written? She'd have to pick something amazing to compete with that. Jaw set, she marched down the hallway, passing a number of rooms where loud trombone blasts and clarinet scales accosted her ears. At the end

of the hall she found a vacant room, stole inside, and sank onto a chair next

to the piano. Her case hit the floor with a thud. The bare, windowless walls closed in around her.

How would she attend Johann Conservatory if Professor Chang didn't consider her qualified? The New York professors were even more rigorous than those here. She needed to practice more. Three hours a day wasn't enough. Nothing and no one was going to keep her from New York—not her family and not Professor Chang. She had to win that scholarship from the concerto competition. It was her ticket to freedom, independence, and the chance to finally be her own person.

As she ran a few scales and arpeggios, the familiar notes flowed in rapid succession under her fingers. She wasn't so bad after all. She turned to the page in her scale book with ascending double stops. Her hands froze. She couldn't bear to look at more chords. But she had to. It was the only way.

The first few notes she deemed passable, but as the level of difficulty increased, her fingers struggled to reach their necessary positions. This was getting worse. Her heartbeat quickened, and her muscles tightened. The violin let out a deafening squawk, and she shoved it into its case.

The door creaked open, and Jerry poked his head in. "Am I interrupting?" Without waiting for an answer, he entered and sat on the piano bench next to her chair.

He said nothing, but instead ran his fingers over the keys. The somber tones of "Für Elise" serenaded her, and she closed her eyes. The plaintive motif echoed the cry that pounded in her heart. When the music stopped, she looked up to find Jerry watching her.

"So are you going to tell me what's going on?" He folded his arms.

She gulped. "Your mother—"

"Oh no." He rolled his eyes. "What has she done now?"

"She doesn't think my Bach is Johann caliber." A sob formed in Victoria's throat. "She—"

The muscles in Jerry's arms flexed with tension. "Don't listen to her. She always finds a way to stomp on people's dreams."

"But she's right. The chords aren't in tune. She flinched every time I played."

"So, don't go to Johann." When she looked into his eyes, did she detect a hint of pleading? Or had she imagined it?

"No, I still want to go. I need to focus, that's all."

Jerry's face fell. "Did you talk to my mom about the details of the concerto competition?"

Victoria hesitated. "I didn't get a chance to ask her. While your mom demonstrated the 'Chaconne,' I looked at a couple of pictures in her case. Then she freaked out that I was looking at those instead of listening to her." As Victoria took a deep breath, the scent of rich, woodsy cologne wafted from his neck.

He passed a hand through his mop of black hair. "You said you looked at her pictures. Which ones?"

"One was of you as a little boy, holding your cello." She smiled, and he inched closer to her. A warm sensation rose to her cheeks.

"And the other was of two violinists dressed in red, your mother and some other woman. She looked like a younger sister or cousin." She peered into his eyes. "I wondered if you had an aunt. I've never heard you mention one, but I thought maybe she lived in China or something."

Jerry swallowed. "Yeah, I bet my mom didn't like you asking about that. What did she do?"

"She slammed her case shut and told me I needed to focus." Victoria grimaced at the thought of the previous exchange.

Jerry stood up. "I see. I'd better leave you to it, then." He tugged open the door.

"Wait, Jerry. You didn't answer my question. Who was the other woman in the picture?"

But the door had already clicked behind him.

Chapter 7

Saturday morning, Victoria set her violin down on her bed and stretched her fingers. After a grueling two-hour practice session on the Bach, she needed some fresh air. Outside, Louisa lay sprawled on the hammock in a green hooded sweatshirt, nose buried in a book— as usual.

"What are you reading?"

Louisa held up the novel. "*Little Women.*"

A smile spread across Victoria's face. "Haven't you read it before?"

"Yes, but it's my favorite."

Victoria laid down next to her sister. "If you had a choice, would you be a March sister from *Little Women* or a Bennet sister from *Pride and Prejudice?*"

The hammock swayed as Louisa popped to a sitting position. Victoria gripped the edges to keep from falling off.

"Well, Jo March has amazing literary ambition and doesn't care a bit about fashion." Louisa's voice quickened with excitement. "Elizabeth Bennet is witty, classy, and doesn't mind getting her feet dirty. She reads a lot and plays piano, like me." Louisa's forehead crinkled. "It's a tough decision. Who would you choose?"

Victoria stroked her sister's long brunette hair and stifled a laugh. Louisa took this so seriously. Not a typical fourteen-year-old, for sure. "Well, like both Jo and Elizabeth, I can't wait to experience adventure beyond this town. Think of Jo dashing around New York or Elizabeth at the Pemberley estate. How exhilarating!"

Louisa fell silent for a moment. "Yes, I guess they both leave their families behind."

"Isn't that the point?" Victoria raised her gaze. "They leave home to achieve new levels of accomplishment."

A frown spread across Louisa's face. "At least in Jo's case, I thought family helped her find success, not hinder it."

Victoria shrugged. "Maybe you're more like Jo and I'm like Elizabeth. You're an amazing writer. For my part, I can't wait to leave this place and experience something new. I just wish I could take you with me." She planted a kiss on Louisa's head.

She laid back on Victoria's chest, and a flowery scent wafted from her hair. "Thanks, Victoria. I'm going to miss you."

The familiar twinge cut through Victoria.

"I almost forgot." Louisa jumped up from the hammock. "Earlier Marie said she wanted to have a movie night. We'd better go inside."

"All right." Victoria's aching muscles protested leaving the comfort of the hammock, but Louisa had already sprinted halfway to the house.

"Maybe we can watch *Little Women.*"

"You're here." Stella jumped up from the living room floor where she was painting her nails. Her vibrant pink T-shirt matched her manicured fingers. "Now we can start the movie."

"I really should practice. I still need another couple of hours."

"Don't be a party pooper, Victoria," Stella retorted.

"Okay, I'll stay for a few minutes." Victoria settled into the plush navy couch facing the TV. "Which movie do you want to watch? Louisa plopped next to her. "I just told you. *Little Women.*"

"We've watched that about a hundred times." Adrienne's loud voice carried from the kitchen. A moment later, she emerged wearing an apron imprinted with French cafés and Eiffel Towers. Marie followed, strands of dirty blonde hair hanging from her ponytail. She carried a plate of chocolate chip cookies.

"If we want a sister flick, how about *Pride and Prejudice?*" Adrienne sprawled on the love seat. "I'm dying to see the new version."

Louisa scrunched her lips in protest. "Let's take a poll. We each have to decide if we'd rather be a March or a Bennet sister. Whichever family gets the most votes determines the movie."

"Ooh, I like it." Stella waved her bright pink fingernails back and forth like a fan.

"Victoria, since you're the oldest, why don't you start?" Marie said as she set the plate of cookies on the coffee table.

"Yeah, Victoria," Adrienne said. "You're lucky to choose between the two most beautiful sisters—the lovely Meg March or the demure Jane Bennet."

Victoria scratched the back of her head. "I didn't realize we had to pick our corresponding birth order sister. I would have picked Elizabeth Bennet." She glared at Adrienne. "Meg is sweet but not ambitious, as she just wants to get married and have babies. Not really my style, is it? But Jane travels to London to visit her aunt and uncle, so I think I'll choose her."

Victoria had always dreamed of exploring London. Maybe she'd have a chance to visit during graduate school. She visualized herself hopping on a double-decker bus to see Big Ben and the Houses of Parliament, strolling along the River Thames…

"Good choice," Stella said. "Besides, Jane ends up with fun, rich Mr. Bingley, but Meg marries that poor, boring Mr. Brooke." She stuck out her tongue. "But Mr. Bingley is much more exciting, with all his fancy balls." She raised her arms and twirled a pirouette, then sank onto the love seat next to Adrienne.

Marie laughed as she fixed the stray pieces of hair back into her ponytail. "All right. One vote for *Pride and Prejudice.*" She hurried to the kitchen and returned with the bag of leftover chocolate chips. As she sat on the floor she tossed one chip on the table as a counter for the votes.

"I'm next." Adrienne grabbed a cookie. "It's tough to choose between Jo March and Elizabeth Bennet—"

Victoria rolled her eyes. "That's because they're both main characters. Lucky second-born sisters."

"Jo's a writer, which I'm not," Adrienne continued, "and she has no sense of fashion." Her eyes darted to the French apron she had yet to remove, then looked up again. "But Elizabeth marries Mr. Darcy, my favorite romantic character, so I choose her."

Stella's blue eyes sparkled. "Adrienne, if you're Elizabeth, who's Mr. Darcy?"

Adrienne laughed. "I would imagine a tall, dark, handsome European."

"Aw, come on," Marie groaned. "Pick someone we know."

"Oh all right." Adrienne straightened her shoulders. "Let's see. I'll have to choose someone attractive, serious, and accomplished."

An image of Jerry in his handsome tux came to Victoria's mind. Why couldn't she stop thinking about him? She was being ridiculous.

"I guess I'd have to say Jerry."

"What?" Victoria exclaimed, leaping from the couch. The blood rushed to her face, and a fainting sensation made her sit back down.

Adrienne frowned. "You don't think he's attractive or accomplished?"

"I do, but—"

"Then what's the problem?" Adrienne raised her eyebrows.

Stella jumped up and down, a flurry of pink. "Victoria's jealous that you get to marry Jerry."

Victoria chucked a pillow at Stella. "That's not it," Victoria lied. "I don't think Jerry seems very British." It was a lame excuse, confirmed by Marie's pointed look.

"That's two for *Pride and Prejudice*." Marie tallied another chocolate chip on the table. "Louisa, how about you?"

"Jo March."

Adrienne frowned as she set down her half-eaten cookie. "Louisa, you can't be Jo. You have to choose between the younger ones, Beth and Kitty. How about Beth? She's sweet, shy, and plays piano, like you."

Louisa's face fell. "But Beth dies. Is that how you see me? Sick and frail?"

"Of course we don't see you like that," Victoria patted her back.

"Besides, you shouldn't be Beth—she's the third sister," Marie said. "That's my spot."

"But I don't want you to die either." Louisa's green eyes darkened.

"I'll take my chances. My other choice is Mary Bennet." Marie grimaced. "She's such a prude that, let's face it, I'm better off as Beth."

Louisa laughed. "Okay. But who should I be?"

"You can be Jo." Victoria said pointedly. "No one cares about the birth order. *Miss Elizabeth Bennet* didn't pick her anyway." Adrienne's nose raised a few inches.

Eyes darting between Victoria and Adrienne, Marie pulled out two more chocolate chips and placed them on the opposite side of the table. "We're tied—two for *Pride and Prejudice* and two for *Little Women*."

"What are we voting on?" Mom asked as she entered the room.

"Which sister story we like better: *Pride and Prejudice* or *Little Women*," Marie said. "Which mom would you choose, Marmee or Mrs. Bennet?"

"You're definitely Marmee." Louisa reached for Mom's hand.

"Yeah, Mrs. Bennet is a nut job," Marie laughed.

"What about me?" Dad appeared in his medical scrubs. "Who would I be?"

"Mr. March or Mr. Bennet?" Louisa asked.

"I have no idea who they are." Dad chuckled. "You're the bookworm, Louisa. Which one do you like better?"

"Mr. March is absent most of the time, whereas Mr. Bennet is witty." Louisa scratched her head. "I guess I'd have to pick Mr. Bennet for his humor."

"Great. We're still tied." Marie snatched the other half of Adrienne's cookie. "Stella, who do you pick? Lydia Bennet or Amy March?"

Stella laughed, a light, tinkling laugh. "Do you have to ask? Lydia is so scandalous, running off with that scumbag Mr. Wickham. Amy March is fashionable and moves to Paris where she marries heartthrob Laurie. It's so romantic." She batted her eyelashes.

"Hmmm, maybe I should have been Amy," Adrienne mused. "She's an artist and speaks French, like me."

"You can't change your mind," Victoria said. Her sister had some nerve. "Besides, you're the one so hung up on the stupid birth order."

Adrienne folded her arms across her chest.

"Who would be Laurie?" Louisa looked at Stella.

"Isn't it obvious?" Marie exclaimed. "Eddie."

Louisa nodded. "Yeah, he's like our brother."

"Ugh." Stella scrunched her nose. "There's no way I'm marrying Eddie someday. He's such a nerd."

Marie jumped to her feet. "What's wrong with that? I'm glad he's smart."

"Then you marry him," Stella said.

"You forgot, I'm the one who *dies*." Marie swooned onto the couch on top of Victoria and Louisa.

"Get off." Louisa giggled as she pushed Marie to the floor.

After clambering back to her feet, Marie tossed out another couple of chocolate chips. "It looks like we have a winner—*Little Women*."

Louisa beamed. Adrienne scowled.

"I'll make popcorn." Victoria stood up and stretched her legs before heading to the kitchen, where she tossed the popcorn bag into the microwave.

A few seconds later, Marie joined her. "So, Jerry's Mr. Darcy, huh?"

"No, he's not." Victoria wished she could steady her racing heart.

"Really?" Marie turned on the oven and pulled a pizza out of the freezer. "I'm not stupid. I saw how you blushed when Adrienne mentioned him. You're jealous."

"I am not. I don't want her clinging to him all the time, that's all. Can't she choose the new Texan guitar player, Matt whatever-his-name-is?"

Marie laughed as she grabbed the popcorn bag out of the microwave. "Just keep telling yourself that." She dumped the mounds of fluffy kernels into a bowl and pulled butter and cheese from the fridge.

Victoria frowned. "What are you doing?"

"Spicing things up a bit." Marie dropped the ingredients into another container, then grabbed garlic salt and another seasoning shaker from the cabinet. "It's Italian popcorn."

"What's that?" Victoria wrinkled her nose.

"I promise it's good. Sometimes you have to try an old standby with a new twist to really appreciate it."

She zapped the mixture in the microwave for a few seconds, before dribbling the yellow substance over the popcorn. "Taste it."

"Here goes nothing." Victoria dipped her hand into the messy mixture, then raised a couple bites to her mouth. A blend of the familiar popcorn taste and exotic seasonings danced on her tongue.

"Good, right?" Marie popped a handful into her mouth, and placed the pizza in the oven.

Victoria grinned. "Delicious."

"You have to try it, before someone else snatches it up." Marie scooped up the bowl. "And I'm not just talking about the popcorn."

Chapter 8

Jerry jolted to attention as Mr. Vatchev rapped his baton on the music stand. "Silence." The chatter and racket from the orchestra abated. "The Fall Concert is in a couple of weeks, on Halloween, so it's imperative we take maximum advantage of every rehearsal." His gaze swept the concert stage like a hawk in search of prey. He turned to Victoria. "Where's Adrienne?"

Victoria shrugged. "I don't know."

"Coming." Adrienne's voice squeaked from the rear of the stage. Her hair stuck up in every direction. She wore sweats and no makeup. Poor girl. Probably overslept. Jerry gave her an encouraging smile as she clambered around several violists to reach the vacant seat at the stand adjacent to his.

The conductor's eyes shot daggers in her direction, then examined the score in front of him. "Today we turn our attention to the last two movements of Berlioz' 1830 *Symphonie Fantastique*—'March to the Scaffold' and 'Dream of a Witches' Sabbath.'" A pregnant pause ensued as Adrienne fumbled to remove her viola from its case. Mr. Vatchev cleared his throat. "Like Vivaldi's *Four Seasons* a century before, Berlioz championed program music, the fusion of sound and story."

One of the clarinetists raised her hand.

"Yes?" Impatience rose in the conductor's voice.

The clarinetist perched herself on the edge of her seat, instrument in her lap. "In preparation for my solo in the third and fourth movements, I researched the life of Berlioz."

"Overachiever," Adrienne whispered to Jerry.

He rolled his eyes.

The girl straightened her shoulders and continued. "Is it true Berlioz composed the work while on drugs?"

Franklin, seated next to Victoria, laughed so hard his instrument almost slipped to the floor. Jerry groaned.

The maestro waved the girl off with his free hand. "Allegedly so. In this epic adventure of love and loss, an artist becomes obsessed with a woman he considers the feminine ideal. After taking a powerful drug, he dreams that he murders her in a fit of jealous rage."

One of the flutists clutched her instrument so tightly her fingers turned white. "It sounds like a Shakespearean play."

"Yes." Mr. Vatchev nodded. "Berlioz's affinity for Shakespeare inspired many of his compositions. In 'March to the Scaffold,' the artist is condemned to death for his crime. He approaches the guillotine and then—" The conductor raised his baton above his head, then sliced the air like a blade.

Gasps rippled across the orchestra.

Franklin's eyes gleamed red with insatiable interest. "He gets his head chopped off?"

"Yes." Mr. Vatchev's slender fingers stroked the baton like Voldemort with his wand. "If you listen to the chords at the end, you can hear the blade fall."

Jerry gagged.

Raising two fingers to his mouth, Franklin pretended to take a drag off a cigarette. "Yeah. Sounds like Berlioz was high on something."

Franklin would know all about that. The sickly stench of pot hung on him like a cloak.

The conductor nodded. "He probably took opium, a drug known to cause hallucinations."

A diabolic smile spread across Franklin's face. "Cool."

The muscles in Jerry's stomach tightened. Why did musicians find such a fascination with drugs? Maybe they were trying to compensate for something broken deep inside. Or maybe the pressure of performing drove them to it? He winced. Could Victoria handle the pressure of Johann Conservatory? Or would it break her, like it did so many composers? And Aunt Margaret. A lump formed at the back of his throat. He had to protect Victoria from that fate. If he ever *did* ask her out, could he convince her to stay?

###

After a run-through of the two movements, Victoria's arms ached with fatigue. The conductor closed the score. "That's enough for today. At our next rehearsal, we'll focus on Vivaldi's 'Autumn,' with soloist Professor Chang, and Saint-Saëns' 'Danse Macabre.'"

Yet more confirmation of the maestro's morbid obsession. She caught sight of Jerry and rolled her eyes. He grinned in return.

Mr. Vatchev picked up a pile of papers off the podium. "Don't forget, the Fall Concert is your last chance to sign up for the concerto competition." He handed a flyer to Victoria with the words "Belton Concerto Competition" printed in bold. Franklin snatched one and stuffed it in his folder.

Like a wand in the hand of a wizard ready to cast a spell, the maestro's baton pointed straight at her. "Victoria, please prepare the solo part of the Saint-Saëns for our next class. You'll need to acclimate yourself to its unusual tuning."

Her breath caught in her throat. What unusual tuning? "I, uh, assumed Professor Chang would play the solo."

Mr. Vatchev shook his head. "Not on this piece. She'll be backstage preparing for 'Autumn.' This one is your responsibility."

Victoria's heartbeat quickened with excitement. "Yes, sir."

"Good. I'll see you next week." The conductor descended the podium and strode off stage.

"Yeah, Victoria," Franklin said, voice dripping with disdain. "I'll sit as concertmaster for this one. We wouldn't want anything to … interfere with your solo." He tightened his grip on the bow clutched in his hand. "One wrong note and your chance to win the concerto competition will be—" He snapped his fingers. "I've been practicing my concerto for months. What about you?"

"I…" Victoria lowered her eyes.

"That's what I thought." His harsh laugh pierced the air. "You haven't even started. Been too busy babysitting your giant family?"

"Lay off it, Franklin." Jerry stood behind Victoria, his bow inches from Franklin's chest. How long had he been there? "She's been practicing all summer. More than I can say for you." His eyes scanned Franklin's gaunt face. "You were stoned for at least half of it."

Franklin met Jerry's gaze, his features hard, bloodshot eyes flashing. "You wouldn't know anything about it. Don't want to get in trouble with Mommy, do you?"

Jerry raised a clenched fist, but Victoria grabbed his wrist.

"Just back off, Franklin," Jerry said through gritted teeth.

Franklin pushed Jerry away. "All right. But we'll see who's the best player this spring at the audition. Victoria can't stay on top forever." He laughed a cold, cruel laugh.

Victoria stood on the front porch and inserted her key into the lock. Why did she allow Franklin to get under her skin? He was all bluff—jealous she'd beat him out for concertmaster. But why was he so competitive? To compensate for something else?

As she opened the front door, the halting sounds of an incompetent piano student accosted her ears. This was the last thing she wanted to hear right now. The kid clearly hadn't practiced. How infuriating. Victoria stepped inside and set down her case with a thud.

After the piano music stopped, Mom's heels clicked into the entryway. "Good work today. Try to get in a few more practice sessions this week." A little girl and her mother waved as they opened the door. "See you next week," Mom said before the door clicked shut behind them.

She turned to Victoria. "How was your day, sweetheart?"

"Fine."

"That bad?" Mom frowned. "Do you want to talk about it? I can brew tea. I found a new flavor the other day—a chocolate caramel infusion."

Victoria's mouth watered. "Sounds delicious."

Once they entered the kitchen, Mom pulled a round black canister and two mugs from the cupboard, one with the words "World's Best Mom" imprinted on it and the other "I Love Music."

Mom scooped a few of the leaves into a tea ball. "Did you rehearse the Berlioz? I love the *Symphonie Fantastique.*"

"You do?" Victoria arched an eyebrow. "It's a far stretch from your light Italian art songs. Gruesome, if you ask me."

Mom laughed. "You forget that I was an opera singer before I became a mother. I wouldn't call Wagnerian operas 'light.'" She ran her hand through her golden hair. "You're right. I do prefer the joyful nature of Mozart. However, the dance scene in Berlioz's second movement reminds me of heaven with the two harps." She strummed the air with her fingers.

"It all goes to pot from there. Literally. Berlioz was on opium when he wrote it, so his main character's high for half the work."

Mom sighed as she placed the mugs in the microwave. "Yes, it breaks my heart that so many musicians fall into that path."

"I don't understand." Victoria leaned on the marble countertop. "What drives them to it?"

After a moment's hesitation, Mom spoke. "I can't say for any particular individual, but the pressure of performing weighs on some people. The desire for perfection, the obligation to put on a good show, the need to recreate the same dramatic intensity night after night—all of these factors affect a person's well-being." When the microwave beeped, Mom retrieved the drinks.

"How did you do it?"

Mom dropped the tea ball into the "I Love music" mug and handed it to Victoria. "By the grace of God."

Victoria raised her lips to the steaming liquid as Mom continued. "I prayed God would give me the strength to fulfill His plan for my life."

"And He did?" Warmth flooded Victoria's body as the chocolate-caramel goodness trickled down her throat.

"Yes. He walked with me every step of the way. Even when surrounded by people held captive by drugs, I prayed I could shed a glimmer of light into their dark world." She pulled the tea ball from Victoria's mug and plopped it into her own.

How could her mother have such sympathy toward her fellow musicians, the Franklin Curtises of the world? Victoria's insides churned. Would she possess the strength to carry her through the strenuous life of a conservatory musician? What if she, too, crumpled under the immense pressure of it all?

Her mother took Victoria's free hand in hers. "Victoria." Her voice rang in Victoria's ears like church bells. "You're a musician for a reason. You have the talent and the passion for it. But those aren't enough." Her steady gaze held Victoria's. "You'll never reach artistic perfection." She took a sip of the tea. "The good news is you don't have to."

Chapter 9

Halloween night, the rehearsal room buzzed with a cacophony of sound as the musicians warmed up. Trombones wailed. Drums pounded. Oboes cried.

Jerry took a deep breath then exhaled. Would Victoria listen to him today? His hands trembled as he rubbed rosin on his bow. Like a gymnast in preparation for a bar exercise, he needed to ensure a proper grip. He ran the strands of white horsehair over the rosin a couple more times for good measure.

"Hi, Jerry." Victoria's unmistakable voice spoke behind him. He swiveled to face her. She looked gorgeous in her black dress.

"Are you ready for your big solo?"

"I think so."

As he placed his hand on her shoulder, a tingle radiated down his arm to the tips of his fingers. "You'll be fantastic."

She knelt to remove her violin from its case. "But Mr. Vatchev was right. The tuning for the Saint-Saëns solo throws me off."

"I thought you sounded splendid yesterday at rehearsal."

She smiled. That smile got him every time. "Thanks, Jerry."

He fidgeted with a cufflink on his black tux. "Victoria, I wondered…" He paused.

"Yes?"

"Do you—"

"Please take your places on stage." Mr. Vatchev's deep, baritone voice boomed from the back of the room. He motioned several brass players toward the door. Surrounded by the musicians' black attire, the conductor's khaki pants and white polo shirt stood out like a tuba in a wind ensemble. Why wasn't he dressed in his usual coat and tails?

"Quickly." The maestro waved his arms in an emphatic manner. "It's imperative we rehearse 'Autumn' with Professor Chang and run a few of the difficult passages in the *Symphonie Fantastique* before the concert."

Why did his mother always get in the way? Jerry tugged at his collar to loosen the bow tie. "I guess we'd better go."

"Yeah, I suppose."

Did he detect a hint of regret in her voice?

When Victoria and Jerry reached the stage, he gasped. An elaborate display of pumpkins in all shapes and sizes adorned the front— orange, white, and even an occasional blue. Autumn foliage dangled from the ceiling as if falling from trees. The scent of pumpkin spice radiated from a couple of diffusers at both ends of the stage. A scarecrow smiled at him next to the double basses.

"Impressive, isn't it?" Victoria whispered so close her breath warmed his cheek.

He nodded, unable to speak.

"Break it up." Franklin pushed between them, violin in hand. "Don't you know we have a concert today?"

Jerry glared at him and then meandered to his chair next to the platform where the maestro stood.

A couple of minutes later, his mother's resplendent gold dress swept the floor as she promenaded onto the stage. A comb of jeweled leaves adorned her hair as if to personify the season. Whatever her faults, she possessed incredible stage presence.

Images of Vivaldi's merry shepherds leapt through Jerry's mind as his Mom's bow danced on the strings. Why had she discouraged him from auditioning for the concerto competition? Perhaps he should anyway.

Who else might compete? Of course the phenomenal clarinetist who played the solo in the Berlioz. And the first chair trumpet might give him a run for his money. Adrienne would be formidable competition if she signed up. Perhaps his technique and practice habits surpassed hers, but, to borrow one of Adrienne's French phrases, she possessed a certain *je ne sais quoi* with her viola that charmed people. The worst thing would be competing against Victoria. The violin goddess might strike him down on the spot. But he didn't need to win. He just wanted the experience of performing a big solo one last time.

###

"Take fifteen." Mr. Vatchev wiped his brow at the end of rehearsal while Victoria scribbled a couple of dynamics into her score. "The concert begins in twenty minutes. Please make sure you're in your seats on time." He shuffled the scores on the music stand. "And don't forget, tonight is your last chance to sign up for the concerto competition." He held up the flyer. "I'll leave the sheet backstage for you."

With everything on her mind, between her solo and the previous encounter with Jerry, Victoria had almost forgotten the competition.

She placed Saint-Saëns' *"Danse Macabre"* at the front of the folder, assembled the rest of the music in the proper order, then rose to leave. Several music professors had already arrived in costume. The flute teacher wore a sleek black jumpsuit with cat ears and a tail. She chatted with the trumpet instructor dressed as a superhero, complete with muscle bodysuit.

Jerry nudged Victoria. "Check out my cello professor's costume."

Victoria squinted. "Where is he?"

"Over there." Jerry pointed to a man who looked like Beethoven. The bushy hair on his wig shot out in all directions.

"Perfect." Victoria laughed. "But I need to hurry. I've got to sign up for the concerto competition."

Backstage, a long line had formed next to the table with the flyer. Oh no. Were all these students signing up for the competition? A glance at the clock reminded her that only a few minutes remained. As concertmaster, she'd have a couple of extra moments backstage before her grand entrance. She wiped her sweaty palms on her dress. The Saint-Saëns solo was such a tricky part to play.

She reached the front of the line, set her violin on the table, and scrawled her name on the list. When she turned around, she found herself face-to-face with Adrienne. Victoria frowned. "What are you doing?"

Adrienne stared at her, a blank expression on her face. "Same as you, signing up for the concerto competition."

"But, but…" Victoria stammered. "I had no idea you were competing. You're not a senior. You can't even go to graduate school yet."

"It doesn't say you have to be a senior. I'm sure they'd let me defer the scholarship to the following year."

Victoria's mind whirred. Why did Adrienne have the audacity to compete against her? Her sister could compete next year. This was Victoria's senior year. She needed that scholarship money in order to move to New York.

The blood rushed to her face as anger bubbled up inside her. Adrienne always stole the limelight. Victoria needed a minute to process, to calm down. The musicians had already filed onstage, and the concert lights dimmed.

She snatched her violin from the table and stepped onstage. Her mind clouded as though filled with smoke. She couldn't breathe and could barely see due to the bright lights. Her foot hit something hard, which caused her to stumble. She clutched her violin in a vice-like grip. A pumpkin fell off the edge and crashed to the floor. What in the world? Smoke billowed on stage. She hadn't imagined it. Maybe the concert hall was on fire!

Her heart raced as she peered through the smoke at the smashed pumpkin which lay next to a black box. A fog machine. Who'd come up with such an infernal idea for a classical concert?

After a shaky bow, she pointed to the oboist for the tuning note. Victoria played her open A string and the other musicians followed suit. Time for the grand surprise. After everyone else had finished, instead of tuning her highest string to an E, she would lower it to an E ♭ . But when she reached for the peg, the string was already completely slack. What had made it slip? Unnerved, she cranked it into place.

Smoke continued to fill the room as Victoria took her seat. An eerie red spotlight appeared on the left side of the stage to reveal a man dressed as Voldemort. The audience gasped, then erupted into applause for the maestro. He strode to the podium, black cape billowing behind him, baton at the ready. After his bow, he extended his hand to Victoria. Startled by his changed appearance, she leaned back in her seat.

"Shake his hand, Vicki," Franklin whispered at her side. "Or are you scared?"

Something inside her snapped. She gripped Mr. Vatchev's hand with all her might, then raised her violin to her shoulder. The shiny varnish reflected the red glow of the spotlight, blinding her eyes. She couldn't think straight. Rage at Franklin washed over her like a flood. Get it together. Time to play the opening tri-tone, the dissonant interval the medievalists labeled "the devil's interval." Her bow struck the upper two strings, and the ear-piercing sound rent the air. She drew her bow for the subsequent chord and let it drop to the strings. A loud pop erupted from her violin as icy, cold steel slashed her face.

Victoria froze. Her cheek burned where the string had struck it. The awkward silence in the concert hall was unbearable. What should she do?

The conductor glared at her through his vampire-like eyes. She glanced at her violin. Sure enough, the E string had snapped in two. Had the force of her stroke caused the break? No time to worry about that now. Think fast.

Franklin leered at her, clearly enjoying her predicament.

One viable option lay before her. She'd seen it once before at a concert when the soloist had faced a similar situation. The corners of her mouth turned upward into a sly smile as she held out her violin to Franklin. "The show must go on," she mouthed to him.

As hoped, Franklin's smirk faded into a look of confusion, his brows furrowed.

"What?" he whispered.

"Lend me your instrument," she mouthed back.

He shook his head. "No."

She flashed her smile again and dipped her head toward the waiting audience. "It's protocol."

His eyes darted to the maestro, who nodded. With a sigh, Franklin traded instruments.

She took a deep breath, tuned the E string to an E♭, and began again.

Chapter 10

"Excellent job." A student carrying a large tuba clapped Victoria on the shoulder. "You pulled that off with a bang." He guffawed as he joined the other brass players backstage.

"Yes, snapping good performance," Franklin said as he sauntered down the hall.

"Lay off her, will you?" Jerry glared at the bassist, then glanced at Victoria. She looked like she might curl up in a ball and hide in the bathroom. Jerry wanted to beat the tar out of Franklin. He'd watched the two of them switch their instruments back after the Saint-Saëns. Thank goodness another violinist had lent her an extra E string to finish the concert.

Jerry reached for her arm. "Want to grab a drink at Café Chocolat?"

"Yes, please. Anything to get out of here."

"I figured. That's why I got this for you." He extended her case to her.

She set it on the table and tucked away her violin. She pulled out the fragments of broken string that protruded from her orchestra folder.

"What do you think would have caused it to break?" She fingered the pieces of string. "I changed the whole set a couple of months ago, just before the start of term. The E should've lasted longer."

Jerry reached for the wiry fragments and examined them for a few seconds. "From the looks of these, the string had already begun to unravel." He handed them back. "How much have you practiced over the past couple of months?"

She shrugged. "A normal amount."

He raised his eyebrows.

"Okay, a lot, but still…"

A streak of blood was smeared on her cheek where the string had slashed it. He brushed her skin, rubbing it away.

"There, all better." He smiled. "I think that's the last of the blood."

She flinched. "What blood?"

"The caked blood where the string hit you."

"Oh, how mortifying. I must look awful." She reached for his shoulder to steady herself. "Let's leave before I'm obligated to talk to anyone else."

"All right." He put his arm around her waist and ushered her to the door.

As the pair stepped inside the café, a strong waft of pumpkin and coffee greeted Jerry's nose. People in costume filled every inch of the place. A swarm of sorority girls in yellow tutus and black leotards hoisted a girl in a tiara and a sash that read "Queen Beta Bee."

Another group of girls in short-skirted white nursing gowns flirted with several boys dressed in medical scrubs.

"Why is that guy wearing a white cardboard scale with '<21' printed on it?" Victoria gestured at the awkward student who'd struggled to walk through the door in his boxy costume.

"Don't you recognize him?" Jerry asked. "He's a freshman trombone player."

Victoria squinted. "What's he supposed to be?"

"A minor scale." Jerry laughed. "Good one."

Victoria chuckled as she stepped up to the counter where Marie, a cowgirl hat cocked askew over her ponytail, poured drinks.

"Howdy, partner." Jerry grinned. "What's with the hat?"

Marie rolled her eyes. "The boss insisted we dress up."

"Where's the rest of your costume?" Victoria eyed Marie's T-shirt, jeans, and sneakers.

"It was either the hat or these cat ears." Marie held up a headband with two furry triangles, which she settled on Victoria's head.

"Meeeooowww." Jerry said.

She punched him playfully on the shoulder. "Where's your costume, Jerry?"

"I don't do costumes—only tuxedos." He straightened his bow tie. "But you look purrrfect. Just no cat fights, all right? I don't want to clean more blood off you tonight."

"What?" Marie leaned forward on the counter.

Victoria shuffled her feet. "My string broke in the middle of—"

"Bonjour."

Jerry turned at the sound of the familiar voice.

Adrienne struck a pose, hand on hip, faux pearls draped over her black concert dress. A cloche hat hugged her temples, and black Mary Jane heels adorned her feet.

Jerry laughed. "Who are you supposed to be?"

"*Je suis Coco Chanel.* Can't you tell?" Adrienne twirled, the little black dress clinging to her hips.

Victoria shrugged. "I see nothing out of the ordinary."

Jerry chuckled as he removed his tux jacket.

"Do you want a pumpkin spice laté, *Mam'selle Coco*?" Marie tipped her cowgirl hat.

Adrienne shook her head. "No, I'll take a double shot of espresso and a croissant."

Victoria scrunched up her nose. "That'll keep you up half the night. Too much caffeine. I'd like a caramel apple cider."

"And for you, Jerry?" Marie asked as she poured Adrienne's double shot.

"Plain coffee's fine." He leaned on his cello case as he examined the desserts. "And a slice of pumpkin bread."

"Good choice." Marie smiled. "I made it earlier today. It's to die for."

Victoria pointed to an empty table next to a couple of guys, one dressed as a train and the other as an elephant with giant ears. "What in the world?"

"Let me guess." Jerry stroked his chin. "Engineers."

"That's hilarious." Adrienne laughed. "Eddie would love it."

After they settled into green vintage chairs, Victoria rounded on Adrienne. "When did you decide to sign up for the concerto competition?"

Adrienne's fingers traced the felt trim of her hat. "When Mr. Vatchev announced it in class. How amazing to perform a solo in front of hundreds of people!" Her eyes glazed over in a dreamy fashion. "Imagine gliding onstage in a fabulous gown, all eyes on you—the chance to play a solo with the orchestra."

"I'm not sure I'd go so far as to wear a sparkly gown," Jerry said as he unlatched his cufflinks.

Victoria giggled, then turned to her sister. "Do you already have a song in mind, Adrienne?"

"Yes." She twirled her string of faux pearls. "Berlioz's *Harolde en Italie*."

Victoria scratched her head. "Never heard of it." She looked sexy in those black cat ears.

"I *loved* Berlioz's *Symphonie Fantastique*." Adrienne's eyes twinkled with excitement. "So, I researched to see if he'd written anything for viola, and I found *Harolde en Italie*. Of course, I listened to the work right away, and it was perfect. It fits me like a glove. It's about the composer's journey through Italy. I can imagine myself traveling through Europe. What a wonderful adventure!"

Jerry took a deep breath. If Adrienne set her mind on something, she wouldn't give up without an argument. There might be a cat fight after all. He'd better not mention that he'd signed up, too.

The cowgirl hat caught his eye as Marie brought over a tray of steaming drinks.

"Victoria, what happened with your solo?" Marie passed Jerry his coffee.

"My E string broke."

Marie nearly tipped the drinks off the tray but leveled it just in time. "Your string broke during your solo? How dreadful."

Victoria scowled. "Yes. Let's continue to relive it, for good times."

"Do you know why it happened?" Adrienne held the tiny espresso cup to her lips. "Was the string old?"

Victoria sighed. "It looked worn."

"Why didn't you change your strings before the concert?" Adrienne bit into the flaky croissant. "I saw Franklin restring his backstage before we went on."

Victoria took another sip of the warm cider. "I changed mine a couple of months ago. They should've—wait, what did you say?" Her cup froze midair. "Franklin changed his strings? How? Where?"

Adrienne rubbed her chin, bangles clanking together on her wrist. "By the table with the signup sheet. I can't believe you didn't see him. He was standing right behind you."

Jerry's mind raced with the chronology of events. He'd talked to Victoria right before she'd signed up. She'd set her violin on the table. Franklin wouldn't have dared change her string literally behind her back, would he? His blood boiled at the thought. He wouldn't put it past him.

Adrienne glanced at the clock, then popped up. "I'd better go." She smoothed the folds in her dress. "My art class is throwing a costume party tonight. I've already missed half of it because of the concert, but I want to make an appearance." Her dress swished at her sides, and her heels clicked as she hurried away.

"Can you believe it?" Jerry pounded his coffee on the table. "I bet Franklin swapped your good string for an old one."

Marie took a sip of the cider. "Surely not. Why would he do that?"

Jerry pursed his lips. "Because he's pure evil."

"Or jealous," Marie muttered.

"Either way, he won't get away with it. He can't have the last say." Victoria drummed her fingers on the table. "Somehow, I will win that competition. I'll practice so much Franklin and Adrienne won't stand a chance."

Jerry took a sip of coffee. Definitely not the time to tell her. Cat claws would attack for sure.

Chapter 11

As Victoria creaked open the front door, a whirlwind of notes assaulted her ears. The minor key of the piano piece lent an ominous tone to the atmosphere, appropriate for the night. The level of difficulty surpassed that of a novice. Must be Mom. For some inexplicable reason, the music drew Victoria, as if calling her to join the musical frenzy.

Darkness encased the room like a curtain. A lamp in the corner and a candle next to the piano served as the sole sources of light.

Though the notes flitted like bats moments before, they faded into nothingness.

When Victoria reached the piano, she drew a quick intake of breath at the sight of the musician. "Louisa, I thought you were Mom."

"Mom and Dad went out tonight—some party with the other piano teachers." Louisa's green eyes flickered in the candlelight. Apple cinnamon emanated from the tiny wick.

"When did you learn to play like that?" Victoria searched for a score on the piano, but found none. "Last time I listened to you perform, you played 'Mary Had a Little Lamb' at Mom's student recital. Now you could pass for Mom." Victoria rested her hand on Louisa's shoulder. "What piece was that, anyway? Chopin?"

"Yes, his 'Valse in C# minor.'" Louisa lowered her gaze to the keys. "I like to practice when everyone's gone or on the keyboard with headphones in my room."

Victoria frowned. "Why don't you perform for people more often? You're fabulous."

Louisa rubbed her hands on her black leggings. "I guess I like to play for myself. Makes me nervous to perform for other people."

Victoria nodded. "I think it does for everyone." She sank onto the plush couch. "Except maybe Adrienne. She lives for the limelight. Did you know she's trying out for the concerto competition, too?"

"She never told me." Louisa slipped onto the couch next to her. "What're you gonna do?"

Victoria shrugged. "Figure out how to win."

"Have you picked a piece yet?" Louisa hugged a fuzzy decorative pillow to her chest.

"No." Victoria sighed through gritted teeth. "But Adrienne already has—a work by that quack-job composer Berlioz."

"So, pick a piece." Louisa stood up, moved to the nearby bookshelf, and scanned the folders. "Pedagogy, Arias, Sonatas. Here we go—concertos."

Victoria shook her head. "I bet they're for piano."

"Not all of them." As Louisa rummaged through the scores, she passed several to Victoria. "Beethoven, Tchaikovsky, Mozart. Mom has several for violin."

Victoria rifled through the pile. "Some of these are mine from high school, but not all. Why would Mom have old violin concertos?"

Louisa raised an old score whose cover hung by a thread. "From Gigi."

"How do you know?" Victoria looked up from the growing stack.

"Because this one has the last name scrawled across the top." Louisa pointed.

Victoria rubbed her chin. "I didn't know Gigi played violin."

"Maybe they're from when our aunts studied violin." Louisa handed her the last couple of scores.

"I'll take a look at them tomorrow." Victoria yawned as she added the music to the large pile. "Perhaps I'll find a good one to play for my lesson next week. Who knows what Professor Chang will say about it?"

Sweat dripped down Victoria's brow as her bow sawed over the strings in her teacher's studio. She'd spent the previous forty-five minutes of her lesson on the last two pages of the Bach "Chaconne." This piece would be the death of her.

After the last note faded away, Professor Chang walked to her desk, heels clacking. "Better."

Victoria glanced at her professor's open case, but she shut it with a snap. She probably didn't want her to ask about the picture again.

"Professor Chang?" Victoria's voice squeaked, mouselike even to her own ears.

"Yes?" The professor turned around. A charm on her necklace glistened in the light from the window—a silver half-moon engraved with two Chinese symbols.

Victoria squinted. If only she'd paid more attention when Jerry tried to teach her Chinese. She'd never been able to focus with him next to her. For a few moments, she'd even thought he was going to ask her out before the concert on Halloween. And the feeling of his arm around her waist as he'd escorted her from the building had made her cheeks burn. But she couldn't date him. Not with New York hanging in the balance. Time to concentrate on something else. Ah yes, the necklace. The first character looked like a fusion of the letter L and the number 7, and the second resembled a ladder with three rungs. What did those mean? Maybe she *could* ask Jerry.

"Well?" Professor Chang asked.

Victoria shuffled her feet. What were they talking about? Professor Chang pursed her lips like Adrienne when she spoke French. Finally, Victoria remembered. "I need more details about the concerto competition. Can the scholarship money be used for any music graduate school?"

"Yes."

"Including Johann Conservatory?"

"Yes."

A sense of relief flooded over Victoria. This could work. "What song should I choose?"

Her teacher's features remained motionless, as though she wore an impenetrable mask.

Okay. Victoria took a quick breath, tucked her violin under her chin, and decided to play Mozart's *Violin Concerto in D Major*, her favorite work from high school. The lightness of the piece lifted her spirits like a bird above the trees. What a refreshing change from the melancholy "Chaconne."

Over the past couple of days, she'd been amazed how fast she'd re-mastered the piece. Her fingers found their way around the violin as if on autopilot, in spite of the six-year gap since she'd last performed it.

Her breathing quickened as she approached the cadenza—the most difficult part of the concerto. A sting of pain shot through her pinky as it contorted to reach the triple stops.

In spite of a few cringe-worthy chords, she finished with a flourish and breathed a sigh of relief.

"Not bad, but no."

Victoria knit her brow. "What do you mean, 'no?'"

"Your performance was beautiful." Professor Chang walked to the music stand and examined the score. "But it won't win a concerto competition."

"Why not?"

"You need a different concerto."

Victoria bit her lip. "What's wrong with Mozart?"

"The Mozart concerto is light, organized—perfect."

"Exactly. So, what's the problem?"

"It lacks the emotional depth of the Romantic era. You need a concerto that will cut you to the core—a work that expresses your greatest desires and deepest regrets." She placed a hand over her heart, then gazed out the window, a far-off look in her eyes.

Victoria wiped the rosin dust from her strings. What a load of nonsense. Mozart's genius generated his well-structured works. No one could deny his brilliance. In contrast to his adherence to prescribed norms, the vulnerability of the Romantic-era compositions made Victoria's insides churn like a blender. Who would want to put their deepest desires and regrets on display for the whole audience to see? Not her. She glanced at her teacher. "Do you have a concerto in mind?"

Professor Chang turned away from the window as though forcing herself back from a reverie. "No, Victoria." Her eyes softened, and for a moment a trace of Jerry's kindness rang in her voice. "Only you can decide which work expresses your soul."

Victoria held her gaze for several moments. "Like the Tchaikovsky for you."

Professor Chang fingered the pendant on her necklace. "Yes."

Inside her room, Victoria tossed the assortment of concertos onto the red comforter.

Bach, Vivaldi, Mozart, Beethoven, Lalo, Mendelssohn, Sibelius, Brahms, Bruch, Barber. Several of them she'd already played. Maybe she should play one of those? She flopped on her four-poster bed. Why was this decision so hard? Pick a piece already.

Footsteps padded up the stairs, and the door burst open. Adrienne flew in and sprawled on the bed like a cat. "I'm exhausted. The Berlioz is killing me."

Victoria frowned. "I'm surprised you're practicing on a Saturday. Nothing better to do?"

"I'm done for now. I've already put in two hours." Adrienne sauntered to the dresser and rummaged in the middle drawer.

"Get out of my stuff!" Victoria jumped to her feet and sprinted to the dresser.

"I need to borrow one of your shirts." Adrienne examined a gray one but discarded it on the floor.

"Leave my shirts alone. Don't you have a bedazzled Eiffel Tower one in your own closet?"

Adrienne rolled her eyes as she tossed another shirt on the floor. "It's in the laundry, along with your 'I'm an ork dork' tee."

Victoria picked up the clothes and refolded them on the bed, running her hand over the fabric to smooth the wrinkles.

"Why do you have an enormous string in your drawer? This can't be for violin." Adrienne held up the circular wire—a cello string Jerry had given Victoria a few years ago. He'd twisted it into a bracelet and slipped it over her wrist. Her heart fluttered at the recollection.

"Where are you going tonight, Adrienne?" Victoria asked.

"Dinner with fellow art students." She grabbed a bottle of perfume and sprayed herself. "Then I'm meeting Jerry afterward."

"What?" Victoria's entire body went rigid, as though turned to marble. Adrienne couldn't be serious.

"He wanted to meet." Adrienne held up Victoria's favorite black shirt—a lacey V-neck with billowy sleeves.

"Like a date?" Victoria's head was spinning now. She clutched her bed frame.

"I don't know." Adrienne examined herself in the mirror, then pulled red lipstick from her pocket and traced the curve of her lips.

"But … you can't." Victoria stammered. Her heart raced like the end of a symphony. Not Jerry.

Adrienne spun around. "Why can't I? He's my friend as much as yours."

Victoria glared. "Because he's *my* Jerry."

Adrienne's ski-jump nose shot in the air. "You don't own Jerry. You're not even dating."

Resist the urge to punch her. "I don't think you're his type."

"And you are?" She arched her eyebrows. "What if he's decided Miss 'bossy, uptight, I'm-moving-to-New York-and-leaving-you-all' isn't his type?"

Victoria lunged at her, but Adrienne darted out of the way. Anger washed over her like a tidal wave. "Why do you take everything I care about? Jerry, the concerto competition—"

"You can't monopolize the concerto competition." Adrienne planted a manicured hand on her hip. "I want to compete, and you can't stop me."

Victoria grabbed a pillow off the bed and threw it at her. "Get out of my room! And don't ever come in here again."

"Fine. You didn't have anything attractive for a date anyway." She stormed out of the room, and Victoria slammed the door.

Chapter 12

Victoria sank onto her bed. If only the covers would swallow her. How could Jerry do this? She wasn't surprised if Adrienne stabbed her in the back, but Jerry—the steady, levelheaded one in their trio? Surely he hadn't fallen for Adrienne. But he'd asked her out.

As Victoria ran her hand along the comforter, a coiled wire brushed against her palm—Jerry's cello string. Not a fancy gift, but one she treasured. A tear slid down her cheek as she slipped it over her wrist. He'd given it to her after the last high school orchestra concert her senior year—a day she'd never forget.

That moment replayed in her mind. At the end of the concert, he'd pulled her aside backstage. "You know we'll still be friends after you graduate, don't you?" He'd bent over, unwound his A string, and slipped it over her wrist. Then he'd kissed her on the cheek. "Don't worry, no strings attached." He'd winked as he gestured at his cello. Always one for humor.

Shake it off. Time to focus. She was moving to New York. Jerry could go out with whomever he wanted. Except Adrienne.

The sound of beginner piano music blasted upstairs. Victoria cringed. Why did Stella have to practice now? She'd never be able to concentrate. Not here. She needed something to take her mind off Adrienne and Jerry. A good swim at the student rec center might do the trick. She'd practice at the music school afterward.

Yes, that would be best. After a deep breath, she gathered up her music, instrument, swimsuit, and gym bag. When she reached for the doorknob, the string bracelet gleamed in the light. She sighed and tucked it away in her dresser drawer.

As Victoria entered the rec center, she swiped her ID card. Few music students set foot here—not usually the athletic types. For her, swimming was a life source—a way to rejuvenate.

In the locker room, she slipped on her swimsuit and stuffed her clothes into the gym bag. She crammed it in the locker along with her violin.

Several noisy students congregated in the hot tub. Steam rose from the water. A couple of bleached blondes in string bikinis snuggled next to shirtless frat boys with six packs.

The lap pool, however, was empty. Victoria dove in. The cool water hit her face, and goose bumps pricked her body. She stretched her arms in front of her, palms cupped, and moved them in a wide, circular motion for the front crawl.

As she kicked her legs, she drew strength from the powerful force. For several moments, nothing mattered but the swim stroke. The water washed away all other thoughts. An athlete who worked to keep her muscles strong for her craft, the endurance required for three-hour orchestra rehearsals made a swim feel like a breeze.

After a half hour, she paused to catch her breath. A lanky guy— eyes bloodshot—in Hawaiian swim trunks sauntered in, surrounded by several others. Franklin.

"Look who it is, little Vicki Pearson," he hollered.

She groaned.

"What're you doing here?" he asked as he tugged off his tee. "Surprised you don't have to babysit your little sisters tonight." He laughed, and the others joined him.

"Leave me alone, Franklin. I'm busy." She turned back to the lane in front of her.

"Ready for auditions Monday? I've practiced the passages all week."

Victoria's breath caught in her throat. With the Fall Concert, graduate school audition material, and now the concerto competition, she'd forgotten about orchestra auditions. What if she lost her position as concertmaster? Victoria tilted her head from side to side in an attempt to pull herself together.

"Almost." She swam to the ladder and hoisted herself out. "I'm headed to the music school now to practice."

"You don't want to join us?" Franklin pointed to the hot tub.

"No." She grabbed her towel and rubbed herself dry. "I have work to do."

"Party pooper."

She rolled her eyes.

"Did you know Monday is a blind audition? The faculty will put up a screen so the judges won't recognize us while we play. It will all come down to skill. Hope you're ready." He sneered, then crawled into the hot tub with his buddies.

###

Victoria winced at the page covered in inky black notes. She should have looked at these orchestra passages sooner. Auditions were bad enough, but a blind one? What if she bombed and the judges moved her to last chair? She played better with an audience present, but what about behind a screen? Would it be similar to these awful, white walls in the practice room? It was like practicing in a jail cell.

She played the page one note at a time. So many irregularities, with sharps and flats written all over the place. Half of the notes were positioned on ledger lines high above the staff. She squinted to make them out.

After the initial run-through, she turned on her metronome to keep the beat. Time to speed it up.

The obnoxious click of the device pounded in her brain like the incessant beep of a dying smoke detector—enough to drive anyone crazy.

In the middle of her sixth repetition, a blast of noise erupted from the next room.

She resumed the music, but her fingers fumbled to regain their previous pace.

The shriek of an electric guitar sliced the air. She covered her ears with her hands. This is a classical music school, not a rock concert venue.

Victoria exited and stomped to the adjacent room—the last one at the end of the long hallway. With a shove the door opened, and a blast of drums and electric guitar filled her ears.

"What's going on? I—" Victoria stared at the ensemble in front of her.

Several musicians filled the spacious room. A guitarist with shaggy blond hair wailed into a microphone. Behind him, the top of a guy's head bounced to the beat of drums.

And beside him stood Jerry. On bass guitar.

Victoria's jaw dropped open. What was he doing here? Wasn't he out with Adrienne?

She looked at the person next to Jerry, but the music stand blocked her view.

The band stopped as they all looked at her.

"Hey, Victoria, isn't it?" The guitarist stepped toward her, hand extended. "I'm Matt."

Victoria frowned. "Matt who?"

"Matt Deiter. From the coffee shop." He swept a stray wisp of sandy blond hair from his eyes. "Your buddies are awesome musicians."

"What?"

"Yeah, Jerry's a killer bass guitar player. Eddie can whack a drum better than anyone I know. And Adrienne"—he gestured at the music stand—"is quite the fiddler."

Victoria's mind was about to explode. Eddie Carter, the engineer, had set foot in the music building? And Jerry, classical cellist Jerry, played bass guitar? And Adrienne on fiddle?

"Not *fiddle*. Viola." Adrienne stepped away from the music stand and looked at Victoria, daggers shooting from her hazel eyes. "What're you doing here?"

Victoria's tongue unfroze. "I was about to ask you the same question."

"I'm jammin' with the guys." Adrienne ran a hand through her hair. "Is that a problem, or do I need a permission slip?"

Jerry coughed. "We didn't expect you, Victoria."

"Clearly." She fixed him with her gaze.

"Awww, lighten up, Vicki." Eddie poked his head from behind the drum set. "This is fun."

Victoria's hands shot to her hips. "I'm trying to practice for orchestra auditions, and your 'fun' rock music is so loud I can't concentrate."

Eddie snorted.

"What's so funny?" Victoria narrowed her eyes.

"You call this rock?" Eddie laughed. "Not even close."

"Country—"

Matt waved his hand. "Pop."

"Whatever. It's interrupting my concentration. Jerry, I'm surprised you're not practicing, too."

"Oh, don't worry." Matt laughed. "He practices his concerto non-stop. He's gonna win that competition."

"What?" Victoria's eyes shot to Jerry.

He looked away. "I never said I'd win it."

"I don't care what you do." Her words reverberated throughout the room. "Or who you do it with. Just keep it down and let me practice in peace." She slammed the door.

Back in her practice room, tears welled up as she stared at the orchestra music in front of her. How could Jerry betray her like this? It was bad enough he'd asked her sister out, but now he'd joined a band with Adrienne, Eddie, and some cowboy. Did she know him at all?

Worst of all, he'd signed up for the concerto competition without telling her. In addition to Franklin, Adrienne, and everyone else, Victoria would compete against Jerry—the best musician at Belton and her best friend—or *former* best friend.

A knock on the door interrupted her reverie. "Victoria, can I come in?" Jerry's unmistakable voice.

"I'm practicing."

"No, you're not. I haven't heard a note for the last several minutes." He cracked the door open and stepped inside.

She wiped her eyes. Mascara streaked the back of her hand. "What?"

"I want to talk—"

"I don't want to talk to you. You signed up for the concerto competition and didn't bother to tell me?" She glared.

"Look, Victoria—"

"You have as much right to compete as I do. I thought, after all these years, we were good enough friends to share things with each other... But I guess not."

Jerry hung his head.

At that moment, Adrienne burst inside. "Jerry, we're all waiting on you. We've got to finish the set list tonight."

"Adrienne, give me a few minutes. I need to—"

"Please, Jerry." She touched his shoulder.

"Victoria, can we catch up later?" Jerry pleaded.

"Go." Victoria forced the word out. "Don't keep *the band* waiting. Besides, I need to practice."

She picked up the violin and began to play. Jerry opened his mouth, but Adrienne yanked him out the door.

Chapter 13

"Girls, time to go." Dad's voice carried into the living room. "I told Papa and Gigi we'd be there in half an hour."

Victoria lowered her violin. She couldn't leave. Not now. Not with so much to practice for auditions tomorrow. She'd stayed up half the night at the music school, but she needed more time. This morning she'd already slaved away for two hours on the orchestra passages, but they were far from perfect. Calluses had formed on the tips of her fingers from the strings, and her bow arm ached from overuse. But she didn't want to stop until everything was flawless. Anything to keep her mind off Jerry's betrayal.

Stella stood in the doorway, a vision in purple and hot pink. "Are you ready?"

Victoria's eyes scanned her sister's sundress. "More than you. It's fall, why are you wearing that?"

She laughed. "I wore it to church this morning—which you missed, by the way— because it's cute. And you look Goth in all black. It's not like you have a concert today."

"What's wrong with black jeans and a matching shirt?" It matched her dismal mood. "I guess I'll go with you."

As the two made their way to the kitchen, the delicious scent of pumpkin filled the air. Marie was bent over the oven, removing a rectangular baking dish.

"What'd you make?" Stella asked.

"Pumpkin bars." Marie set the dish on the stove.

"What's in them?" Stella stood on tiptoe to peer into the pan.

"They're a fall dessert, with pumpkin pie filling, cinnamon, nutmeg, and cloves." Marie wiped her hands on her jeans. Flour peppered her flannel shirt.

Stella reached out her hand to pinch off a piece, but Marie swatted it away. "Not yet, silly. You'll have to wait until lunch. I promised Gigi I'd bring dessert."

Louisa entered in her nightgown, stifling a yawn. "Hey." Her fluffy slippers padded the floor as she moved to hug Victoria.

"Louisa, it's 12:30. Why are you in your jammies?"

She shrugged. "I needed a nap after church.

Victoria gave her sister a tight squeeze. "We're supposed to be at Papa and Gigi's by 1."

"What?" Louisa squinted, her eyes blinking at the bright light.

"Were you up late reading again?" Victoria asked.

Louisa nodded.

"Go change before Mom or Dad sees you."

"All right." Louisa shuffled out of the room.

Victoria opened the door to the fridge and retrieved the cranberry juice. She poured a glass and took a sip. The tart liquid revived her after her lengthy practice session.

"Where's Adrienne?" Stella asked.

"In our room." Marie cut the pumpkin dessert into rectangles.

"I'm here." Adrienne breezed in, short hair sticking out in all directions. "Sorry, I overslept."

"Why were you out so late?" Marie's blue eyes twinkled.

Color rose to Adrienne's cheeks. "Band practice."

"With Jerry." Stella giggled.

Tears stung Victoria's eyes. How were the others so oblivious to her pain?

Mom waltzed in, the shiny beads on her tank top matching her sandals. "Are we ready to leave? Where's Louisa?"

"I'm coming." Louisa hurried down the stairs, a book in hand.

A half hour later, the Pearsons pulled up to the old farmhouse. White with green trim around the windows, the A-frame building stood alone in the field like a lighthouse in a dark sea. Victoria crawled out of the car and pulled her coat closer. Orange and yellow leaves crunched under her feet, and more leaves flew through the air as Stella twirled through the yard, practicing her pirouettes. Marie balanced the pan of pumpkin bars in her hands while Louisa carried a bowl of salad.

Victoria and Adrienne walked side by side in icy silence. Victoria hadn't spoken a word to her traitorous sister since the previous night. What would she ask? How was your date? Did you have fun at band practice?

Now Victoria needed to practice for her orchestra auditions to keep her chair. Why did Gigi pick today to invite them to lunch?

Ahead of her, Dad and Mom climbed the steps to the front door. Mom pushed the doorbell, and melodious Westminster chimes filled the air. The door swung open to reveal Gigi framed in the archway.

"You're here." She flung her arms wide.

"You look radiant." Mom pulled Gigi in for a hug.

"Bonjour, Gigi." Adrienne kissed her on the cheek. "Did you sew a new outfit?"

Gigi's turquoise skirt matched her bright eye shadow, and the rose brooch pinned to her lapel was the same shade of magenta as her lipstick.

"Oh, I threw it together." Gigi waved her hand aside, jewels sparkling on several fingers. "It didn't take long to sew. Nothing like those taffeta gowns I made when you girls were little."

Adrienne fingered the blouse's fabric. "Lace is *haute couture* now. Everyone's wearing it."

"Where's Papa?" Marie raised her hand to her eyes to block the sun.

"He and Eddie are working in the field. They've been at it since sunrise." Gigi pointed a ruby-studded finger at the tractor inching its way through mounds of dirt. "It's supposed to rain later. Papa's anxious to finish planting before everything turns to mud. Thank goodness he had Eddie's help. We couldn't have asked for a better neighbor out here. I'd better call them to lunch."

How did Eddie get up that early after his late-night band practice?

"I'll get them, Mom," Dad said, then strode toward the field.

As the girls filed inside, Adrienne shot Victoria a frigid stare. This would be a long lunch.

Victoria removed her coat and hung it on the stand. Photos of Mom and her nine brothers and sisters and their kids decorated the wood-paneled entryway walls. Pictures of swimmers, dancers, musicians, birthday parties, and holidays covered nearly every inch of space from floor to ceiling. Victoria's eyes fell to a photo of Adrienne and her in matching red sequined dresses, hair pulled back with enormous gold bows that covered most of their heads. Much to Victoria's surprise, they were smiling at one another over their instruments.

If only they could become that close again. She shook her head. Impossible. Everything had changed. Adrienne had Jerry, and she had… New York.

"Victoria, *cherie*, are you coming?" Gigi poked her head in from the dining room. "Hurry along. We're waiting on you."

After one last glance at the picture, Victoria joined the others at the long wooden table.

By now, the men had returned from the field. Papa sat at the end of the table. His overalls covered a flannel shirt, and he wore thick leather boots. His callused hands were rough from a lifetime of hard work, and his eyes shone with kindness.

"Let's pray," he said in his rich, bass voice. "Dear God, thank you for bringing us together as a family. Bless this food which we are about to eat and the conversation we share. Amen."

Steam rose from a large porcelain bowl in front of Victoria. An aroma of cooked vegetables and broth filled the air.

"Gigi, this looks delicious." Marie held a large spoonful to her mouth.

She chuckled. "It's not much, but it'll do." She slathered butter on a slice of bread. "Victoria and Adrienne, your mother tells me you're performing in the concerto competition this spring. What will you play?"

Victoria swallowed. "I, uh… haven't decided yet. I wanted to wait until after orchestra auditions tomorrow."

Gigi took a bite of bread. "Why not choose one of Bach's concertos? I love to perform his works at church. You and Adrienne could play his double violin concerto. A sister duet would be a showstopper."

Victoria laughed. "Gigi, we played that as kids. It would never win a concerto competition. Besides, Adrienne doesn't play violin anymore. She plays viola."

"You don't think I can play violin?" Adrienne arched an eyebrow. "Try me."

"I have a couple of your aunts' old violins here. Why don't you give us a little concert when we're done with lunch?"

After they'd finished the delicious stew and pumpkin bars, Gigi hurried from the room and returned with two violin cases.

Victoria rolled her eyes.

Mom pulled her aside. "Just do it."

Lips pursed, Victoria removed one of the violins from its case and situated the shoulder pad. She drew the bow across the strings and cringed. The tonal quality of the instrument left much to be desired. Probably a cheap student instrument discarded by her aunts when they upgraded to their professional ones.

Adrienne removed the other, then tuned it as well.

This would be interesting. She hadn't played violin in years.

"Do you need music, girls?" Gigi patted her curls. "I'm sure I have the score somewhere."

"I have it memorized." Victoria wiped dust from the wood. "But maybe *Adrienne* does."

Her sister's nose rose in the air. "I think I can handle it."

Victoria frowned. "Are you sure? I know violin isn't your cup of tea."

Adrienne's gaze hardened. "Positive." She tucked the violin under her chin and began to play.

Victoria's heart skipped a beat as her sister's fingers flew over the strings. How could she play this fast, by memory, and not on her primary instrument? Victoria was so taken aback she almost missed her entrance. She gritted her teeth. Two could play this game.

Her violin part sailed over Adrienne's in perfect rhythm. Although a decade had passed since they'd played the piece together, childhood muscle memory served them well.

Bach's competing melodies pitched the two violinists against each other in a battle for dominance. Adrienne played a series of rapid notes while Victoria kept the steady beat down below. A few bars later, they switched. Adrienne's bow moved over the strings with such ease, as though years of playing the larger viola had rendered the small violin easy by comparison.

As they neared the end of the movement, Adrienne turned to face Victoria. Both sisters were breathing hard. Their eyes locked as they raced to the finish line. The last note rang out in unison.

In a small enclave at the back of the house, Victoria scanned shelves crammed full of music scores. Her mind still reeled after their dueling duet. As much as she hated to admit it, Adrienne was a powerhouse performer. And because the two had similar musical training, they'd blended well together. A perfect duo.

Victoria returned her gaze to the shelves. Gigi lacked nothing in literature or music scores. Church organ music, piano sonatas, soprano arias, violin concertos. It wasn't hard to see where Mom had developed her musical taste—and herself, for that matter. Music ran in their blood.

"Are you looking for something in particular?" Gigi placed her hand on Victoria's shoulder.

"I wanted to see which violin concertos you have." Victoria traced her fingers along the spines of several scores. "My professor says it has to be Romantic." She pulled a few from the shelves to examine them. "Whose was this?" Victoria handed Gigi a particularly dilapidated score.

Gigi squinted at the writing. "It looks like my grandfather's. He was a violinist, you know."

"He was?" Victoria's eyes widened with shock. "I never knew that."

"Oh yes." Gigi nodded. "He was the concertmaster of the symphony in Mirecourt, France.

Victoria's heart skipped a beat. "That's incredible."

Gigi examined Victoria. "You're a lot like him, with your dedication and ambition. You and Adrienne. What's she playing for the competition, by the way?"

"Berlioz's Viola Concerto."

"Viola concerto?" Gigi frowned. "I don't think he composed a viola concerto."

"He did. Something about an artist in Italy."

Gigi nodded. "*Harolde en Italie.* But that's not a concerto, *cherie.*"

Victoria's jaw dropped. "It's not?"

"No, it's a symphony with viola solo. Belton Symphony performed it years ago while my children attended."

This was the best news she'd heard all week. Adrienne was dumb enough not to select a concerto for a concerto competition? Incredulous.

Gigi sighed. "I never understood why she switched instruments. She was such an accomplished violinist. Your duet earlier was heavenly, absolutely stunning." She clasped her hands to her chest. "You two play so well together. Sisters in harmony—it warms my heart."

Victoria fidgeted with the scores in her hands. She couldn't tell Gigi how distant they'd grown over the years. It would break her heart.

"I still picture you two in those pretty red Christmas dresses, playing 'Silent Night.'" Her eyes glistened. "Like two little angels."

Not so angelic anymore.

Once they returned home, Victoria hurried upstairs to her room, the Saint-Saëns score and her instrument in hand. Why was she drawn to this composer, in spite of the flop of playing his violin solo at the Fall Concert?

She climbed onto her bed and scoured the sheet music for other clues about the previous owner. All this time, she'd figured it belonged to one of her aunts. But it was her great-great grandfather's music. Although not as famous as Tchaikovsky or Beethoven, Victoria had heard the Saint-Saëns concerto performed at recitals with piano accompaniment. Now was the time to give it a try. She rosined the bow and placed the violin under her chin. With several powerful strokes, the opening bars bellowed from the instrument. The pent-up tension from the past several days poured over the strings as the bombastic triple stops reflected the anger exploding inside her.

As she reached a difficult fast passage, her fingers struggled to maintain tempo. These notes would require significant practice and repetition to master. Difficult but—with sufficient dedication—attainable.

After the turbulent opening, Victoria relaxed as she entered the sweet, lyrical section of the piece. Images of golden wheat fields filled her mind while peace washed over her like a refreshing swim on a summer day.

All too soon, she jerked from her reverie at the return of the theme—this time, the level of difficulty heightened. Her muscles tightened as she braced herself for the ending. The fast runs came in rapid succession, followed by a series of double stops.

When she neared the climax, her bow moved faster and faster, and the fingers of her left hand climbed higher and higher up the instrument. Adrenaline flooded her body for the final note of the arpeggio as she reached a pitch only dogs could hear. Then she drew her bow for the last two chords.

Breathing heavily, she set down the instrument. This was it—the perfect work for the concerto competition.

Chapter 14

"We're finished for today." Mr. Vatchev folded the score on the music stand in front of him. "I'm sure you're all aware that we must cut rehearsal short today to allow time for chair auditions. I hope you've all signed up for a time slot. This year we will have blind auditions, so the other judges and I will sit behind a screen while you play your passages. We won't permit talking because we don't want you to give away your identity. The placements will be conducted on merit alone—not seniority."

Victoria eyed Jerry, who fiddled with the music on his stand, apparently unmoved.

A young flute player raised her hand. "Does this mean a freshman has a chance to sit first chair, not just seniors?"

The conductor nodded. "Yes, if the younger musician plays with superior caliber. We will judge based on accuracy of notes, adherence to prescribed dynamics, articulation of sound, and tempo."

Victoria shuddered. She'd mastered the first few requirements, but due to her lack of focus, she hadn't reached the maximum speed. How much would they mark her down?

"Also," the maestro continued, "if you plan to participate in the concerto competition in April, please send me your music selections so I can verify that we have access to the orchestral accompaniments."

Victoria smiled as a flood of relief washed over her. At last she'd made progress in this area. She raised her hand. "Mr. Vatchev? Does the selection have to be a *concerto* for the *concerto* competition?"

He furrowed his brow. "What do you mean, Miss Pearson? Of course it has to be a concerto."

"That's what I assumed, but I know some people may want to play something else."

"Like a sonata?" He peered over his glasses. "Those are chamber works, not orchestral."

Victoria shook her head. "Obviously. But what about a solo for orchestra that isn't a concerto?" She turned her head toward Adrienne, who stared at her, eyes wide.

"If you mean a single movement showpiece, that won't be eligible." The maestro laid his baton on the stand. "The other competitors will be playing multi-movement concertos."

Victoria's pulse quickened. "What about a symphony with solo instrument?"

The color drained from Adrienne's cheeks.

A frown creased the conductor's features. "There aren't many of those. I suppose," he said as he stroked his mustache, "if the work meets the requirements of a concerto, and is of sufficient length, it would be allowed."

A smug grin spread across Adrienne's face. She rose to leave and brushed past Victoria without a word.

"What was that all about?" Jerry stood next to Victoria, cello case in hand.

Victoria lowered her eyes.

"I presume you didn't choose a concerto but something else instead?" Why else would she have asked the conductor such a specific question.

"Of course it's a concerto." She hardened her jaw. "I'm not an idiot."

"Then why did you ask Mr. Vatchev all those questions?"

"Because your *girlfriend* wants to play a symphony rather than a concerto."

He stepped backward. "My girlfriend? Who are you talking about?"

"Don't play dumb with me, Jerry." Victoria folded her arms. "I know you asked Adrienne out Saturday night."

He shook his head. "No, I didn't." What had caused her to think that?

Victoria took a step closer to him, hands on hips. "She told me you did. Then I found you two together at that stupid band rehearsal."

Jerry glared at her. "First of all, just because you don't like the band doesn't make it stupid. Not everyone is as single-minded as you when it comes to musical taste. Also, I didn't ask Adrienne on a date. The guys wanted a violin or viola part for a couple of songs. I thought of you first, but I knew you'd been a little … stressed recently." He fidgeted with his cello. "I didn't want to add another thing to your plate, so I suggested Adrienne. Matt protested at first, due to her lack of improv skills, but I told him if I wrote out parts for her, she'd be fine."

Victoria's cheeks turned crimson. "You didn't go out with her?"

"No." He hoisted his case onto his back. So she *did* care. "To be honest, I think that was a pretty low blow to try to ruin her chance at the competition after she's worked so hard. What did you decide to play, anyway?"

She straightened. "The Saint-Saëns Violin Concerto in B Minor."

Jerry's heart stopped. Not the Saint-Saëns. Now she'd never forgive him.

Victoria's eyes crinkled. "What's wrong with that?"

He shook his head. "Nothing. Don't worry about it. Good luck on your audition this afternoon."

"You, too," she called after him as he hurried away.

###

In the dingy hallway outside the audition room, Victoria slipped on gloves to keep her fingers warm. The orchestra auditions were running forty-five minutes late, which allowed too much time for her hands to grow cold. The committee had decided to hear the violins last. The cellists had finished hours ago.

Jerry. She cringed. Why had she misjudged him? She'd known Adrienne wasn't his type. He'd asked her to play in their band, not out on a date.

Fine. Victoria's schedule didn't allow time for band practice, anyway. Still, deep down, a small part of her cried in protest. Why did Jerry want to join a band with all he had on his plate right now, between his medical studies and finishing his music degree? And why did her choice of the Saint-Saëns concerto upset him?

The audition room door opened, and Franklin sauntered out.

"Hi, Vicki. A little cold, are you?" He motioned to her gloved hands. "It's even colder inside."

Victoria peeled off the gloves. "I'm fine."

"I think it went pretty well." He tucked his thumbs into his skinny jeans and leaned against the wall. "I sped through that last passage in a couple of minutes."

"I didn't ask, but thanks for the info."

"The white screen is enormous. It felt like a hospital."

Victoria squeezed her eyes shut to block out the image. He wanted to scare her, but she wasn't going to let him.

A squeak of the door and a voice announced, "Next violinist, please."

Head held high, she brushed past Franklin. You can do this. Just relax.

She took a deep breath, then exhaled. The large screen split the room—she on one side, the judges on the other.

"Please begin whenever you're ready." The thick Russian accent of the voice behind the screen belonged to the maestro.

Victoria placed her music on the stand and opened to the first audition passage. At least this one was marked *Adagio*. The relaxed tempo worked in her favor and slowed her heart rate.

The second passage, quicker than the first, required several high notes, which her fingers struggled to reach due to the cold.

The last passage sent a shiver down her spine as she approached the rapid runs with extra sharps and flats. A few notes into the passage, she sensed the tempo was off. Her nerves had pushed her to play faster than she'd rehearsed. Her heart raced, and her palms began to sweat. She moved her hand to shift, and her fingers slipped out of place.

She froze. What should she do? End there, several bars early, and on such a bad note? Or begin again? If she asked the judges, she might give away her identity. Best to start again—slower.

After the last note died out, she lowered her instrument. This time she'd played the passage well, except for the tempo. Would her debacle the first time cost her the position of concertmaster? If Franklin played as well as he boasted, it was a strong possibility.

"Thank you." Mr. Vatchev's voice carried over the screen. "You may leave."

The curtness of his reply didn't bode well.

Chapter 15

As Victoria opened the front door to the house, familiar music greeted her ears. She crossed the entryway to the family room, where Louisa sat snuggled under a blanket on the couch, eyes glued to the TV.

Victoria laughed. "I see you've changed your tune since our last sister movie night." She pulled another blanket from the basket by the sofa, then scooted next to her sister. The warmth of the cover thawed her frozen fingers.

A frown wrinkled Louisa's forehead. "What do you mean?"

"You decided to watch *Pride and Prejudice* after all. I thought you were a diehard *Little Women* fan."

Louisa burrowed further into her blanket. "Why can't I like both?"

"You can." Victoria raised her eyebrows. "But you claimed Elizabeth Bennet 'didn't do much besides read and play the piano.'"

With a twinkle in her eye, Louisa smiled. "Perhaps I was prejudiced. Besides, I like to read and play the piano. They're two of my favorite hobbies."

A quick glance at the screen showed Mr. Darcy about to make his awkward first proposal.

Louisa grimaced. "I hate that they're so mean to each other in this scene. I want them to get along." She dropped her gaze. "But I suppose they must lose their pride to experience the joy of companionship."

The corners of Victoria's mouth twitched. Such an astute girl for her age.

The little scholar leaned her head against Victoria's chest. "How'd your audition go?"

Victoria's stomach muscles clenched. "Not well. I played under tempo, I messed up at the end, and had to repeat the whole passage. I wouldn't be surprised if Franklin takes my spot as concertmaster."

Louisa looked up, eyes filled with concern. "I'm sure you were great. Try not to worry about it."

"Thanks." Victoria gave her a tight squeeze. "I should've practiced sooner to familiarize myself with the passages."

"You've had a lot on your plate. Do you know how Adrienne did?"

Adrienne the traitor. "I have no idea."

"Are you still mad because Jerry asked her out?"

"Well…" Victoria fumbled with the blanket in her hands. "It turns out he didn't ask her on a date."

A confused expression creased Louisa's face. "Why did Adrienne say he had?"

"He'd asked her to play in a band with Eddie, some guitarist named Matt, and himself."

"I'm surprised he didn't ask you."

"Me, too. He figured I was too busy."

"You have been stressed. Maybe it's for the best."

"I suppose." Victoria shrugged. But why did a part of her cry out in protest? It's not like she *wanted* to be in a band. "They have a concert tonight at Café Chocolat."

"Don't you think," Louisa said, a note of pleading in her voice, "that since those two aren't a couple, you and Adrienne should patch things up?"

The clenched muscles in Victoria's stomach twisted into a firm knot. "Adrienne made me think they were a couple to annoy me." She took in a deep breath, then expelled it. "At least Jerry wasn't implicated."

Louisa's green eyes sparkled. "Maybe he'll ask you out now."

Victoria shook her head. "I doubt it. Not based on what he said this afternoon." Her cheeks burned at the recollection. *That was a low blow, Victoria, after she's worked so hard.* The sting of his reproach knifed her in the gut.

The door to the room burst open, and Stella flounced in. Her blonde curls bounced up and down as she skipped around the room. Marie followed close behind, apron in hand.

"Do you work tonight?" Victoria asked.

Marie nodded. "You all should come. The guys' band is playing."

Victoria pursed her lips. "With Adrienne."

"Yes." Marie paused, a look of confusion on her face. "It should be better than last time. Jerry wrote out the parts for her."

"Come on, Victoria." Stella tugged on her arm. "It sounds like fun, and I'm in the mood for hot chocolate."

Victoria frowned. "But it's a school night."

"Aw, don't be such a party pooper." Marie gave her a pointed look. "Let her come. You don't have to stay for the whole set."

"All right." Victoria peeled herself off the couch. "If Mom and Dad don't mind."

"Mom has rehearsal, and Dad got called back to the hospital," Stella said. "They won't know."

"I'm not sure it's best to hide it from them." Victoria folded her arms. "But I guess it couldn't hurt to bring you along."

"Yessss!" Stella jumped up and down with excitement. "Give me a couple of minutes to change clothes."

###

In spite of it being Monday night, people crammed into every corner of Café Chocolat. A strong scent of espresso filled the air. Victoria glanced at the stage where the guys were setting up. The guitarist, Matt, wore a checkered flannel shirt and cowboy boots, while Eddie sported a T-shirt and jeans. Victoria's eyes moved to Jerry, who plugged several cords into the amp. His black T-shirt emblazoned with flames and dark jeans seemed a far cry from his tux. But somehow, it still suited him.

She scanned the stage. No sign yet of Adrienne. Maybe she got cold feet.

Behind the counter, Marie was already taking orders. She'd left before they did because Stella's "couple of minutes to change" had taken a half hour. When she'd finally descended the staircase, her sequined pink dress and ballet flats had sparkled in the lamplight.

Louisa stepped up to order. "I'll have a salted caramel hot chocolate and a mint truffle."

Stella stood on tiptoe. "And I'll have a raspberry mocha."

Marie laughed. "No, you won't. The last thing you need is coffee. But I can make you a raspberry hot chocolate if you'd like."

"Okay."

"And for you, Victoria?" Marie reached for the tea bags.

"Chamomile."

An impish grin spread across Marie's face. "Partying hard tonight."

"I need to calm my nerves after those blind auditions. What genius came up with the bright idea that we should play in front of a screen?" Victoria grimaced.

"On that note, I'll throw in a couple more truffles." Marie winked. "Looks like the band's about to start. You guys better find a place to sit."

Victoria spotted a small circular table and chairs off to her right. She waved Stella and Louisa to follow her.

Behind his trap set, Eddie played a drumroll as Marie climbed on stage and faced the audience. "Ladies and gents, thanks for your presence here tonight. Let's give it up for the band Drum and String." The coffee shop erupted with hoots and hollers.

Matt took a bow, then strummed his guitar with a rapid motion. Jerry jumped in with a catchy bass line. For a moment, Victoria caught his eye. He gave a slight smile and then lowered his gaze to the guitar. Was he still mad at her from earlier?

Marie brought over the drinks and handed them to her sisters. Seconds later, Matt's powerful baritone filled the room. Warmth spread through Victoria's chest as she sipped her tea. The addition of bass guitar certainly heightened the intensity. But where was Adrienne?

After their third song, Matt grabbed the microphone. "For this next number, let's give it up for our violist, Adrienne Pearson!"

Applause greeted her as Adrienne emerged from backstage and took her place at the mic. She scintillated in her sequined gold top and skinny jeans, paired with spiky-heeled jeweled sandals.

When Adrienne drew her bow across the strings, the audience fell silent. She was playing from memory. The music sounded familiar, like a classical viola piece. Adrienne began with a soft tone, then grew to a powerful crescendo. Eddie joined her with an explosion of drums, followed by the blast of guitars. Everyone cheered as Adrienne took a step back to make room for Matt at the mic.

###

At the end of the first set, Stella sprinted to the stage. "That was awesome!"

Matt grinned. "It looks like we've found our number one fan. What's your name, little miss?"

"Stella Pearson."

He chuckled. "I might have guessed. How many of you Pearson girls are there?"

"Five. I'm the youngest." Stella propped a hand at her waist.

"Are you a musician, too?"

Her blue eyes sparkled. "Yes. I'm a singer."

"And dressed for the part, I see. What do you say we bring you up for our next song?"

"Really?" She jumped up and down with excitement.

"Sure." He waved her up on stage. "Let us know what you want to perform."

As Matt helped Stella, Jerry hopped down and pulled Victoria aside. "Hey, thanks for coming tonight. It means a lot."

She shrugged. "The girls wanted hot chocolate. Actually, Stella wanted coffee."

"That would be disastrous. She's already bouncing off the walls." His eyes moved to the table where Louisa sat, book in one hand, hot chocolate in the other. "I see Louisa is in her happy place."

"Yes."

Jerry moved next to Victoria, so close his body heat warmed her arm. "I'm glad to see you're out and about tonight. I wasn't sure you would be, after the audition results."

"What? They've already sent them?" Victoria's hand fluttered to her chest.

His eyes widened. "You haven't seen them yet?"

She shook her head. This couldn't be good.

Victoria bit her lip. "I'm afraid to ask. Did Franklin take my spot as concertmaster?"

Jerry averted his eyes.

She took a deep breath. "I figured he might. I didn't play well. He'll never let me hear the end of it. I hate sitting by him."

Wrinkles creased Jerry's brow. "The good news is you won't have to."

"Why not?" A surge of panic flooded her body.

He wrung his hands. "You're fourth chair."

She staggered backward as the force of the information registered. "But… who took second and third chairs? Franklin and I are the only senior violinists."

"A couple of juniors, or maybe one of them is a sophomore. I'm not sure."

The whirring sensation in her head made the room spin. She plopped onto a chair.

Jerry followed suit and enveloped her in his arms. "Maybe it's for the best. You've had too much stress. Now you won't have the pressure of concertmaster on your shoulders."

The muscles in her body tightened. She scooted away from him. "You're a cellist. You don't understand how hard I've worked to become concertmaster. Johann Conservatory won't even look at me if I'm fourth chair."

"You're right." He pulled his arm away and stood up. "Cellists don't understand what it's like to be a concertmaster. We're not given that opportunity."

Chapter 16

The next day, Victoria lowered her head to hide her face as she made her way to her seat for rehearsal. Fourth chair. If only the stage held a hidden trap door for her to disappear. She slipped next to the girl in third chair, a junior in her violin studio. Without a word, Victoria extricated her violin from its case and warmed up with a scale.

"Look who it is, Vicki Pearson." Franklin cackled. "How does it feel not to play in the inner circle?"

She pursed her lips. "Better, now that I don't have to sit next to an arrogant scumbag."

He scowled, then took his place as concertmaster.

The somber opening of Corelli's *Christmas Concerto* reflected her dismal mood. How had she managed to lose her position? She'd worked her whole collegiate career to become concertmaster, only to have it snatched away by her arch-nemesis. Her vision blurred as she struggled to hold back tears.

The lump in her throat threatened to choke her at the sight of Jerry in his usual place as principal cellist. She missed sitting across from him. His smile always boosted her spirits. But now their relationship was falling apart. Not that they'd ever been a couple or anything, but even their friendship was crumbling to pieces.

After the close of the last movement, the maestro set down his baton. "Good work this morning. We should be ready for our Christmas concert next month. Take fifteen."

Victoria set her instrument on the chair and hurried offstage. Once behind the curtain, she dashed into the nearest dressing room and closed the door. Tears, which grew into sobs that rent her entire body, streamed down her cheeks. She gave way to the flood of emotion and collapsed onto the floor.

A quiet knock jolted her to attention. "Go away," she said between sobs.

In spite of her protest, the door creaked open, and Jerry stepped inside.

She wiped her eyes. "I don't want to see anyone."

He sat next to her, a hint of cologne filling the air.

"Can we talk about this?" He turned her head to face his.

"About what?" She sniffed.

His gaze penetrated hers. "This. Your chair. Us."

The tears flowed again. "Oh, Jerry, everything's falling apart. I know it sounds stupid, but I can't bear to sit fourth chair. It's humiliating."

He moved closer and put his arm around her shoulders. "I know. I'm sure it's hard."

"But you don't understand. You're still principal cellist."

"But I *do* understand disappointment." When he squeezed her tighter, she nestled into him. He paused, and she basked in the warmth of his embrace. "Every time I play, I face the reality that next year I won't have this opportunity anymore. Instead, I'll be far away, studying for medical school."

She peered up at him. "I thought you wanted to go to medical school."

He shook his head. "No. Mom and Dad want me to go to medical school. It was never my dream. I'd rather pursue music."

She blinked several times to clear her sight, then turned to face him. "Why don't you?"

"Dad says musicians don't earn enough money. He wants me to follow in his footsteps and be a radiologist."

"What does your mom say? Surely she's supportive of your musical dreams."

"No." He looked at the floor. "She complains about how little money the music faculty makes. All these years she's hounded me to practice, but now she forbids me to continue with music after college."

Victoria's jaw dropped. "You're kidding. How could she say that?"

He shrugged. "She's jaded, I guess."

"But why?" Of all people, why would Professor Chang dissuade her own son from his musical dream?

"Perhaps not the best field of study." Her shoulders slumped. "After my last audition, I wish I could quit. If fourth chair is the best I can achieve here at Belton, there's no way I'll be accepted to Johann Conservatory."

"You might be surprised." A fraction of the tension in her body melted away as he rubbed her back. "Maybe you need a different approach."

"What do you mean?"

He moved his hands to her hair and massaged her scalp. She relaxed into his intoxicating touch.

"You've practiced alone for so many hours, I think the solitude gets to you. You're a perfectionist and way too hard on yourself. Why not allow more time to collaborate with others?"

She paused. "Like with you? I'd like that."

He wrapped his arms around her. They were getting dangerously close to crossing out of the friendzone. "And Adrienne."

Heat rose to her cheeks. "I still think Adrienne wanted to show off for you."

"Victoria." He spun her around to face him. "I swear, nothing happened between her and me."

She took a deep breath. "I believe you. But I don't trust her."

"Can't you two get along? You could be a dynamic duo if you'd set aside your differences and work together."

Victoria shook her head. "She sabotages my performances every time and always tries to attract attention to herself. It drives me crazy."

He lifted her chin with his finger. "Did you consider that maybe she needs *your* attention? You need to embrace your family."

Her breath caught in her throat as his proximity held her senses captive. She reached out to stroke his cheek. "And maybe you should stand up to yours.

Chapter 17

A gust of wind ruffled Victoria's hair as the Pearsons piled out of the SUV at Gigi and Papa's house. She drew in a deep breath and inhaled the cool, crisp November air.

"Girls, don't forget to grab the violins and viola," Mom said as she pulled up her fur-rimmed hood. "It's chilly, and we don't want the wood to crack."

Gigi had insisted they bring the instruments for entertainment after the meal. As Victoria popped open the rear door to retrieve her violin, Gigi bustled outside.

"Happy Thanksgiving," she exclaimed. Turquoise-lined bracelets clanked on her wrists, and a large matching stone graced her right hand. She wore a heavy-beaded necklace of many colors and feathered earrings, which dangled to her shoulders.

"Papa and I are elated to have you all here for the holiday." She squeezed Victoria in a tight hug.

"We're glad to see you, too." Mom enveloped her mother in her arms. "You look radiant."

A delicious aroma of herbal seasoning and roasted turkey greeted Victoria when she stepped inside the farmhouse. In the corner, one of her uncles threw several logs on the fire.

The front door burst open, and Eddie emerged, a large pan in hand, followed by his mom and sister. "Happy Thanksgiving, everyone. I've brought the sweet potato casserole. Marie, where do you want me to put it?"

Marie turned from the sink and flashed a smile. "Did you make that all by yourself?"

He placed a hand on his little sister. "I might have had help."

"Now that you're all here, let's eat." Papa motioned for everyone to take their seats, then bowed his head. "Dear Heavenly Father, thank you for the bountiful harvest you have provided. Thanks for the family and neighbors who are with us here today. Help us to love one another and to live in harmony with each other. Amen."

A chorus of " amens" swept the room.

Harmony. That's what Victoria needed today. She plopped a scoop of Papa's famous mashed potatoes onto her china plate.

"Want some turkey?" Papa handed her an enormous platter. She forked over a slice, then passed the turkey to Marie. Victoria ladled gravy over the meat and took a bite. Savory goodness danced on her tongue.

"Everything is delicious, Gigi," Marie said between bites of green bean casserole. "You're an amazing cook."

Gigi's eyes sparkled in the light. "I'm looking forward to your pumpkin pie."

"Me, too." Eddie winked.

Marie's face flushed. "I just threw it together."

"We brought whipped cream, too," Stella said as she spooned in a bite of mashed potatoes.

"You can't beat that." Eddie laughed.

Half an hour later, Victoria pushed back her plate. She was as stuffed as the bird on the platter. Gigi knew how to feed a crowd.

"Who wants pie?" Marie held up the pan.

"Me," echoed several voices around the table.

The doorbell chimed. Victoria scanned the room. Who could that be? Everyone was here.

Gigi opened the door, and Victoria's jaw dropped. Jerry.

"You made it." Adrienne popped out of her seat like a jackrabbit.

Jerry stared at the crowd in front of him, his hand resting on his cello case. What a way to celebrate the holiday. Much better than eating alone at the apartment.

"What ... why are you here?" Victoria stammered.

"Adrienne invited me. She said Gigi wanted us to play our quartet. Mom's performing in New York this weekend, and Dad is on call, so I figured why not?"

Adrienne placed a hand on her hip. "You're late. Didn't I tell you noon?"

He shook his head. "No, you said one."

"I said we'd play at one."

"It's not a problem." Gigi ushered him to a chair at the table. "We've got plenty of food left."

Jerry's stomach rumbled. His family never did anything for Thanksgiving.

A minute later, Gigi shoved an enormous plate piled high with food in front of him, which he snarfed down, then polished off a slice of pumpkin pie. She and Grandma would hit it off, for sure. Maybe they could meet next time she visited.

Gigi's face radiated with culinary pride. "Why don't the musicians warm up while the rest of us clear the dishes? I can't wait for the performance."

Jerry, Adrienne, Marie, and Victoria moved to the living room.

"What song did you have in mind, Adrienne?" Victoria asked as she removed her violin from its case.

"I thought we're supposed to play Christmas trios," Marie said as she rubbed amber rosin over the bow hair.

Adrienne scrunched up her nose. "It's not Christmas season until tomorrow. I've brought something more *apropos* for the holiday." She passed out several parts.

Victoria's eyes widened. "You've got to be kidding. Dvorak's *American String Quartet*? We haven't played that since the chamber music competition last spring."

"Scared you don't remember it?" Adrienne situated a shoulder pad on the back of her viola.

"No. I'm sure you chose it for the opening viola solo."

Please don't let those two fight today. Not on Thanksgiving.

"What do you think, Marie?" Victoria asked.

"It's tough, but I love it." She smiled. "It bridges the gap between my two music worlds—classical and fiddle."

Adrienne looked at Jerry. "What about you?"

He laughed. "I'm game, considering that's what you told me to play. I've practiced."

Victoria sighed. "Oh, all right. But no judgment, since I haven't looked at the part in half a year."

Adrienne faced the rest of the family for the announcement. "Today, in honor of Thanksgiving, we want to play *The American Quartet*. The composer, Dvorak, wrote this piece during his sojourn to the American Midwest. He developed a love of American folk music which stemmed from African-American spirituals and Native American songs. It is our honor to carry on these traditions today." She took her seat, then raised her instrument. The rich alto of the viola lent itself well to the folk tune. She played with such emotion, as though the people's stories resided within her.

The music filled Jerry with a sense of belonging and cultural pride. In this country, people came from all over the world to live together in harmony. As Victoria picked up the theme in a higher register, he pictured Native Americans running through trees, hunting buffalo, and cooking corn over an open fire.

When the theme passed to him, he closed his eyes and played by memory. His bow leapt on the strings as if to perform an indigenous dance with the early Americans. This was his first real Thanksgiving, after all.

When he finished, his eyes moved to Victoria, who was watching him intensely. He smiled, and she reciprocated. Maybe he was crazy, but did he detect a sense of longing in her gaze? With a snap, her eyes returned to the page. A slight blush crept over her cheeks.

She must've lost her place because Marie jumped to the first violin part. Perfect Victoria had missed an entrance because she was looking at *him*.

The melody soared from Marie's instrument like a caged bird finally given the chance to fly. This style of music seemed natural to her, as though she were born to perform it. Even Victoria didn't appear to mind the shift in roles, but instead smiled at her little sister, the master fiddler.

When Marie had finished the theme, she called out the measure number, and with renewed vigor, Victoria resumed her usual role as first violinist. This time, the melody flowed through her fingers like water from a stream, as though she enjoyed the communal dance.

When the work drew to a close, the rest of the family and guests burst into applause.

"Pure beauty," Eddie's mom said, hands clasped to her chest.

"I loved it." Papa gave Marie a squeeze. "Made me think of your fiddle tunes."

Gigi patted Jerry on the back. "A true testament to the American spirit. The world is more beautiful when we work together as a family."

That last word, along with Gigi's maternal touch, melted something deep inside Jerry.

If only he could be a part of this family—Victoria's family. Instead, he was stuck with his busy dad and obstinate mother who was plagued by her own past. Could he dare dream of being a part of this family someday?

Chapter 18

Holiday lights twinkled outside Victoria's bedroom window while soft Christmas music emanated from downstairs. She moved to her dresser and pulled out the string bracelet from Jerry. Ever since Thanksgiving, things had shifted between them—in a good way. He'd been exceptionally attentive to her, or perhaps she'd just started to notice. Did he possibly want to be more than friends? Did *she* want to be more than friends? No, it would never work. She'd be leaving for New York in a few months and had no idea where he'd end up for medical school. If only he'd audition for Johann Conservatory. Then maybe—

"It's Christmas Eve!" Stella bounded into the bedroom, decked out in a red velvet Santa dress with white fur trim.

Victoria giggled. "Don't you look festive."

"I've got to be fabulous for my solo tonight." Stella scrunched up her nose. "Victoria, you can't wear all black on Christmas Eve. It's depressing."

"I always wear black when I perform."

Stella ran a hand through her blonde ringlets. "You don't have to. This isn't an orchestra performance."

Victoria frowned. "I know, but—"

"I'll be right back." Stella dashed out the door.

A smile played at the corners of Victoria's mouth. She loved the annual Christmas Eve concert. Every year after the church service, the family gathered for dinner and a show. Papa and Gigi used to host it at their house until the group grew so large they exceeded its capacity. After that, they'd rented the church fellowship hall and extended an open invitation to everyone. Church members would stick around after service for the potluck meal and show.

"Here you go." Stella's voice jolted Victoria back to the present. "I found this amazing red belt and matching heels."

Victoria laughed. "Where did you get these?"

"From Adrienne's closet." Stella tossed the accessories on the bed.

A groan escaped Victoria. "I can't wear them. Not after I told her never to borrow my stuff again."

Stella waved her hand to the side. "Adrienne won't care. She wants the members of the string quartet to look festive."

"Oh all right." Victoria slipped the thick belt over her black dress and slid her feet into the red satin pumps, complete with bows.

Her sister eyed her from head to toe. "Much better."

Louisa entered, wearing a forest green shift dress with flowy sleeves. Her long hair hung in loose tresses down her back. She kicked off her flats and plopped onto the bed. "I'm so glad it's Christmas Eve— my favorite night of the year."

"Me, too." Victoria snuggled next to her. "Are you ready to play your Christmas piano music tonight?"

"You know I hate to perform in front of people."

"Don't worry." Victoria patted her on the shoulder. "It's background music for dinner."

"I hope no one will notice." Louisa shuddered.

"You'll be great," Victoria said. "I have full confidence in you."

Marie poked her head in. "Are you girls ready? Mom says it's time to leave."

"Tell her we're headed down." Victoria rose and the others followed suit. When she entered the hallway, she almost bumped into Adrienne.

"Watch it," Adrienne said. Her eyes narrowed. "Why are you wearing my shoes?"

"Stella insisted I needed color." Victoria scanned her sister's outfit. A short, green velvet dress which hugged her curves was paired with sparkling three-inch heels. "You think Mom will let you wear that to perform?"

Adrienne smirked. "She'll like it better than Marie's jeans and T-shirt. She hates when we wear jeans to church."

Marie rolled her eyes. "Oh all right. I'll change, but only because it's Christmas." She scurried back to her room and returned a couple minutes later in black slacks and a red flannel shirt."

Arms crossed, Adrienne huffed. "Still too casual."

"Still too tight," Marie retorted.

Jerry entered the fellowship hall at the church. The sight took his breath away. Poinsettias adorned each table, accompanied by bowls of votive candles and paper snowflakes. Twinkle lights dangled from the ceiling over white-tipped Christmas trees. A winter wonderland.

"Ho, Ho, Ho," a jolly voice said as a man dressed as Santa Claus greeted several of the Pearsons.

Marie threw her arms around him. "Papa, I mean, Santa." She chuckled.

"Have you been good this year?" His faux mustache twitched.

"Of course." She flashed an impish smile.

Eddie appeared in a green-and-red elf costume, authentic from the top of his hat to the tips of his pointy shoes. "She's always good." He winked.

"Eddie." Marie giggled. "You look hilarious."

He pulled a sheet of paper several feet long from his pocket. "Looks like you made the nice list."

Adrienne scurried over. "That's debatable. She almost wore jeans to church."

"How shocking." Eddie's fingers flew to his mouth in mock surprise. "But by the look of your ensemble, Adrienne, I'd say you're on the naughty list."

Jerry couldn't hold back a laugh. Eddie was spot-on.

Adrienne stuck out her tongue.

"That's enough, you two." Gigi approached in full Mrs. Claus attire, carrying a basket. "I need you to help me pass out these candy canes."

Jerry turned around to see the magical stage with a giant Christmas tree on one side and a nativity scene on the other. A backdrop of snowmen and gingerbread figures adorned the back wall.

His gaze moved to Victoria, who was setting up chairs for the quartet. A red belt accentuated her waist, and her red heels made him do a double take. Since when did she wear stilettos? He set down his cello and hopped onstage.

"Merry Christmas, Victoria."

Her eyes lit up. "Merry Christmas, Jerry."

"You look beautiful—so festive."

"You, too." She moved closer and fingered his red-and-white-striped tie. "I didn't see you arrive."

"Of course you didn't." He clipped on a pair of candy cane cufflinks. "There are at least a hundred people here. You Pearsons go all out for Christmas."

"Yeah." She laughed. "That's what happens when you come from a big family."

"I wouldn't know." He dropped his gaze to the floor. "Usually it's just Mom, Dad, and me, and they're busy most of the time."

She squeezed his hand. "You can be a part of our family anytime."

His eyes met hers. "You don't know how much that means to me."

A blush colored her pretty cheeks. Definitely something was happening between them.

Marie plopped her instrument on a chair. "Let's get this show on the road. I can't wait for our opening number."

As soon as the four of them were ready with instruments in hand, Jerry plunked out a jazzy bass line to "Deck the Halls." A couple of bars later, Victoria and Adrienne joined in with the familiar tune. Marie grinned as she added the harmony, making funny faces as she did. They continued with "March" from Tchaikovsky's *The Nutcracker Ballet*. Several of the young boy cousins in soldier uniforms clambered on stage and marched to the beat.

Next, the quartet played "Waltz of the Snowflakes," as the little girl cousins twirled around in fluffy white tutus. One snowflake almost fell offstage. That was close.

For the conclusion of the Tchaikovsky medley, Stella tiptoed on stage to perform "Dance of the Sugarplum Fairy." She moved with such grace and confidence in her pointe shoes that Jerry couldn't help but admire her talent for such a young age.

At the close of the song, the dancers and quartet members moved to a side room offstage which still offered a view of the performance.

"Ho, Ho, Ho," Papa bellowed as he climbed onto the platform. "Welcome to our annual Christmas program. If only I could find Mrs. Claus to lead us in song."

"I'm here, I'm here." Gigi bustled to the piano in her Mrs. Claus costume.

"Excellent." Papa chuckled. "Now where are my carolers?" A choir made up of Victoria's mom and her nine siblings filed behind him. The voices of the ten carolers broke out in four-part harmony to "Santa Claus is Comin' to Town."

Backstage, Jerry leaned close to Victoria. "Your family's incredible. Is everyone musical?"

Victoria tipped her head to one side. "I guess most of us are."

He gaped at her. "All of you?"

She gave him a playful shove. "Don't act so surprised. Gigi's a huge advocate for music education."

He nodded. "Of course. They're fun."

"If you think this is entertaining, wait until the next number." Victoria set her violin on a nearby table and grabbed a large gray sheet with a hole in it. "Adrienne, Marie, it's time." Victoria slipped her head through the hole.

"What in the world?" Jerry gaped.

"It's a hippo costume."

"You're kidding."

She wagged a finger at him. "Never repeat this to anyone at Belton."

He raised an eyebrow. "No promises."

Marie pushed past them. "Let's get this over with." She crawled underneath the sheet. "I'm the middle. Adrienne, get in behind me."

Adrienne rolled her eyes. "Absolutely not. No way I'll be the backside of the hippo, especially in these heels."

Jerry guffawed. "You're supposed to be what?"

She shook her head. "I won't do it. I'll be the front." She yanked the sheet off Victoria and slipped it over her own head. "You take the rear."

Victoria crossed her arms. "No."

"Somebody has to do it," Adrienne's voice rose.

"I'll volunteer for the honorable position." Eddie must have snuck up behind them. With a flourish, he took a dramatic bow. "Santa's elf, at your service."

"Great," Victoria said. "Crawl in behind Marie. And don't forget to act the part."

"Never fear, Eddie is here." He poked Marie in the side, then took his place.

Eddie, always the showman.

"No funny business," Victoria warned. "Now for the finishing touch." She picked up an enormous gray cardboard box and stuck it on Adrienne's head.

Jerry jumped backward. Two Styrofoam blue eyes with pipe-cleaner lashes stared creepily back at him. "That's terrifying."

Victoria nodded. "I thought so, too, the first time I saw it. I'm glad Stella is the one who has to sing with it now. It used to be me."

He snorted. "You sang with that hippo?"

"Yes."

"I can't see out of this thing." The cardboard muffled Adrienne's voice.

"There's a hole in the bottom where the mouth is located." Victoria waved a hand beneath the hippo's jawline. "Hurry. Stella's about to start."

Victoria guided the hippo to its place backstage as Stella sang the opening to "I Want a Hippopotamus for Christmas."

Halfway through the song, Victoria gave the hippo a slight shove onto the stage, and the audience roared with laughter. Stella grabbed hold of the hippo face and planted a smooch on its gargantuan nose.

"You used to kiss that monstrosity?" Jerry whispered to Victoria. She spun around. "I, um, yeah."

He raised his eyebrows. "You're full of surprises tonight."

"What's the matter?" She pursed her lips. "Are you jealous?"

He gazed at her mouth, then back at her eyes. "Maybe."

His cheeks burned. Where could he find mistletoe? He took a step toward her, and she closed her eyes.

A moment later, something shoved them both into the wall. The giant hippo had returned backstage.

"Watch where you're going." Victoria pushed the monstrosity away from her.

"I can't see," Adrienne mumbled under the box.

Victoria stepped back to let the hippo pass.

"That was, um, interesting." Jerry wiped his forehead.

"Yeah, it's—"

A loud noise erupted behind them. He spun around in time to see the table which held Victoria's violin topple to the floor.

Chapter 19

"No!" Victoria yelled as she rushed for the instrument.

Too late. It hit the ground, then the table collapsed onto it with a heart-wrenching crack. She snatched it from the floor. A strangled cry escaped her lips. The fingerboard had smashed into the body of the instrument, which split down the middle.

"It can't be broken. Not now. Not my senior year." She crumpled to her knees.

Jerry dropped next to her and held her close.

Adrienne yanked the cardboard hippo off her head and crawled out from under the sheet. She gasped. "Victoria, I'm so sorry. I couldn't see. I'm sure insurance will cover it."

Rage surged through Victoria's veins and burned from the inside out as the full force of the situation hit her. "You think insurance will cover this? I'm pretty sure this falls under the category of 'gross negligence.' What would I say, a girl in a giant hippo costume knocked it over? They'd never take me seriously."

Adrienne lowered her eyes. "I suppose you're right."

"This wouldn't have happened if you hadn't worn those ridiculous heels," Victoria cried. "Now look what you've done."

Adrienne's eyes widened, her jaw set. "Look what I've done? I wouldn't break an instrument on purpose. That was you. Don't you remember? Let me refresh your memory." Adrienne straightened her shoulders. "We'd both performed our violin solos for the Belton Young Artists Competition. After an intense round of judging, you came in second, and I won first."

Victoria groaned. Please don't share this story. Not in front of Jerry.

"I'd hoped you could be happy for your little sister. But of course not. Instead, when you heard the results, you flew into a rage, grabbed my precious violin, and whacked it against the wall."

Victoria's cheeks burned as humiliation enveloped her like a shroud. Her hands turned clammy. She'd spent years trying to forget that moment, and now it was in the open for everyone to hear.

Adrienne's nostrils flared. "After that, I vowed never to compete against you again. I even switched to viola to differentiate myself from you. Instead of Victoria's little tagalong, I became my own person. But you never accepted me—the real me. And you never learned to control your temper."

Icy silence filled the air. Victoria froze. What could she say? It was all true. Mortification crashed over her like an ocean wave. "I was the reason you never wanted to play the violin again?"

Adrienne nodded.

Victoria closed her eyes as the children's choir began to sing. "Silent Night, Holy Night. All is Calm, All is bright." How ironic.

Several moments passed before she opened them again. Adrienne still stared at her, as well as everyone else in the room, including Jerry.

"I'm sorry," Victoria said weakly, a crack in her voice. "I never should have—"

"Girls, it's time." Mom peeked her head backstage. "Grab your instruments."

Victoria blinked. "But I—"

"Here, take this." Marie shoved her own violin into Victoria's hands. "Now go."

Adrienne scooped up her viola, then Victoria and Louisa followed her onstage.

Their mother's voice rang out through the microphone. "This next song holds a special place in my heart. It's one I've treasured since childhood. Written by composer Adolphe Adam in 1847 to the French poem 'Minuit Chretien,' the hymn tells the story of our Savior's birth. I hope you enjoy the music as we perform 'O Holy Night.'"

Louisa made her way to the piano while Victoria and Adrienne took their places next to each other. After the piano's opening bars, Mom's soprano floated through the air. "O holy night, the stars are brightly shining; It is the night of our dear Savior's birth!" Her silver dress sparkled in the shimmering light like the stars about which she sang.

Adrienne's viola joined her with the harmony as Mom continued. "Long lay the world in sin and error pining, Till He appeared, and the soul felt its worth."

Victoria closed her eyes and let the music wash over her. *Dear God, I've made a mess. I haven't loved my brother, or in this case my sister, as myself. Please help me to change, to remedy past wrongs. Give me the strength.*

"O night, divine. O night divine." Mom's conclusion of the stanza cued Victoria. She lifted the instrument to her shoulder. With a nod to Adrienne, they began the next verse together.

"Truly He taught us to love one another; His law is love and His gospel is peace."

The lyrics reached a deep corner of Victoria's soul, one she'd ignored far too long. As she pulled her bow across the strings, the notes blended like angel voices in perfect harmony. She drew a deep breath, and a sense of peace filled her heart.

Mom's sweet voice continued to ring through the hall. "Chains shall He break for the slave is our brother, And in His name all oppression shall cease."

God, break the chains that have kept us apart, and help us to love each other as You love us.

"Sweet hymns of joy in grateful chorus raise we, Let all within us praise His holy name."

The violin's descant blended with the soprano and the viola's rich alto like a prayer to Heaven.

As Mom approached the climactic high note, she turned to face her daughters. "Christ is the Lord! O praise His name forever! His pow'r and glory evermore proclaim!"

Worshipful silence stole over the audience as the notes trailed away. The power of the moment surpassed words.

Several seconds later, vigorous applause broke out. Mom covered her heart and took a deep bow, then she extended her arms to her daughters, and they all bowed together.

###

"That was surreal." Marie clapped Victoria on the back when she returned backstage. "I loved it."

"Thanks." Victoria smiled.

Jerry approached, and Victoria dropped her gaze.

"Divine." He caressed her cheek with his fingertips. She lifted her eyes to his. "That was the best I've ever heard you perform."

"Really? It was only a simple hymn."

He brushed a strand of hair from her face. "I said you and Adrienne would make a dynamite duo if you ever learned to work together."

She leaned into his palm. "You were right."

"Hurry. Time for the finale. Hurry," Stella exclaimed.

Victoria grimaced. In the wonder of the moment, she'd forgotten they were short an instrument.

"Go on," Marie said, as if reading her mind. "No one listens to the second violinist anyway."

Victoria shook her head. "This is yours. You can play the first violin for a change."

Marie's eyes widened. "Are you sure?"

"Of course." Victoria handed over the instrument. "After your solo in the Dvorak string quartet, 'Jingle Bell Rock' should be easy. Besides, it's more your style. I'm a classical girl."

Marie beamed. "Thanks, Victoria."

As the other musicians took their places onstage, Victoria picked up her cracked violin. She ran fingers along the broken wood. It wasn't a Stradivarius, but it was hers. And now it was smashed like her dream of playing concertmaster.

Two slender arms wound their way around her waist. "Good job tonight," Mom whispered. "I'm proud of you."

Victoria wiped a tear from her eyes. "Thanks. But you deserve the credit. You were the soloist."

Mom turned to face her. "I wasn't talking about the song."

"You weren't?" Victoria blinked.

"No. I'm proud of how you apologized to Adrienne."

"How'd you know?"

"Louisa told me. I'm also proud that you let Marie play first violin for a change."

Victoria shrugged. "She deserves the chance every now and then. Besides, it's her violin." She buried her face in Mom's chest. "I don't have one anymore."

Mom ran a hand through Victoria's hair. "Don't give up. Dad and I will help you get a new instrument after the holidays."

Victoria shook her head. "No, Mom. You guys have already done so much. I can't ask that of you." *Not the caliber of violin Professor Chang would require. Probably a Stradivarius.*

###

Victoria peeled off her gloves as she crossed the threshold into the house to the smell of gingerbread, mingled with cinnamon and cloves, wafting through the air.

Marie hung her coat in the closet. "Want some hot chocolate?"

"I do." Stella discarded her boots, hat, and gloves on the floor.

Mom frowned. "No hot chocolate for you until you pick up your things."

"Oh, all right." Stella scowled as she bent to retrieve her clothes.

Victoria moved to the music room where a Christmas tree stood in majestic glory in front of the bay window. Golden balls and crystal ornaments hung from verdant branches. White lights twinkled amidst the pine needles. At the top of the tree, a porcelain angel dressed in satin and diamond-tipped wings clutched a violin beneath her chin.

Stella and Adrienne entered arm in arm and sat together on the plush sofa. Marie followed with a tray of seven mugs of hot chocolate. She placed it on the glass coffee table, snatched a mug, then sank onto the floor in front of the fireplace. Louisa moved to the table, grabbed her hot chocolate, and scooted next to Marie. With a glance at the couch, Victoria sighed, scooped up two mugs and handed them to Adrienne and Stella.

Adrienne extended her hand for the drink. "*Merci.*" Their eyes met, and a hint of a smile played at the corners of Adrienne's mouth.

It was a start. Victoria retrieved her own hot chocolate and sat next to Stella.

Last of all, Dad and Mom took their seats in the large armchairs like a king and queen on their thrones.

"Since it's Christmas Eve, let's take a few minutes to remember the reason for the season." Dad opened the well-worn leather-bound family Bible. "I'll begin with Luke 2. *[1] And it came to pass in those days...that all the world should be taxed... [4] And Joseph also went ... [5] to be taxed with Mary, his espoused wife, being great with child. (KJV)*"

Every time Dad introduced a new character in the Christmas story, the girls took turns placing it in the stable on the fireplace mantle. Marie beamed as she carried in the mother Mary, while Stella sang "Angels We Have Heard on High" with the angel clasped in her hands. Victoria's heart melted at one of her favorite Christmas traditions.

"Excellent job, girls." Dad reached for another antique book and settled back in his chair. "*The Night Before Christmas (1823),* by Clement Moore." He donned a Santa hat and pulled out a pair of spectacles. " 'Twas the night before Christmas and all through the house, not a creature was stirring, not even a mouse."

If only Santa would bring her a new violin. How could she practice without one? How long would it take her to find a new one? Would it even be good enough to win the concerto competition?

"Merry Christmas to all, and to all, a good night." Dad closed the old book, while Mom handed each of the girls red-and-green plaid fuzzy pajamas. "Time for bed. Santa can't come until you're asleep."

Adrienne rolled her eyes. "Mom, we're not little kids anymore. There's no need for the charade."

Mom's hands flew to her hips. "Then you know better than to cross Mrs. Claus on Christmas Eve. Put your jammies on and get some sleep."

Victoria chuckled. "Good night, Mom."

"Wake up!"

Victoria's eyes popped open as a giant flurry of fleece landed on top of her.

"Stella, what in the world?"

"It's Christmas! I can't wait to open my stocking."

Victoria rubbed her eyes. "What time is it?"

"Seven." Stella jumped off the bed. "I've been up since six, but Mom told me I couldn't wake anyone up until now. I want to peek in my stocking." She sprinted from the room.

Victoria slid out of bed and shuffled to the landing. Would Adrienne be up at this hour? Probably not.

The delicious aroma of cinnamon and cloves permeated the air. Her stomach rumbled. Mom's famous cinnamon rolls. Garland encircled the banister to the staircase and sparkled with twinkle lights.

In the kitchen, Mom bent over the oven and pulled out a pan of golden rolls.

"Merry Christmas." Victoria slid her arms around Mom's waist.

"Merry Christmas, dear. I hope you slept well." Mom wiped her hands on her Mrs. Claus apron and gave her a hug.

"I did, until Stella jumped on me."

Mom laughed. "She's excited."

Beyond her, Marie stirred a large pot on the stove, steam floating upward.

Victoria breathed in the spicy aroma. "That smells delicious, Marie. What is it?"

"I wanted to try this wassail recipe. Cranberry and orange juice, spices, and rosemary."

"Sounds festive."

"It's ready now." Marie reached for a snowman mug, ladled in the crimson liquid, and passed it to Victoria.

The zesty spices reinvigorated her as they danced on her tongue.

Louisa shuffled in and swiped a strand of long hair from her eyes. "Merry Christmas, everyone."

"Good morning, Louisa. Do you want to help me decorate the cinnamon rolls?" Mom handed her a spatula with snowflakes printed on it.

"Sure." Louisa yawned.

"I arranged them in a circle to look like a wreath. We'll use red and green frosting for holly." Mom set two bowls of icing onto the counter.

Stella burst into the room, dragging Adrienne by the hand. "Time for presents!"

"Breakfast first." Mom pulled out a set of porcelain snowman plates. "You can set the table."

Stella's bottom lip protruded, but she obeyed.

"Good morning, Adrienne." The words sounded unnatural from Victoria's mouth. This would take practice.

"How can anything this early be good?" Adrienne blew a wisp of hair from her eyes and turned on the coffeepot.

The back door opened. Dad entered and scraped off his boots. "Hello, girls. Looks like we got our white Christmas." He wiped a few snowflakes from his coat.

"Merry Christmas, Dad." Stella ran and flung her arms around his neck. "I love you."

He grinned. "I love you, too."

Mom placed fruit salad on top of the poinsettia-embroidered tablecloth. "Everyone, sit down. Time for breakfast."

A circle of iced cinnamon rolls formed the perfect wreath as a centerpiece. Dad took his seat at the table and bowed his head. "Dear God, thank you for this wonderful Christmas morning. We are so grateful for the birth of your son, Jesus. I pray we may enjoy this special day when we can all be together as a family. Amen."

"Amen," the girls echoed.

Victoria glanced at Adrienne, who examined her plate. Hard read. Victoria took a cinnamon roll and bit into the soft bread. Delicious. The sweet icing melted in her mouth.

Dad turned to Stella. "I hear someone's ready to open presents."

"Yes." She giggled. "I can't wait. Eat fast, everybody."

A few minutes later, they cleared their dishes and returned to the music room where five stockings hung from the mantle, one for each girl. Victoria grabbed her red one and peered inside.

"Makeup," Adrienne said as she waved a blush brush in the air. "Check out this eyeshadow and lipstick. Santa has good taste."

Marie nodded. "I love my new lip gloss. So natural." She tore open a chocolate Santa wrapper and popped the candy in her mouth.

"I got makeup, too." Louisa held up a tube of mascara. "I have no idea how to use this thing."

"You'll get better with practice." Adrienne applied crimson red lipstick to her own mouth. "You should use it now that you're in high school."

Louisa didn't look convinced.

Stella tipped her stocking upside down and shook everything out. Candy canes, chocolates, and a green envelope fell to the floor. She pushed the candy aside and held up a small tube. She scrunched her nose in protest. "Chapstick? That's it? Why didn't I get cool makeup like everyone else?"

Mom pursed her red lips. "Probably because Santa knows about the no-makeup-before-you're-thirteen rule."

"I'll be thirteen this summer."

"Then next year Santa might bring you some."

Stella rolled her eyes.

"What's in the envelope?" Adrienne asked. "Do you other girls have them, too?"

Victoria rummaged in her stocking. Sure enough—a green envelope. What could it be? Maybe tickets to a symphony concert?

Dad scooted to the edge of his chair. His eyes sparkled with excitement. "Everyone, open them together on the count of three. One, two, three."

Victoria tore open the envelope and gasped.

"Tickets!" Stella squealed and threw her arms around Dad's neck.

Victoria squinted at the paper in hand. "To where?" A vacation? Dad's smile widened. "New York."

She jumped to her feet. "Are you serious? When do we leave?"

"Our flight's at six tomorrow morning." He arched his eyebrows in a down-to-business sort of look. "We'll need to leave at four-thirty."

"Ugh." Adrienne sank onto the couch. "Who wants to be up that early?"

Mom frowned. "Those who want a trip to New York, that's who."

"I can't believe you're taking us there." Victoria ran to Dad and kissed him on the cheek.

He enveloped her in his arms. "I figured, since you're set on moving there, we'd better check it out with you."

Tears threatened to spill. "Thanks, Dad."

Chapter 20

Traffic lights flashed. Yellow cabs honked in the street. The scents of ethnic food, sriracha, and espresso mingled in the air. Victoria took a deep breath as she stepped out of the taxi outside the hotel. How could she absorb all the flavor of New York at once? The city that never stops. The Big Apple.

"I can't believe we're here." Marie's blue eyes grew wide as she took in the site.

"I wanna go to the ballet," Stella squealed next to her. "It's the best."

The Pearsons followed the bellhop to the center of the lobby where a giant waterfall cascaded over rocks into a small basin. Luxurious couches beckoned them. When Victoria sat down, an elegant chandelier hanging from the ceiling caught her eye.

Moments later, Mom's stilettos reverberated off the marble floors. "We're checked in. You girls head up to your room while Dad and I wait for the bags." She handed out keycards. "We're in room eleven and you're in twelve on the seventh floor."

"Perfect." Adrienne grabbed her key and headed toward the elevators. The others followed suit.

Inside the room, Victoria surveyed the space—two queen-size beds, a cot, TV, desk, and a breathtaking view overlooking the skyscrapers. She was finally here, in the city of her dreams.

Adrienne wrinkled her nose at the sight of the cot. "Who has to sleep on that?" She pointed.

"One, two, three, not it." Stella flopped onto one of the large beds.

"But Stella," Victoria said, "you're the smallest."

"I'm always stuck on the cot or the floor." Stella's bottom lip protruded. "That's why this time I said, 'not it.'"

Victoria shook her head. "That doesn't count—"

"Aww, let her have the bed. I don't mind." Marie plopped onto the cot.

"I'll bunk with Stella." Adrienne set her purse on the bed next to Stella.

Louisa turned to Victoria. "I guess that leaves you and me." She climbed under the covers and lay her head on the pillow.

"It's not time to sleep yet." Victoria laughed.

"But I'm so tired." Louisa yawned. "That early flight killed me."

Minutes later, Dad, Mom, and the bellhop entered.

"Here are the suitcases." Dad and the hotel employee pulled them off the cart and set them beside the beds.

"Thank goodness they made it, unlike the last vacation." Stella moaned. "I had to wear the same dress for three days in a row."

"*Quelle horreur.*" Adrienne struck a tragic pose.

"Dad, do we have an itinerary?" Victoria grabbed the pad and pen off the desk, ready to take notes.

"Tomorrow, I thought we'd visit the Statue of Liberty, Ellis Island, and Times Square. After that, I figured you girls could decide what you'd like to see over the next few days."

"Great." Victoria could hardly hold back her enthusiasm. " I'll start planning the rest." She couldn't afford to waste a moment exploring her soon-to-be-home.

The following morning, Dad woke everyone up at a quarter to seven. "We need to be at the boat tour by 8:30 to see the Statue of Liberty." His early-morning doctor schedule kicked in, even on vacation.

Once on the boat, Adrienne leaned against the railing. "It's really a French statue," she lectured, "designed by Frédéric Auguste Bartholdi and built by Gustave Eiffel in 1886, the same engineer who built the Eiffel Tower for the World's Fair in 1889."

"Nice to have our French history tour guide with us," Mom said, giving her a squeeze.

At Ellis Island, while Victoria learned amazing stories of immigrants who had braved the Atlantic Ocean to find a new life in America, her thoughts turned to Jerry and his family. He'd been born in the United States, but Professor Chang had immigrated from China to New York to study music at Johann Conservatory. What an exhilarating experience that must have been, to leave her family behind and start a new life in such an exciting city. And to think, in only a few short months, that would be her.

A couple hours later, her heart still pounded with the energy of New York as they strolled around Times Square.

"What do you think of the Jumbotron?" Dad pointed a finger at the enormous screen, while Mom clasped his other hand, her fur coat wrapped tight around her frame.

"It's huge." Victoria pulled her own wool hat over her ears to block out the wind as a slight chill stole over her.

Stella gaped. "That's the biggest screen I've ever seen."

"Where are the hot dog vendors?" Louisa scanned the streets. "I'm starving."

"There's one," Dad pointed.

"We could grab those for lunch, then head to Café Lalo for dessert and drinks," Marie suggested.

"What's that?" Victoria asked. "Like Lalo the composer of *Symphonie Espagnole*?"

"Spelled the same, yes." Marie's blue eyes sparkled. "It's one of the most famous cafés in the city."

Dad glanced at a map. "Looks like we can stroll through Central Park to get there."

"Perfect," Mom said. "I'll need to walk off that hot dog."

"But it's cold," Stella protested.

"Then I suggest you zip up your coat." Mom reached out and zipped it for her.

Sure enough, the frigid air filled Victoria's lungs as they hurried through the park. Since it was December, the trees were bare, and the grass brown. Maybe she should have visited in the fall. Was it always this icy?

By the time they finally reached the café, Victoria's fingers tingled from the cold, in spite of her leather gloves. Thank goodness she didn't need to play her violin today. How did the New York musicians manage this weather?

Mom squinted as she examined the sign. "Honey, wasn't this the café in the movie *You've Got Mail?*"

"Which movie?" Dad scratched his head.

"The film where the girl owns a local bookstore and the guy owns the big box store."

"Sounds like one of your romantic comedies," he laughed. "They all blend together to me."

"I quote it all the time," Mom said.

Adrienne nodded. "True. She does."

"The one about the cute bookstore?" Louisa squealed. "We should definitely check out an indie bookstore while we're here."

"Agreed," Mom said.

Inside the café, display cases filled with decadent cakes, elegant pastries, and scrumptious pies beckoned them.

"I see why you chose this place." Victoria nodded to Marie. "Right up your ally."

"It's even more French than Café Chocolat," Adrienne exclaimed. "Check out that *tarte aux fruits*. It looks to die for."

Once everyone had ordered, they squeezed together around an antique table toward the back of the café.

"What a fabulous first day." Victoria bit into her Chocolate Raspberry Delight. The rich fusion of cookie crust and raspberry mousse created the perfect combination. "Thanks so much for bringing us here, Dad and Mom."

"I'm glad you're having fun, sweetie." Dad patted her arm. "What's on the agenda for tomorrow, New York girl?"

"Can we visit the Met?" Adrienne interjected. "I'm dying to see the French impressionist paintings."

"Absolutely." A large smile spread across Dad's face. "I studied several of the paintings for an art history class in college. They're incredible."

Mom reached for Dad's hand. "I also want to visit the Empire State Building."

"Is this because of that movie again?" Dad asked.

She giggled. "A different one, but the same actors."

"No wonder I can't keep them all straight."

"We should also take the girls to see Carnegie Hall. Remember when I sang there with my choir?"

"How could I forget? You were the stunning soprano soloist in a gold evening gown surrounded by a sea of black choir robes. Definitely the prettiest one there." He planted a kiss on her cheek.

Mom's face blushed a deeper shade of pink.

Victoria nodded her assent as she took another bite of the delicious dessert. "I definitely want to see Carnegie Hall and the Met. But I don't want to run out of time to visit Johann Conservatory."

"Don't worry," Dad took a sip of his coffee. "That's why we came. I promise we'll get there."

The following day, they managed to visit the Met, an indie bookstore, and Carnegie Hall as Dad's attempt to keep everyone happy. On top of that, he even surprised them with tickets to the ballet that he'd purchased online several months before. Stella was over the moon with excitement as she watched the dancers twirl across the stage.

"Tomorrow, we should visit Rockefeller Center," Adrienne suggested as they were leaving the ballet.

"Ooh, I'd love to skate." Stella clasped her hands to her chest. "It's like dancing, but on ice."

"You should check on ticket availability," Mom suggested.

"Let's see," Adrienne pulled out her phone. "We could get tickets for an appointment tomorrow at 9 a.m."

Marie moaned. "Nothing later?"

Adrienne shook her head. "No, it's booked the rest of the day."

"But I want to visit the conservatory," Victoria asserted, hands on hips. At this rate they'd never make it.

"I promise we'll visit the conservatory," Dad reassured her. "There's still plenty of time. We'll go skating in the morning and visit Johann in the afternoon."

"I sure hope so," Victoria muttered.

###

The next morning, a heavy fog hung over the city as they headed toward Rockefeller Center.

"I hope we can still see the tree," Mom said, clinging tighter to Dad's arm.

"Don't worry." He patted her hand. "It's covered in so many lights you won't be able to miss it."

Victoria's stomach muscles tightened as she slid her feet into the rental skates. When was the last time she'd been on ice? Probably middle school. Her heartbeat quickened as she stepped tentatively onto the rink.

Seconds later, Stella whizzed past, hair flying behind her from the breeze. What a natural. When had she fit skating lessons into her packed schedule? Her talent for dance translated well onto the ice.

"Need help?" Marie skidded up next to her. "I could hold your hand."

"Nope, I'm good." Victoria grabbed the plastic partition to steady herself. "Just out of practice."

"Okay." Marie skated off.

After an indeterminable amount of time, Victoria finally made it to the tree. Balls and ornaments decorated nearly every inch of the enormous pine, which shimmered with light.

Dad and Mom approached, skating hand in hand.

"Isn't it beautiful, honey?" Mom's eyes sparkled like the tree as she leaned her head against his shoulder.

"Yes, incredible." He scanned the tree. "It must be at least eighty feet tall.

"I've never seen anything like it." Louisa beamed up at it.

They turned to see Stella twirl on the ice, a vision in her pink marshmallow coat.

"Wonderful, dear," Mom exclaimed.

Dad nodded. "Looks like the skating lessons are paying off."

"Victoria, stop clutching the railing and come join me," Stella yelled. "You look like an old lady."

"Ha ha, no thanks," Victoria shook her head. "I can't afford to fall and hurt myself this close to my audition."

"I'll join you," Adrienne said as she hurried up to Stella.

The two bustled off, hand in hand, toward the far end of the rink.

"Shall we take another spin?" Dad asked Mom.

She smiled. "I'd be delighted."

Marie held out her hand to Louisa. "Shall we take another spin as well?" she asked in her best Dad impersonation.

Louisa giggled. "I'd be delighted."

Victoria sighed as they skated away. If only she could let loose and not have to worry about the audition. But that would be irresponsible. She couldn't allow a few minutes of fun to further jeopardize her future. How could she ever handle finding a new instrument and recovering from an injury?

She putzed back toward the other end of the rink, where Stella and Adrienne were skating.

"Let's spin," Stella said as she reached to hold both Adrienne's hands.

"I'd better not," Adrienne protested. "I'm not as good as you."

"Don't worry, you'll be fine."

Slowly, the two of them started to spin together in a circle.

"Isn't this fun?" Stella asked.

"Too fast," Adrienne yelled, as Stella increased her speed.

By now, the two were a blur of color. A second later, Adrienne's toe pick caught the ice, she slipped, and stretched out a hand to catch her fall. Stella, still wobbly from spinning, lost her balance and toppled onto her.

Adrienne collapsed to the ice. A painful scream pierced the air like a shard of glass.

As though on autopilot, Victoria scrambled across the ice. Her stride increased as her older-sister protective nature clicked on. She had to reach her.

Adrienne continued to scream. Seconds later, Victoria slid her arm around Adrienne's waist. With the extra effort to hold another person up, she had more difficulty keeping her balance. Victoria glanced at Adrienne's wrist. Blood flowed from her sister's arm like water down the side of the boat. Victoria's head spun and her vision blurred.

Stella sat on the ice, frozen in shock.

"Get Dad," Victoria yelled.

In a daze, Stella stood up and skated in search of Dad. Could he get there in time?

In the meantime, Victoria pressed her fingers to Adrienne's wrist to stop the flow of blood. She needed Dad. Now.

A minute later, Dad zoomed up, concerned lines etched across his forehead. His gaze fell to her arm. "Help me get her off the ice."

With Adrienne wedged in between them, the two of them skated off the rink and hurried to the nearest bench.

Victoria cradled her sister in her arms. "Adrienne, are you all right?"

She shook her head. Her face drained of all color. "No. My . . . my wrist."

Dad kneeled next to them, now in full-on doctor mode. He grabbed Victoria's scarf and wrapped it around Adrienne's wrist like a tourniquet. "I've got to stop the blood. Call a taxi. We need to get her to the hospital."

Three hours later, Victoria, Marie, Louisa, and Stella found themselves in the hospital waiting room.

Stella sank into one of the chairs. Louisa pulled a book from her bag, stared at it, then put it back.

Victoria paced back and forth. "I can't stand it any longer. What's taking so long?"

"Dad's there," Marie said. "He'll know what to do."

Stella whimpered from the chair. "I can't believe this happened. And it's all my fault. I shouldn't have spun her so fast. Do you think she'll be okay?"

Louisa took a seat next to Stella and pulled her tight. "Let's pray for her. Dear God, please be with Adrienne. Help her not to lose too much blood. Give the doctors wisdom."

"And let her be okay." Stella sniffled.

Louisa nodded to Victoria.

Her throat tightened. She hated to pray out loud. The sound of her own voice made her uncomfortable. What should she say? She kneeled beside the other girls. "Dear God, I pray she isn't in too much pain, and give her a fast recovery."

"And give her the mental strength she'll need for the trials ahead," Marie added.

Stella's face turned as white as the bed sheet. "You don't think she's dying, do you?"

"I hope not." Marie shook her head. "But I doubt she'll play viola anytime soon."

Victoria's stomach churned. She'd been so worried about Adrienne's immediate condition that she hadn't even imagined how this would affect her sister's music career. Why had she been so hateful toward her last semester? Now she'd give her own right arm for Adrienne if she had the chance.

"What can we do?" Stella's blue eyes searched her face.

Victoria's gaze dropped to the floor. She was the oldest, in charge of protecting her sisters. She should have the answers. But she didn't.

Marie straightened her shoulders. "Regardless of her condition, it's our job to encourage her—rebuild her self-esteem. Are you with me?"

Victoria and the others nodded their heads in assent.

After what seemed like an eternity, Dad clicked open the door. "They had to operate."

"What?" Marie's eyes bulged.

"It must've been pretty bad," Louisa said.

Dad nodded. "Yes, a compound fracture. She'll wake up from the anesthesia soon. I'm sure she'll want to see you all, but it might be best to visit her one at a time. Remember, she's weak and medicated, so keep your visits short."

"I'm going." Marie stood up to leave with Dad.

By now Stella was bawling with hysterics, while Louisa tried to comfort her. Victoria fidgeted in her own folding chair. What should she do? How long until her turn?

Fifteen minutes later, Dad joined them and motioned to Victoria.

She took a deep breath to steady herself, stood up, and walked to room 112. When she knocked, Marie opened the door.

"She's awake now," Marie said. "You should have a little time with her before the meds kick in again." She gave Victoria's hand a quick squeeze and exited the room.

Adrienne sat upright on the bed in a light green hospital gown, propped up with pillows and connected to an IV. Her hair stuck up in random patches all over her head. Victoria's gaze fell to Adrienne's left arm wrapped in bandages. "How are you?"

Adrienne's face turned white. "They said it will take several weeks to heal. Even then, I may not make a full recovery." She looked away.

A knot formed in Victoria's throat. She reached to grab Adrienne's good hand. What could she say?

When Adrienne turned back to look at her, tears pooled in her blue eyes. "I might not play viola again." She burst into sobs.

Victoria scooted closer and cradled her sister in her arms. "Don't jump to conclusions. They don't know that yet, do they?"

Adrienne wiped her eyes. "No. They couldn't give me a definite answer one way or the other. At any rate, it'll be weeks."

Silence stole over the room. Victoria stroked Adrienne's wispy hair. "I'm so sorry. I know how much the concerto competition means to you. Maybe you'll be better by April."

"You would've won anyway." Adrienne sniffed.

Victoria clasped her hand in both of hers. "I'd give up the concerto competition right now if it could make you well again. If only I could take your place."

Adrienne shook her head. "No. You need your arm for your audition here. I was the one stupid enough to skate with Stella. There's nothing we can do."

"We can pray." Victoria bowed her head. "Dear God, please heal Adrienne's arm. Keep her safe, and if it's your will, help her make a full recovery. Amen."

A sob escaped Adrienne's lips. "Thank you." She nestled her head on the pillows. "Your support means a lot. It's all I ever wanted."

Victoria choked back tears. She planted a kiss on Adrienne's forehead. "I'm here for you, no matter what happens."

Chapter 21

Jerry couldn't focus on the music. He should practice his concerto, but instead, he opted for running aimlessly through his scales. When would Victoria get here? She'd flown back from New York today, and he wanted to hear all about it. That wasn't true. He didn't *want* to hear her gush about the city. Why did she and his mother have an obsession with New York, anyway? If it wasn't for that, he would have asked Victoria out months ago. But if she really wanted to move to New York, he wouldn't stand in her way.

A glance at his watch said five till nine. Thank goodness she was usually punctual. In the meantime, he'd practice the etude his teacher had assigned for his next lesson.

Minutes later, he jolted from the knock at the door. "Come in."

The heavy door creaked open, and Victoria stepped inside.

She plopped onto the piano bench and set what appeared to be Marie's violin case on the floor. But something was wrong. Her puffy eyes said it all.

"What happened?"

"Jerry, it's awful." She sniffed.

"The conservatory?" He allowed a half-hope to surface.

She shook her head. "No. We never made it to visit Johann. Adrienne had an accident."

Jerry's mind raced. "What kind? A car accident?"

"We were skating at Rockefeller Center when she and Stella spun out of control. Adrienne fell to the ice, and Stella collapsed on top of her."

Jerry winced. "Is she okay?"

"She's stable now, but she lost so much blood. I saw her bone protruding from her wrist." Victoria crumpled as sobs overtook her.

Jerry slid next to her on the bench, and she buried her face in his chest. The flowery smell of her shampoo filled his senses.

She peered up at him. "What if we'd lost her? And after I'd been so horrible."

Another wave of sobs overtook her. He pulled her close and wrapped his arms around her.

"Victoria, it wasn't your fault. And now that she's stable, you don't have to worry."

"I don't know. She's so shaken. They said she might not play viola again."

Silence. What could he say? It was bad enough he had to face the idea of giving up music, but Adrienne? It would kill her.

"Do they know that for sure?" he asked, stroking her back.

"No, they don't know anything for sure right now. We just have to wait and see how she heals."

"She's not going to handle that well, I imagine. Do you think I should visit her?"

Victoria leaned back and searched his face for several moments. "You care about her, don't you?"

"Of course," he answered. "We've been friends for years."

Victoria lowered her gaze. "I see."

He slid his thumb under her chin and raised it so he could look her in the face. "I care about her as a friend."

Her brown eyes bore into his. "Is that how you see me?"

How could he respond? Yes, he cared about Victoria as a friend. She'd been his best friend for several years. But no, he didn't care about Adrienne the same way he did Victoria.

He held her gaze. "No."

Confused lines wrinkled her forehead. "But I thought we were friends."

He inched closer to her on the bench, her intoxicating proximity nearly overwhelming him. "We are, but—" He leaned forward and pressed his lips to hers. He'd longed to do this. For years. He was kissing Victoria.

A few seconds later, she pulled away. "I... I don't know what to say."

He tightened his embrace. "Say you want to kiss me again."

"I do. I mean, I don't know."

"What do you mean?" He held his breath. What if she didn't feel for him the same way he felt about her?

She stood up. "How is this going to work? I'm leaving in a few months. Besides, your mom would never approve."

"Forget Mom. We'll keep it a secret." He pulled her back onto the bench. "She doesn't need to know."

Victoria frowned. "That'll never work."

"Of course not long term." He drew his face inches from hers. "Just for now, while we're sorting this out."

She held his gaze. Did he detect a hint of longing in her eyes?

He reached out to stroke her cheek, then wound his hand to the back of her neck and drew her to him. This time, she lingered for several more seconds as his lips met hers—a good sign.

Victoria's heart leapt when she woke up the next morning. Jerry Chang had finally kissed her! Had it been a dream? The soft brush of his lips against hers, his hands running through her hair, the enticing smell of his cologne.

The door creaked open. Dressed in flannel pajamas and fluffy slippers, Louisa squeezed in and halted mid-stride. "Oh, I'm sorry, Victoria. I thought you'd be up by now." Her green eyes met Victoria's. "What're you grinning at?"

Victoria sat up and propped her back with a pillow. "Nothing."

Louisa plopped next to her and leaned against an extra pillow. "I know you better than that. Give me the scoop."

"Can you keep a secret?"

She raised her eyebrows. "Better than anyone. What's up?"

"Well…" Victoria snuggled deeper under the covers. "Jerry and I—"

"He asked you out!" Louisa squealed. "I knew it."

"Uh…" Victoria bit her lip. He *hadn't* asked her out. What were they? A couple? A secret couple?

Louisa frowned. "You are dating, aren't you?"

Victoria twisted the comforter in her lap. "I don't know. We're still trying to figure things out."

"What happened?"

"He kissed me."

A squeal erupted from Louisa. "He did? How exciting! What was it like?"

"What do you mean?"

Louisa giggled. "Timid, sweet, passionate?"

Victoria yanked the pillow out from behind her and bopped Louisa's stomach. "I'm not going to kiss and tell."

Louisa pulled out her own pillow and whacked Victoria's back. "Victoria and Jerry, sittin' in a tree…"

The door opened just as Victoria flung her pillow at Louisa. Marie smirked from the doorway. "A pillow fight? How old are you, five?"

"Fourteen." Louisa chucked the pillow at Marie, who danced a step to avoid it.

"When you're done playing slumber party, I've got breakfast ready. Quiche and fruit salad."

"Sounds delicious," Louisa said.

The scent of bacon caused Victoria's mouth to water. "Thanks. We'll be down in a minute."

"Good." Marie closed the door behind her.

Louisa hugged her knees to her chest. "Do you think Jerry will kiss you again? What did you do afterward?"

"Matt and Eddie showed up for band practice and insisted we join them."

"Ugh, boys are oblivious. Couldn't they tell you two needed a moment alone?"

Victoria rolled her eyes. "Of course not. I broke away as soon as I heard footsteps outside the door."

Louisa frowned. "Why don't you want people to find out?"

"It's still new." Victoria traced a seam along the comforter with her fingers. "And his mom's my professor."

"You think she'd care?"

A knot tightened in Victoria's gut. "Probably. She'd think a relationship between us would get in the way of our careers. She didn't even like me leaving for New York for vacation instead of staying to practice."

Louisa's jaw fell open. "You're kidding. Doesn't she know you needed a break?"

"No. She thinks holidays are a great time to catch up on work, not gallivant around." And make out with her son...

The door burst open. "You girls coming?" Marie asked. "I don't want the quiche to get cold."

Louisa slid from the bed and pulled Victoria with her. "We'd better go."

Two days later, the barren white walls of the hallway did nothing to inspire confidence as Victoria stood outside the door to Professor Chang's office. After several deep breaths, Victoria willed herself to turn the knob.

"Hello, Victoria." Professor Chang's voice betrayed a hint of coldness. She tapped her fingers on the desk in front of her. "I'm glad you're back from vacation. As you know, we have a lot of work to do before your conservatory audition next month."

Victoria swallowed. Her teacher was still mad. How much did she know?

"Let's start with the second movement of the concerto." Professor Chang's dark eyes flashed. "I hope it's improved since your last lesson."

Victoria's hands trembled as she pulled Marie's violin from its case. If only she had a better instrument. Instead, she'd downgraded. What a disaster. Try to relax. Think of a peaceful place.

As she began the opening bars, images of Jerry flooded her mind. Unlike the volatile nature of the first movement, the second floated through the air as if on ocean waves. She'd listened to the piece so many times she could hear the flute part soar with the violin, like two birds in song at the first sign of spring. Her muscles loosened while the music evoked images of the sea, the Statue of Liberty standing tall in the Atlantic Ocean. Her fingers cascaded over the instrument like foam on the beach. In her mind, she strolled along the harbor with Jerry, hand in hand. Her stomach fluttered as he drew her close, leaned over, and placed his lips on hers. Elation bubbled inside when the music swelled. Her fingers continued to dance, then she pulled her bow in deliberate strokes to the climax. She paused for a moment with her bow poised at the tip to bask in the warmth of the moment. Then, slowly, her bow resumed its motion, and she brought the movement to a close.

After the last note died away, she turned to Professor Chang in anticipation of her critique. But instead of a stern expression, Professor Chang sat with eyes closed, a faint smile on her face. After several more moments of silence, she opened her eyes. "Now *that* was the work of an artist. Bravo."

Victoria's heart skipped a beat. Had her teacher given her a true compliment?

"However, this violin is abysmal. Where on earth is yours?" Professor Chang took the instrument to examine it. "I'm suspicious of a crack in the seam." She held it sideways, righted it, and then peered through the f-holes. "The soundpost needs an adjustment, and I'd suggest a new set of strings." Professor Chang ran the bow over the G, D, A, and E strings. "This is a student violin, not fitting for a soloist on stage." She set the violin on her desk. "The orchestra will overpower you."

Victoria's heart sank. How could she find an adequate one in time? Maybe she should ask Mom and Dad for help.

Professor Chang retrieved her own Stradivarius violin and held it out to Victoria. "Try this for comparison."

Victoria froze. Play a Strad, the most famous violin of all time? Her hands trembled as she reached for the Italian instrument. She clutched the wooden neck with such a tight grip her knuckles turned white. Whatever you do, don't drop it. After a couple of deep breaths, she recommenced the second movement.

"Not that one." Her teacher shook her head. "Play the first movement."

The opening bars filled the room with the force of a kettledrum. The strength of the instrument took Victoria's breath away. No wonder the Stradivarius had earned its esteemed reputation.

"See?" Professor Chang arched an eyebrow.

"Fabulous." Victoria nodded as they traded their instruments back. "But I don't own a Strad."

"Of course not." Professor Chang tucked the violin in its case. "But you can't compete on a student-grade violin. I believe you have a strong chance to win the concerto competition and attend Johann Conservatory, but you need to do everything to boost your chances. No more vacation or other distractions." She shot Victoria a pointed look. "If you want to be accepted, you must focus. Keep your eyes on the goal."

A knot twisted inside Victoria. She forced a reciprocal grin. "Thanks. I appreciate your vote of confidence."

"I want to hear the third movement at your next lesson. But not on that instrument."

Victoria winced. "Yes, professor." Where in the world would she find something like a Stradivarius by next week? Even with her parents' help, she could never afford *that*.

Chapter 22

Jerry's mind raced as he stirred the shrimp and vegetables, then checked on the rice that simmered in the adjacent pot. Victoria had agreed to a dinner date. Tonight. She'd be here in thirty minutes. Perhaps he could win her over with his amazing culinary skills.

"Jerry," his mom called from the living room, "I'm headed to rehearsal." She poked her head into the kitchen. "No need to wait up. This'll be a long one. Also, can you pick your father up from the airport in the morning? He gets in at 8:10, and you know I'll need my sleep after tonight."

Jerry nodded. With both of his parents gone, he'd have plenty of time with Victoria.

A half-hour later, the doorbell rang. He paused, smoothed his polo shirt, and opened the door. Victoria stood there, a shy smile on her face. Wow, she looked good in that pair of skinny jeans and black sweater. She'd even thrown on a pair of heels.

"Hi, Jerry."

"Hey, Victoria." His heartbeat quickened. "Come in."

She followed him inside, and he guided her to the living room.

"Smells amazing. What are you making?"

"Shrimp stir fry."

"Ooh, sounds good. Do you need help?"

"Sure, you can keep an eye on the rice." He handed her a wooden spoon.

She stirred the pot for several moments. "How do I know it's done? Sorry, I'm not much of a cook. Mom and Marie do most of that at our house." A slight flush crept into her cheeks.

"That's okay. I do most of it here." By now the rice had absorbed the water in the pot, so he reached for the spoon, then scooped the rice into a bowl. "Why don't you take this to the table, and I'll get the shrimp."

"Sounds good." She smiled as he extended her the bowl. "Thanks for inviting me to dinner."

"My pleasure."

They'd hung out a million times before, but never here. And never on a date. What should he say? "Hey, I know Matt hopes Adrienne will be able to play with the band by the time of our concert, but if she's not, we'd need another string player. What do you think?"

Victoria frowned. "I don't play viola."

"Doesn't matter," he insisted. "I wrote the part in treble clef. You can read it."

"I suppose. But let's pray Adrienne recovers." She scooped a bite into her mouth. "Ooh, this is delicious. I can tell you're pro."

"Thanks. I just threw it together." That wasn't true. He'd agonized over the meal for an hour, then spent two hours at the grocery store to make sure he had the exact ingredients. He raised a piece of shrimp to his mouth and took a bite. Not bad.

Victoria set down her fork. "Your mom thinks I need a new instrument."

Jerry continued to chew. Did they have to talk about his mom on the date?

"She let me play her Stradivarius, and it sounded phenomenal. There's no way I can buy an instrument to compare with that."

"Mom has these crazy lofty ideals for everyone, but sometimes she can't see reason. Of course you can't afford one. She only has one because a rich donor gave it to her after coming to one of her concerts."

Victoria fiddled with her napkin. "Still, she's right. I do need *something* now that mine is broken, and Marie's would never suffice for a soloist in a concert hall. I'd never stand a chance at winning the concerto competition, and I've been practicing three hours a day on top of all our rehearsals. I absolutely love the Saint-Saëns. It's phenomenal." She took another bite. "Oh, I almost forgot. What are you playing for the competition?"

He looked down at his plate. Did he dare tell her? On their first date? No. That wouldn't go well. He didn't want to risk her wrath. "Um...I'm still trying to decide."

Her jaw dropped. "Jerry, the audition is in two months. You're running out of time. You'd better decide fast. Does your mom know yet that you're competing?"

"No. I'd rather her not find out until the last minute. She thinks I need to focus on my studies."

She reached for his hand. "You don't have to go to medical school. It's your choice, not theirs."

The touch of her fingers on his sent a ripple of excitement through his body. "I know. But I don't want to be a disappointment."

"To them? Or yourself?"

He swallowed. Good question.

The next morning, Victoria couldn't stop thinking about her date as the family drove to church. Was she crazy to consider starting a relationship this close to graduation? But Jerry had been amazing. Everything about the dinner had tasted delicious. And those banana fritters drizzled in caramel sauce? To die for. How had she never known about his culinary capabilities? He could rival Marie.

After service, she still replayed every moment of the date as they headed to Gigi and Papa's for Sunday dinner. At the end of the date, he'd walked her to the car and kissed her again. Sweet and slow. They'd lingered several moments together until Professor Chang's silver sedan pulled into the parking lot, and Victoria had quickly driven away. Hopefully her teacher hadn't seen them. She'd never approve.

"I'm so glad you're here!" Gigi exclaimed as the family approached the door. "I was devastated to hear about Adrienne's accident. How are you doing, dear?"

"Not great." Adrienne pointed to the yellow cast on her arm.

"I'm so sorry." Gigi squeezed her tight. "I know this must be painful for you. But come on in. I have something I want to show you." She gestured for them to follow her to the steep wooden staircase that led to the second floor.

"Hold onto the railing," Gigi cautioned. The "railing" was a rope anchored to the wall at the top and bottom of the stairs. "We don't want you to fall down these again, Stella."

"Gigi, I was one year old." Stella laughed.

"Nearly gave me a heart attack." As Gigi reached the top, she stepped onto a mat of green shag carpet.

Victoria's eyes gravitated to the upper point in the A-frame ceiling and then followed the slope down the angle to where it reached the floor. How many hours had she and her sisters spent playing here as kids? The perfect hideout from the grownups, where they'd pretended to be princesses in a high tower, pirates on a ship, and the March sisters' Orchard House from *Little Women*.

Gigi squatted beside an antique metal trunk tucked away next to the wall. She didn't have room to stand. "Let's see what we've got in Maman's affairs from France." She popped open the trunk. "Where are those ballet slippers?" She pulled out several newspapers dating back more than a half-century, a pair of ladies' gloves, several dresses, and a couple of old-fashioned hats.

"How cute." Adrienne donned an oval-shaped hat and batted her eyes in a coquettish manner behind the lace front piece, a hint of her old self peeking through.

"That was Maman's. I remember when she wore it to a party." Gigi removed a china doll and several French books. "Here they are." She held up a pair of pointe shoes. "Stella, these are for you. They belonged to Maman as well. She was a professional ballerina at the *Opéra Garnier* in Paris for several years, you know."

Stella beamed as she fingered the satin slippers. "How beautiful."

Next, Gigi pulled out a vintage fringe dress and a long rectangular case.

"What's that?" Victoria pointed at the latter. It couldn't be ... could it?

"That belonged to Grandpère Leclair. Open it." Victoria examined the case. Two latches fastened it at the front, which sprang open at her touch. A maroon velvet cloth blanketed the interior. Her heartbeat quickened. Hands shaking with excitement, she lifted the material with care. Her breath caught in her throat. Underneath the velvet covering lay an antique violin.

She gasped. Unlike her former instrument crafted within the last century, this one showed numerous signs of age. The outer varnish was worn where the musician's hand had held it. Victoria's fingers traced the curves of the instrument. No perceivable cracks, although a trained luthier would need to give it a proper examination. She plucked the strings, so loose they emitted snapping noises rather than notes. Next, she pulled out the bow, its horsehair yellow with age. Several broken strands hung from the tip.

Gigi's face glowed with pleasure. "From what Maman told me, he was an amazing virtuoso who used to accompany her while she practiced."

A sense of familial pride welled up inside Victoria as she held the old violin. Her musical heritage reached back at least five generations. "This is amazing."

"It's yours, if you want it. Your mother told me your other one broke."

"Really?" Victoria's pulse quickened.

"I thought you might like something to remember your family heritage when you move to New York."

"Thanks, Gigi," Victoria gave her a squeeze. A family heirloom. Of course who knew what condition it was in or if it would be playable. But it was hers.

"And girls, feel free to take the clothes and books, too. These don't do anyone much good hiding in a dusty old trunk, do they?"

"*Merci,* Gigi." Adrienne scooped up the flapper dress and hat.

Louisa ran her fingers along the leather bindings of the old books, then cradled them in her arms as everyone headed downstairs.

In the living room, Victoria engaged in combat with the violin. Every time she drew her bow to play concert A, the string unwound, and the pitch sank into nothingness.

"It sounds like a dying cow," Adrienne moaned. She crossed her legs in the recliner, the fringe of her flapper dress dangling over the sides.

"It. Needs. To. Stick." Victoria gritted her teeth as she twisted the peg with all her might. "There." Her jaw relaxed. "Maybe now it will hold."

She played the open A string. Not perfect, but good enough for now. "One string down, three to go."

Adrienne moaned. "This might take all day."

Victoria struggled for a few more minutes. "This will have to do for now. Do we know who made the instrument?"

Gigi shook her head.

Victoria peered inside the f-shaped holes to read the inscription. She squinted at the faded words. No use. Maybe a luthier with a practiced eye would have more success?

As she nestled the violin on her shoulder, she winced at the lack of shoulder pad. This would be a trick to grip it in place. Much to her surprise, the opening line of the Saint-Saëns soared from the violin with ease. Although the instrument needed new strings and a thorough checkup, its rich tone flowed from the strings. Strong yet subtle, the violin responded well to her touch. With no need to apply additional pressure, she allowed her right arm to sink into the bow as gravity took over. Maybe this instrument *could* help her win the concerto competition.

A round of applause erupted from the room at her conclusion.

"*Magnifique*," Gigi said as tears welled up in her eyes. "I'm sure Grandpère would be proud."

"Can you play the hoedown?" Papa asked.

Victoria chuckled. "That's Marie's genre." She extended the violin to her sister.

Marie's face lit up. "You're sharing it with me?"

"I'd be crazy not to, after you've loaned me yours the past several weeks. Give it a try."

Marie began to play a fiddle tune, Papa slapped his knee, and Gigi put her hands together to keep the rhythm. Even Victoria couldn't resist tapping her foot.

A moment later, Papa stood and extended his hand to Gigi. "A dance, Madame."

She rose to join him, pinching the fabric of her skirt like a duchess at a ball. *Avec plaisir, mon amour.*"

Soon everyone was dancing. Dad promenaded Mom across the floor. Eddie, who'd just arrived for dinner, twirled Stella around the room. This family was crazy, but in a good way. As hard as it was to admit, she'd miss them next year.

By now Adrienne was clicking her heels and swinging her hips like a twenties heroine from an F. Scott Fitzgerald novel.

Victoria's eyes returned to the violin in Marie's hands. If only she could have deciphered the inscription. It wasn't a Stradivarius. Too different from Professor Chang's. Besides, people claimed to find those all the time, but more often than not, the instruments were replicas. The timbre of this violin, while pleasant, possessed a different quality than that of the Italian masters.

"Come on." Stella yanked Victoria's arm, which pulled her from her reverie. "Don't be such a party pooper. Join us."

Victoria gave in. Stella had an uncanny ability to lighten the mood.

Chapter 23

The following Saturday afternoon, Jerry rummaged through the fridge. Victoria had come over for lunch at the last minute, and he hadn't had time to prepare anything. Where was the leftover pizza?

"Looking for this?" Victoria, seated at the table, grinned as she held up a plate piled with several slices.

"Yes." Jerry slid into the chair next to her.

"Nothing beats pizza for Saturday lunch. I heated it up while you were upstairs."

"Making yourself at home, I see." He kissed her on the cheek, grabbed a slice, and took a bite. Cheesy goodness melted in his mouth. Seconds later, he finished his piece and reached for another. "What should we do this afternoon before band practice?"

Victoria rolled her eyes.

"You can't back out now. You promised." He reached for her hand and traced his thumb along the lines of her palm. So smooth.

"Oh alright." She pulled her hand away. "But first, I'd like to swing by Mr. Amati's luthier's shop to see if he can fix up Gigi's old violin. I enjoyed playing it the other day—very powerful."

"Worth a shot." Jerry eyed the Valentine's Day candy hearts she'd brought, opened the bag, and popped one into his mouth. "These are addictive."

"I know." Victoria picked out a purple one. Then a pink. "Take these away from me before I devour them all." She shoved the bowl back toward him. "Wanna go with me?"

Jerry's head clouded as the sugar rush kicked in. "Sure." He closed the pizza box and dropped it in the trash. "I need to get a tune-up for Bella, anyway. I'll bring my bass guitar, too, so we can head straight to practice."

"You named your cello?" Victoria laughed.

He cocked an eyebrow. "Sure. She's got a nice form. Like you." He grinned.

A slight flush colored Victoria's cheeks. "You're scandalous."

He pulled her close. "Because of you."

A half-hour later, bells jingled as Jerry pushed open the door to the luthier shop and stepped inside.

Stringed instruments filled every nook and cranny of the small store. Cello scrolls protruded into the narrow pathway. Double basses laid sideways across the hardwood floor. A couple of harps stood in the corner. Violins, violas, ukuleles, and mandolins covered every inch of the walls, while the smell of spruce and maple filled the air.

"It's like we've travelled back in time," Victoria mused. "The sheer number of instruments." She stretched her arms wide.

As Jerry made his way to the counter, he nearly knocked over a cello blocking his path.

A gentleman with wiry gray hair on the sides of his head stood hunched over a deconstructed violin at the end of a long counter. Odd fragments of instruments like chinrests, tailpieces, curved strings, hairless bows, and woodworking tools lay strewn across the entire workspace.

Jerry pressed the shiny bell in front of him. "Good afternoon, Mr. Amati." When the man looked up from his work, his bifocals reflected the light from the window.

A grin spread across his wrinkled face. "Ah, my favorite customers." He set down his tools and hobbled toward them. "What brings you here today?"

Jerry set his instrument on the counter. "I need a checkup for my cello—looking for open seams, an adjustment, new strings, the works."

Mr. Amati pulled out the instrument and examined it from every angle. "Are you satisfied with its tone quality?" He tipped it to the side.

"To be frank, no. Something sounds off. Maybe due to the winter weather."

The luthier inserted a tiny tool through the f-hole and turned it. "There. Try that."

Jerry grabbed his bow and played a few notes.

"Well?" Mr. Amati raised his bushy eyebrows.

"Better." Jerry stroked the neck of the instrument.

"Of course it still doesn't compare to your mother's Stradivarius. Now that's a beauty." Mr. Amati's crooked nose rose in the air. "She brings it to me every year for its annual maintenance."

"She respects your expertise." Jerry resisted the urge to laugh at the guy's bird-like appearance. "You've been in the business a long time."

Mr. Amati's smile revealed yellow teeth. "I learned the trade from my father, who learned it from his father, who learned it from his father." Jerry wouldn't have thought it possible, but the guy's nose rose even higher in the air. "At one point I traced my musical heritage back to the 16th century. Did I ever tell you the story about my ancestor, Andrea Amati?"

Yes, every time.

"Born in Cremona, Italy in 1505, he's considered the earliest violin maker." Mr. Amati adjusted his bifocals so they perched on the end of his nose. "King Charles IX of France commissioned Amati to make instruments for a court orchestra..."

Jerry yawned. The well-known story could continue for another fifteen minutes.

"Mr. Amati, I wondered if you'd look at this." Victoria placed Gigi's case on the counter. "How much work does it need? And what do you think it's worth?"

Mr. Amati's bushy brows furrowed at the sight of the battered case. "What's this?"

"My grandmother found it in an old trunk."

Mr. Amati's throat emitted a guttural sound. "Let me guess. You think you've stumbled on a long-lost Stradivarius." He rolled his eyes. "I can't tell you how many times people come in here with heirloom violins from their great-great uncle twice-removed and hope it's a Strad. Most of the time, they're not worth more than the cheap factory-made student violins." He pushed the case back toward her.

Victoria's smile faded.

Jerry leaned his arms on the counter. "Couldn't you at least see what it needs and maybe give an appraisal?"

Mr. Amati scrunched his nose. "Alright." After unlatching the sides, he held up the instrument and squinted through the f-holes. "Can't tell the maker—the writing's smudged."

"What about the condition?" Jerry pressed.

The luthier examined it from several angles. "Needs a lot of work. I see several small cracks in the seams, although not as many as I'd expect from an old trunk shipped from overseas." He held the violin under the lamp next to the workspace. "The varnish is worn and ought to be refinished, and I'd recommend we replace the fingerboard." He turned the pegs. "And of course, it needs new strings. These look a hundred years old."

"They probably are," Victoria acknowledged.

He set the violin in its case and picked up the bow. "This requires new horsehair, no surprise, and the ivory tip's broken off."

Victoria's eyes filled with tears. Time to wrap it up.

"Thanks, Mr. Amati, for your evaluation," Jerry said. "Let me know how much I owe you for my cello. I can pick it up in a few days."

"Wait a minute." Mr. Amati put his hand on the violin case. "For Victoria, I'll take a closer look and give an estimate on costs of repairs, appraisal, etc. She can decide what to do when you pick up the cello."

Victoria's eyes met Jerry's. "Thank you," she mouthed.

"Anything to keep the Changs and Pearsons happy." Mr. Amati turned and hobbled back to his work.

After a quick wave to him through the window, Jerry and Victoria climbed into his car and drove away.

Victoria pulled sunglasses from her purse and placed them over her eyes, probably to hide the smudged mascara. "That didn't go as planned. If he doesn't think the violin's worth a thing, there's no way Professor Chang will like it. Now I'll have to find a different one."

"Don't jump to conclusions," Jerry said. "Mr. Amati was edgy because the violin wasn't from his shop. He might come around to it."

Victoria sniffed. "I thought Gigi's violin might be spectacular, or at least an upgrade. He brushed it aside like a piece of firewood."

Jerry leaned back against the seat. "I wouldn't give up yet. He needs to look closer at it. If the instrument's worth something, he'd want to know. Imagine the headlines—'Local luthier discovers Stradivarius.'"

"It's not a Strad."

"How do you know?"

"Different tone than your mom's. Darker."

They pulled up to Victoria's house and opened the front door to an explosion of sound.

Instead of Mrs. Pearson's usual beginner piano repertoire, strains of guitars and drums erupted from the formal music room.

Jerry's grip tightened on his bass guitar case as he moved toward the noise.

Dressed in a sequined purple shirt, Stella pranced around in the center of the room, a mic clutched in her hand. She stepped over a mess of wires and squeezed around the mic stands, pedals, and amps that surrounded her.

Matt, decked in a cowboy hat, crooned next to her, strumming his guitar. Marie sawed away on a red electric violin behind them, while Eddie pounded a trap set.

Stella rose on the balls of her feet and twirled. "What did you think, Jerry?"

"Uhhh … cool." He set down his case and pulled out the instrument.

Matt gestured to Stella. "This girl's got talent. She'll be a star someday."

Stella beamed.

Marie checked the intonation on her electric violin. "Victoria, we need you to convince Louisa to play keyboard with us. It would round out the sound."

"Why does she need convincing?" Jerry took his place next to Marie.

"Louisa hates to play in front of people."

"But we need her," Stella insisted.

"I'll see if I can get her." Victoria headed upstairs.

Minutes later, she and Louisa entered the living room.

Louisa bit her lip. "You all know I hate to perform in front of people. Besides, I don't know how to improvise."

"You'll learn." Victoria's eyes met Jerry's before she ushered her sister to the piano.

So she *had* listened to him.

"How do I play a song I've never heard before without sheet music?" Louisa asked as she sat at the piano.

"I'll teach you." A smile played at the corners of Victoria's mouth.

Jerry's eyes lingered a couple extra moments on her lips. Maybe he could teach Victoria a thing or two about improvisation.

Marie set a sheet on the piano, interrupting his reverie. "Here's the chord chart."

Louisa squinted. "How do I know what notes to use?"

"When in doubt, play the root of the chord." Victoria pointed to the music.

Louisa took a deep breath. "I'll give it a shot."

"I'll play with you as well, to give you a better idea," Victoria said.

Matt cleared his throat. "From the top."

After a hesitant start, Louisa's technique grew more confident each time they ran the song, adding her own ornamentation and arpeggios to add flavor.

"Amazing job." Marie clapped Louisa's shoulder at the end of rehearsal. "I knew you had it in you."

Louisa's face flushed. "I guess it wasn't too hard after all."

"You rock!" Matt flashed her a wide grin. "Total pro."

Stella tugged on his T-shirt. "How about my vocals? Was I in tune?"

Jerry chuckled. Apparently Stella had developed a crush on the much-too-old-for-her guitarist.

"Victoria," Jerry called at the end of rehearsal. "I need to ask you something."

Her stomach fluttered. Wow, he looked good in his black T-shirt. Never in her wildest dreams would she have imagined falling for a band guy.

Once the others left the room, he reached for her hand and tugged her into a corner.

"I didn't get to kiss you yet today." He stroked her silky hair, then ran his hands down her soft sweater.

As she leaned into him, his rapid heartbeats thumped against her chest. She breathed in his rich scent, a warm mixture of orange and saffron, and her own heartbeat raced as he leaned in to press his lips to hers.

A warm sensation flooded her body as he wound his arms around her waist, pulling her closer.

"Victoria," Marie yelled.

The couple jumped apart.

"Always interruptions." He sighed.

Yes, always interruptions. Too many family members here to bother them. He needed to move to New York, too.

Marie entered and cocked an eyebrow. Did she suspect? "Adrienne's listening to moody music again. I need you to talk to her. Unless I'm interrupting something."

Victoria glanced at Jerry. "We're done, I think," she stammered. "I'll see what I can do." She mouthed "I'm sorry" to him before heading upstairs. As she stopped in front of Adrienne's room, muffled music seeped through the door, not clear enough for Victoria to recognize.

After a couple of knocks, she turned the knob. Adrienne lay in bed with her eyes closed, her casted arm visible on top of the canary-yellow bedspread. Her face was pale, and her sunken features lacked their usual animation.

The strains of music continued, clearer on this side of the door—Beethoven's Seventh Symphony, second movement—one he'd composed while losing his sense of hearing. How awful to live in a world without music, the rhythmic pulse that drove her own existence.

She laid a hand on her sister's forehead. "Adrienne? How are you?" Victoria brushed a stray wisp of hair from her sister's face.

Adrienne rolled to her side, away from Victoria. "How do you think I am? While the rest of you practice together, I'm shut up here in this room. Alone."

Victoria's heart sank as the plaintive strains of the symphony filled her ears. Unlike Beethoven, Adrienne could still hear. But if she couldn't play... Victoria squeezed her sister's shoulder. "I can't imagine what you feel, but you don't have to go through it alone."

"Yes, I do." Adrienne turned to face her. "No one else can take my place. It's my problem. I'm the one who fell on the ice."

Victoria closed her eyes to block out the image of Adrienne's fall. When she opened them again, a large easel with a half-completed painting caught her attention. She moved next to it for a better look.

"What's this?" She scanned the raised colors on the canvas.

For a moment, Adrienne's eyes lit up, then the look diminished. "It's nothing." She pulled the covers over her face.

The image displayed a woman next to a beautiful river with a large cathedral looming in the distance. "Paris?"

Adrienne nodded. "I'd like to visit someday. Maybe study music. I've always found the French composers fascinating."

Victoria smiled. "Like Saint-Saëns and Berlioz?"

"Yes. And I found another interesting one recently. Joseph Bologne, also known as Chevalier de Saint-Georges. He was a dreamy black composer, knight, fencer, and even a colonel during the French Revolution, in addition to his position as composer and conductor. Isn't that dreamy?"

"Sounds like it."

"You'd love him. He wrote a ton of music for violin, including concertos and several sonatas for two violins."

Victoria squeezed Adrienne's hand. "Maybe we can play one when you're better. Besides, I'm still looking for an eighteenth-century piece to perform for my conservatory audition. I figured something by Mozart."

Adrienne wrinkled her nose. "Too cliché. Definitely check out Joseph Bologne. He's far more fascinating."

"I will. Thanks for the tip." Victoria kissed her on the forehead. "Now get some sleep."

Chapter 24

A week later, Victoria returned to the practice room for the second time that morning. Over the past few days, she'd thrown herself into practice sessions with renewed vigor, albeit with Marie's violin. Adrienne was right. Joseph Bologne's *Violin Sonata in G Minor* proved the perfect fit for her audition requirements. Her sister would make a great musicologist.

A loud ring interrupted her concentration. She glanced at her phone where the name Mr. Amati flashed on the screen.

"Good morning, Miss Pearson." His voice crackled through the receiver. "I wanted to inform you that I have a preliminary appraisal of your grandmother's violin. It turned out to be much more involved than I'd anticipated."

Her stomach did a somersault. In a good way? Or bad? "How late are you open today?"

"I'm only open until noon."

She glanced at the time. Ten o'clock. "I'll be right over."

"Wonderful. I'll expect you soon."

She tucked away the instrument and exited the room.

Jerry poked his head out from the adjoining practice room. "Victoria, what are you up to?"

"My instrument's ready. I'm on my way to pick it up. Wanna come?"

"Of course." He tweaked her nose, but she batted him away. "Mr. Amati called me an hour ago to say my cello is ready, too. Now I can return this one to my professor."

Twenty minutes later, bells jingled as the two pushed their way through the door to the luthier's shop where the musty smell of wood and dust permeated the air.

Jerry choked. "Mr. Amati could use some air freshener or scented candles in here."

Victoria arched her eyebrows. "Candles in a room full of antique wooden instruments?"

"Good point."

"I'll be right with you." Mr. Amati called from his worktable.

Jerry tiptoed around several double basses.

"Try not to bump into anything," Victoria teased.

Jerry grinned, that cute, mischievous smile. She was falling for him, no question about it.

Mr. Amati shuffled toward them, arms wide. "Good morning."

"I'm here to pick up my cello," Jerry said.

Mr. Amati hobbled back to his worktable, grabbed the two cases, returned, and set them on the counter. "Yours should perform better now." When he pulled out the cello, the varnish caught the light. "I've repaired the cracks, made a few adjustments, and put on a new set of strings. The bow has new horsehair but needs rosin." He ran the amber block over the white hair several times, then extended the instrument and bow to Jerry, who reached for them and sat on the only available chair to play. He moved the bow over the strings, but a peg slipped, and the pitch plummeted.

Mr. Amati chuckled. "It's tough to keep them in tune when they're new. Takes time for them to adjust."

"I know." Jerry turned the peg and resumed.

Mr. Amati leaned on the counter. "What do you think?"

Jerry shrugged. "Better. How much for this?"

"The professional grade string set is normally $150, but I'm running a sale for twenty percent off. The new bow hair is $50, plus an additional $50 for adjustments."

"Sounds good." Jerry glanced at the other case. "What about Victoria's violin?"

Mr. Amati's eyes twinkled behind his glasses. "Ah yes. That little beauty surprised me."

Victoria's heart rate accelerated. So it *was* worth something, after all.

His arthritic hands trembled as he lifted the instrument from its velvet interior. "You say you found this in an old trunk?" His grip tightened around the neck of the instrument.

She nodded. "Yes. My grandmother gave it to me."

He peered over his bifocals. "I never knew your grandmother played violin."

"She doesn't. It belonged to her grandfather."

Mr. Amati's gaze returned to the instrument. "I see. Was he, by chance, French?"

Victoria's breath caught in her throat. "Yes." How did he know?

"I figured." He stroked his long beard. "Based on my research, I believe this instrument was the work of the Mirecourt Violin School in France. Although established around the same time as the Italian school, the French luthiers didn't gain much acclaim until the eighteenth and nineteenth centuries."

"Is that when this was made?" Victoria's voice rose with excitement.

Mr. Amati met her gaze. "I believe so, but I haven't determined an exact date. Aspects of the instrument resemble the work of the prestigious nineteenth-century luthier, Vuillaume, including the extended fingerboard established during his era." He turned the instrument over. "But the age of the wood suggests an earlier maker."

He handed the instrument to Victoria, which she cradled in her arms. "It's hard to believe this violin is several hundred years old." Her fingers traced the curves of the antique. "How much work does it need?"

"Due to its age and transport in the trunk, it would benefit from a different fingerboard, a higher bridge, a new coat of varnish, a professional set of strings, and a few other adjustments. The bow, which I believe dates to a similar era, requires new horsehair. All that plus the formal appraisal is approximately $500."

She flinched. "How soon can I get it back?"

"For this gem, I can have it ready in a week."

Maybe if she could pick up a few extra gigs to cover the cost, this just might work.

###

The following week, the February snow fell thick outside the window of Professor Chang's studio as Victoria pulled out Grandpère Leclair's violin. Her audition for Johann Conservatory was only four days away.

Professor Chang pointed to the instrument. "A new violin, I see. May I take a look?"

"Of course." Victoria passed the antique to her teacher.

Professor Chang ran her fingers over the curves of the wood and peered inside the f-holes. Her eyes grew wide. "Where did you get this?"

"From my grandmother." A sensation of pride bubbled up inside Victoria. "It belonged to her grandfather. The luthier said it's probably an eighteenth-century French Mirecourt."

"Incredible." She continued to stare. "I can't believe your family owned one of these. It predates the Romantic-era and Vuillaume instruments, although…" She settled the violin under her chin. "The nineteenth-century masters must have made several adjustments. The fingerboard was extended to allow the high virtuosic notes."

She drew the bow over the strings in several brisk strokes. "The powerful tone is incredible—a huge improvement from that student one."

Victoria beamed. "Thank you."

Professor Chang examined the instrument a moment longer, then handed it back to Victoria. "You're fortunate to own such an heirloom— the French equivalent of a Stradivarius." Her teacher returned to her desk. "Now time for the true test. Let's see how well it handles the Paganini 'Caprice No. 24.'"

Victoria took a deep breath. Of course her professor had chosen for her to play one of the hardest pieces ever written for violin. At first, Victoria's bow leapt over the strings as if dancing, then the notes swirled like the falling snow outside the window. The eerie octaves caused her fingers to ache as she stretched to maintain intonation, followed by a series of perpetual double stops.

Legend claimed Paganini had sold his soul to the devil in exchange for virtuosic prowess. This work was so insane she wouldn't be surprised if it were true. No person in his right mind would write such a delirious piece. But in spite of its diabolical nature, the song possessed a magnetic quality which enticed Victoria. Her eyes closed as the last chord rang out. The instrument resonated with the ominous work, as if the violin, too, had fought its own battle.

Several moments of silence passed as Victoria stood still, lost in the moment, until a slight sob pulled her back from her reverie. She opened her eyes to find Professor Chang hunched over her own violin case, the picture of two red violinists clutched in her hands.

She shouldn't ask about it. The last time that had ended in disaster. But as the tears flowed more freely down her professor's cheeks, Victoria inched closer.

"Professor Chang, are you alright?"

Her teacher's eyes didn't leave the picture. "That was her swan song—the last piece she ever played." She wiped her eyes.

Victoria hesitated, then placed a hand on her teacher's arm. "Who was she?"

Professor Chang fingered a chain around her neck, the one with the Chinese inscriptions Victoria had noticed months before. "My little sister." She sighed. "We performed a duet together, Sarasate's 'Navarra,' before she concluded the program with that Paganini 'Caprice.'" Her fingers clasped the pendant. "She passed away that night."

Victoria swallowed. How horrible! What could she say?

Her teacher traced the edges of the picture again with her fingers. "What I wouldn't give to see her again, to perform together like we used to." She sniffed, returning the picture to her case. "But we can't dwell on that now. You need to focus on your audition. If you perform Friday in New York as you did today, I'm confident you'll be accepted into Johann Conservatory. My old teacher, Professor Heinberg, would be a fool not to admit you. Now go practice your other songs since we ran out of time." She gestured to the door.

Victoria hesitated. "Are you sure you're alright?"

Professor Chang's features hardened. "Of course I'm fine. Go."

Victoria walked slower than usual down the narrow hallway to the practice rooms. No wonder her teacher had never mentioned the picture before—taken the last night of her sister's life.

Images of Adrienne on the ice flashed before her eyes, which pricked her own conscience. She'd been so horrible to her sister last year. What if she'd lost her? Victoria shuddered. Thank goodness Adrienne's fall wasn't life-threatening. But who knew whether or not she'd be able to play again? The doctor had taken the cast off only days before and told Adrienne to take it easy in order to let it heal. Victoria bit her lip. Surely Adrienne would play again, wouldn't she?

Victoria passed several occupied practice rooms before she found an empty one, stepped inside, and knelt to retrieve her violin from its case. She nestled it under her chin and began the opening of the Bach "Chaconne." Unlike the previous semester, her fingers ran through the movement with easy familiarity until a short knock on the door interrupted her concentration.

Jerry stood framed in the doorway, handsome in a blue polo and jeans, the neck of his cello gripped in his hand.

"I thought that was you." Jerry pulled the door shut behind him and set the cello on the floor. "Nice job on the Bach, from what I could hear through the door." Electricity pulsed through him as he slid his arms around her waist and drew her close. He savored the taste of her lips on his, sweet with a hint of spearmint, deepening the kiss over several glorious moments.

All of a sudden, the door flew open, and Franklin burst in, a smirk plastered on his face. "Well, well, what do we have here? A make-out session with the teacher's son?" He raised an eyebrow. "Victoria, I didn't know you had it in you."

Jerry's insides clenched. "This is none of your business."

Franklin looped his thumbs into the pockets of his skinny jeans. "That's fine. I don't care what you two do here in secret. Although"—his bloodshot eyes shone—"I didn't expect to see this side of goody, goody Victoria."

"Nothing happened." Jerry's right hand tightened into a fist.

"Really?" Franklin eyed Jerry. "Look at you, a true knight in shining armor, here to defend your lady's honor." He laughed. "Remember, Victoria, you don't want to form any attachments that might keep you from New York. We all know Jerry wouldn't be caught dead there—like his aunt."

Fist clenched, Jerry shoved him out the door and locked it. Fire blazed in his chest. "That inconsiderate, self-absorbed scumbag." He sank onto the piano bench.

Victoria squeezed next to him. "He doesn't know what he's talking about."

Jerry continued to stare at the floor.

She patted his arm. "I'm sorry about your aunt. I didn't know she'd died until today. Your mom told me at my lesson."

His head jerked up. "Mom told you? I'm surprised."

"Were you close?"

"It all happened before I was born. I'd rather not talk about it." He turned to face her, ran his hand through her hair, then leaned in. But this time she held back.

Jerry placed his hands on her cheeks. "What's wrong?"

She sighed. "You're keeping something from me, Jerry. Why can't you open up to me about your aunt?"

"I just don't like to talk about it."

"And what about what Franklin said?"

His insides churned. "Don't worry about him. Just think about us." He leaned toward her again, but she wriggled away.

"I am. That's the problem."

This didn't sound good. "What do you mean?"

She leaned back and examined his face. "What are we doing, Jerry? We've been sneaking around for almost two months now, kissing in secret—"

"I thought you liked it." He traced his finger over her mouth.

She clutched his hand and moved it away. "I do. But I've got my audition in New York this Friday. If I get in, I'll live there next year. And you—"

His shoulders slumped. "I'll be in medical school." Her proximity to him on the bench made it difficult to concentrate.

"Why don't you audition there with me? I'm sure you'd get in." Her voice rose with excitement. "You're the best musician at Belton."

He shook his head. "No."

She shot him a quizzical look. "Why not? Then we'd be together."

He stiffened "I won't move there."

"But you'd fit in perfectly. Can't you imagine us performing together in the city? We'd start our own chamber group."

"No, Victoria." He stood to his feet, pulse racing. "How many times do I have to tell you?"

Tears pooled in her eyes. "Don't you want us to be together?"

"Of course I do. But I don't belong there. *You* don't belong there."

She jumped up, eyes blazing. "What do you mean, *I* don't belong there? It's my dream. It's always been my dream. Maybe *you* don't think I'm good enough."

"How can you say that? Of course I think you're good enough. I just don't want you to study there. Not under *him*."

"Under who?"

Jerry met her gaze. "Professor Heinberg. He'll destroy you. Like he did my aunt."

Victoria sat back down on the bench. "What do you mean?"

"Her lifelong dream was to be like Mom, to attend Johann Conservatory. She slaved under him for four years, but he killed her dream. Said she couldn't graduate if she didn't measure up."

Victoria's lip quivered. "What happened?"

Jerry jerked open the door. For a chilling moment, his eyes met hers. "Suicide."

Chapter 25

Victoria's head whirred as she drove home, the Paganini "Caprice" still pounding in her ears. The last notes Jerry's Aunt Margaret ever played. What had pushed her to end her life? The teacher at Johann Conservatory? Competition with her sister? So many musicians struggle with mental health. Did Margaret not know about the resources available to her, like professional counselors?

Victoria shuddered. She'd dreamed of attending the conservatory in New York for so many years. She wanted the life of an international soloist like Professor Chang. She wanted to be respected in her field. But what would it cost?

No wonder Professor Chang demanded so much of her students. She didn't want anyone to end up like her sister. Why had she pushed her own son, Jerry, to pursue an alternative career in medicine instead of music? The money? Or to spare him the pain her sister had endured?

Ice stole through Victoria's body as sleet cascaded down her windshield. What if Professor Heinberg crushed her dreams as he did Margaret's? Could Victoria handle the pressure?

She pulled into the driveway and bustled from the car to the house, violin in hand, to avoid the chill of the sleet. Once inside, she peeled off her gloves and hung her winter coat in the closet.

The smell of fresh cookies drew her to the kitchen where Marie hunched over the oven with a tray in hand.

Victoria leaned against the counter. "Hi, Marie."

Her sister spun around, flour caked on her apron. "Hey, Victoria. I didn't hear you come in." Her eyes narrowed as she surveyed Victoria's face. "What's wrong? You look like you've seen a ghost."

Victoria sighed. "It's a long story."

"One that requires hot chocolate?" Marie eyed her.

Victoria nodded. "Yes, please." The warm liquid might thaw the ice that stole through her.

171

Marie stood on tiptoe and pulled two mugs from the cupboard, poured in the milk, and popped them into the microwave for a minute. She turned to face Victoria. "Tell me what happened."

The creases in Marie's forehead deepened as Victoria recounted the story.

"You're worried you'll end up like Margaret if you go to New York?" She retrieved two mugs, stirred in the chocolate powder, and added a dollop of whipped cream to each.

"Yes." Victoria leaned her elbows on the counter. "What if I don't have what it takes to succeed? What if I can't take the pressure?"

Marie nodded. "True. Maybe you don't have what it takes to succeed in New York. Maybe you'll bomb your audition Friday."

"Thanks for your vote of confidence." Victoria rolled her eyes. "Just the encouragement I need now."

"So what?" Marie lifted her mug to her lips. "Do you think success in New York affects how we, your family, see you? You could be a street busker, and I'd love you the same as if you played in the New York Philharmonic." She set down her drink. "In fact, I'd love you more because I could join you as a street musician. Imagine the headline: The Homeless Sisters perform this Friday on 5th Avenue. Bring coffee and change."

Victoria chuckled.

Marie giggled, too. "We'd make a good team." She slid a mug to Victoria. "But in all seriousness, it's not your title that matters. It's the music you play."

Victoria took a sip. Her sister's words warmed her like the rich liquid that trickled down her throat. "You don't think I should audition?"

"Of course, you should audition. It's always been your dream. You'll never know if you don't try. But don't let an uppity conservatory teacher control you. Do your best, and leave the rest in God's hands."

Wise words from a sixteen-year-old.

"Thanks, Marie."

"Hot chocolate always does the trick." She took another sip.

Victoria eyed her. "I didn't mean the hot chocolate."

Marie met her gaze. "I know."

"This is it." Dad pointed to a large sign on the ominous-looking grey building surrounded by orange construction tape.

Victoria, Mom, and Dad had just flown into New York earlier that day, but due to a weather delay they'd needed to head straight from the airport to the music school.

A knot formed in the pit of Victoria's stomach. "That's Johann Conservatory?" Somehow this dismal site didn't resemble the vibrant images she'd viewed online. Blame the weather. Everything was more difficult to see in this unrelenting sleet. The city had seemed more cheerful and vibrant at Christmas than it did in February.

Victoria's hands shook with cold, or anxiety, as she carried Granpère's violin case down the narrow hallway of the music school. The dingy, beige walls peeled in several places, begging for a new coat of paint, and a musty odor permeated the air. Victoria grimaced. This building didn't compare to the glamour of Times Square.

"How do you feel?" Dad placed a hand on her shoulder.

"Nervous." Victoria tightened her grip on the case.

"I'm sure you'll play beautifully." Mom gave her arm a squeeze. "You've practiced so much that you know the music by heart."

Mom's lavender perfume soothed Victoria's nerves a fraction. "I'm glad you're here as my piano accompanist."

Mom's eyes glistened with tears. "My privilege. I'm so proud of you."

Dad motioned to a large door on his right. "Ready?"

Victoria drew a deep breath. "Yes." If only the butterflies in her stomach would settle down.

"Alright. Let's do this." Dad straightened his tie and knocked on the door.

"Come in," a deep voice grunted from the other side.

A gust of cold air swept over Victoria as Dad pushed open the door and ushered her in. She shuddered. No paintings on the wall. No colorful decor and no windows. The room looked like a larger version of the practice jail cells at Belton.

A squat man in a dark suit sat in a spacious armchair, steepling his fingers as beady eyes peered over his glasses. "Victoria Pearson, I presume?"

Her throat went dry. She nodded. Professor Heinberg.

"You may begin with your scales, Bach, concerto, and conclude with the Paganini." His curt tone sliced the air like a knife.

Her stomach jolted. Margaret's song. She hesitated a moment as she scanned the room. A baby grand stood several feet away. The old professor sat in a lone chair behind a desk, the only pieces of furniture in the room.

He rapped on the desk. "Please begin. I have several auditions today."

Mom's heels clicked on the tile as she moved to the piano.

Victoria crouched in the corner and removed her violin from its case. She rubbed sweaty palms on her dark pants and smoothed the wrinkles in her black sweater as she stood. Deep breaths.

When her mother played an A on the piano, Victoria drew her bow over the strings to tune. The sound echoed throughout the room. At least the acoustics weren't bad.

Professor Heinberg nodded for her to begin.

This was it. The moment she'd been waiting for.

Her bow shook as she began the first few notes of the scale. Get it under control. She gritted her teeth and willed her bow to steady itself. As she moved into the Bach "Chaconne," her fingers clamped the strings for the quadruple stops.

She breathed a sigh of relief when the movement came to a close. Not bad, under the circumstances. Time to channel her inner Adrienne for Joseph Bologne's *Violin Sonata in g minor*. Visions of Paris and French revolutionaries flooded her mind as she sailed through the piece, fighting her own battle of sorts, while Mom's fingers flew over the piano keys.

Next, she performed the first movement of the Saint-Saëns *Violin Concerto*, while Mom played the orchestral reduction on the piano. Victoria cringed when she missed the first couple of shifts on the fingerboard. Pretend nothing happened. Keep going. Thank goodness her accuracy improved as the movement progressed. At last, she pulled through the final chord.

Silence. She glanced at Professor Heinberg.

"What are you waiting for?" He scowled. "The Paganini 'Caprice.'"

Panic seized her. She didn't want to end up like Jerry's aunt. She spun toward Mom and shook her head.

Mom flashed a reassuring smile.

Victoria closed her eyes. Play the song. For Margaret, Adrienne, Professor Chang, and Jerry. Eyes still closed, she lifted the bow.

At first, her fingers danced over the strings for the opening theme, followed by the ominous octaves. Her hands ached from the perpetual double stops, but she pressed forward. At last she executed the final chord, heaving a sigh as she lowered her instrument, her strength fleeting away with the notes.

Again, silence reigned.

Several moments later, Professor Heinberg rose from his chair like a giant toad. "The Paganini wasn't bad—a few intonation problems, but you recovered. Same for the Bach. You butchered the Saint-Saëns when you missed your first shift." He cringed. "In spite of your improvement afterward, it wasn't enough to convince me. And who in the world is Joseph Bologne? Why didn't you play a Mozart sonata?"

Victoria swallowed. "He was a contemporary of Mozart, well-renowned throughout France, the black son of a plantation owner and his African slave."

Professor Heinberg snorted. "An illegitimate child—definitely not someone to be considered alongside Mozart, one of the greatest composers of all time. Besides, I've never considered the French composers on par with their German and Austrian counterparts."

Victoria stared at him. What a monster. Why hadn't she listened to Jerry? He'd been right about this man all along.

Professor Heinberg rambled on. "A true violinist would have practiced three hours a day since she was twelve, which obviously isn't the case." His beady eyes peered over his glasses. "However, you have potential, and once we begin your rigorous studies next year, I believe you will catch up if you apply yourself."

Victoria froze—stunned. In his roundabout, condescending way, had he extended her an offer?

"I'm sorry, did you say you've accepted me?"

His features contorted into a confused expression. "Yes, I thought I made that apparent. You need to start work right away. I expect you to come prepared in the fall with the full Tchaikovsky *Violin Concerto* and two additional Paganini 'Caprices.'" Don't waste any more time on the French and illegitimate composers."

Something inside Victoria snapped. Righteous rage pulsed through her veins as she struggled to preserve composure.

"I'm sorry, Professor Heinberg, but you assumed I've agreed to attend next year."

His eyes bulged. Clearly, no student had dared to contradict him before.

"As it is," she continued, "I enjoy performing Joseph Bologne's music and admire his work. A great composer can come from anywhere, no matter his or her origin. Joseph Bologne deserves respect, and I can't study under someone who doesn't afford him common courtesy."

He continued to stare, wide-eyed.

"Thanks again for your time. I know it's valuable, but if you don't mind, I'll escort my parents out to make way for your next potential student."

She spun on her heels, motioned for Mom and Dad to follow, and marched out the door.

Chapter 26

Still in shock, Victoria stepped outside the audition room, leaned back against the white wall, and slumped to the ground. The crisp fabric of Mom's dress swept the floor as she knelt next to her. No one spoke for several minutes.

Finally, Victoria raised her head and glanced at her parents. "Was I crazy to walk out?"

Mom ran her fingers through Victoria's hair. "You played well, and you stood up for yourself. He devalued you as a person, as musicians of different ethnic backgrounds. You wouldn't respect his advice about music, or your career for that matter, if you didn't believe he had students' best interests at heart. I'm proud of you."

"I am, too." Dad folded his arms. "I didn't like how the professor treated you. When that arrogant man talked, he couldn't spare the courtesy to look us in the eyes. Very rude. I wouldn't consider his opinion worth a dime."

Victoria groaned. "But this was my chance to move to New York." Tears stung the corners of her eyes. "I've waited my whole life for this opportunity, but it didn't turn out at all as I'd expected." Sobs overtook her as she buried her face in Mom's arms.

As she drew her close, Mom's lavender perfume filled her senses. "You did what you thought was best. We all make course corrections. It's part of life."

"But I wanted to move here so much," Victoria cried, as images of herself dashing through the city flashed before her eyes— performances with the New York Symphony Orchestra, rehearsals with a prestigious chamber ensemble, a solo debut in Carnegie Hall. But all these visions vanished before her like the last strains of a sonata as a new torrent of tears streamed down her cheeks.

"I'd better find a restroom to wipe the makeup from my eyes before anyone sees me."

Dad nodded. "We'll wait for you. Take your time."

Victoria gave him a squeeze, then strode down the hall.

As she turned the corner, her case bumped into someone.

"Sorry," she mumbled, eyes averted.

"Hello, Victoria. I didn't expect to run into you here."

Her heart froze. She'd recognize that uppity voice anywhere. "Franklin, what … what a surprise." How could this day get any worse?

"Not too surprising." He smoothed the lapels on his jacket. "I knew you'd applied but wasn't sure of your audition date. How'd it go?" His lips curled into a malevolent grin as he scanned her face. "That bad, huh? Don't have what it takes to compete in the big city?"

Her hands tightened into fists. "Franklin, I'm in no mood for your smack talk today."

"No problem. I don't want to be late for my audition, anyway. We need at least *one* Belton student to make a good impression here." He cackled as he brushed past her and disappeared around the corner.

###

After their flight home, Victoria clambered upstairs to her room and fell onto the bed, still in her clothes.

"Ugh, get off me." Someone shoved her over so far she almost fell off the mattress. A second later, Louisa's head popped up from under the covers.

Victoria cocked her head to the side. "So, you've taken over my room since I've been gone?"

Louisa grinned. "Pretty much. That's my only consolation about your move to New York. I get your old room to myself."

"Don't get too excited." Victoria fell back on her fluffy pillow. "I'm not going."

"You don't know that yet." The lines around Louisa's eyes crinkled. "I doubt they've already made a decision. Give it a few weeks."

Victoria shook her head.

"They turned you down?" Louisa gasped.

The door burst open. "They what?" Stella bounded in, Marie and Adrienne at her heels.

Victoria's gaze moved from sister to sister. "I thought you'd all be asleep by now."

"We wanted to hear about New York." Stella giggled. "Did you go back to the ballet?"

"Or Café Lalo?" Marie's eyes widened. "How was your audition?"

Adrienne stood mute, fiddling with her wrist brace. At least she didn't wear the cast anymore. New York wasn't a good topic for her.

"Did you hear what I said?" Marie wiggled Victoria's foot. "How was your audition?"

Victoria dropped her gaze. "Umm, not good."

"You bombed?" Stella scrunched next to her on the bed.

"No, I didn't *bomb*, but Professor Heinberg didn't enjoy my performance. He hated the Bologne *Sonata*—thinks black composers are sub-par and that I shouldn't have played music by him."

Marie rolled her eyes. "That's his problem."

Adrienne raised her fist. "He turned you down because of that? What an arrogant racist. I wish I could give him a piece of my mind."

"No, I refused his offer of acceptance."

Stella gasped. "You did what?"

"I told him I didn't want to study with someone who didn't value composers that are different from those he's used to. Then I stomped out of the room."

Marie clapped. "Really? That's awesome. Serves the pompous idiot right. Now that you're staying, and Adrienne's practicing a little again, we can form our street-busking group." She raised her arms and pretended to play air violin.

Victoria managed a weak smile. "Still, I feel like my career came crashing down in one day."

Louisa leaned her head against Victoria's shoulder. "From what you said, he wouldn't have been a good fit as your teacher."

"I wish Professor Chang would share your viewpoint. Who knows what she'll say at my lesson tomorrow."

Chapter 27

Victoria stood outside Professor Chang's office, eyes closed to pray. *God, please let this lesson go well. I don't want her to hate me for what I've done.*

She straightened her shoulders and knocked.

"Come in." The teacher's curt voice carried from the other side of the door.

Victoria turned the doorknob and stepped inside. A spicy aroma of sesame seed oil and vegetables filled the room.

"Welcome." Professor Chang extended her arms, a wide smile across her face. "You're back. I've brought breakfast to celebrate." She motioned for Victoria to sit, then handed her a bowl.

"Thanks." Victoria set her violin on the floor, then forked a bite of noodles into her mouth. "I'm not used to such a gourmet breakfast— usually cereal or a bagel."

"Today's a special day. I figured we'd celebrate."

Victoria gulped and almost choked on her food. How could she tell the truth?

Professor Chang twirled several noodles with her fork. "Tell me how it went."

Inside, Victoria's head swam Best to jump straight to the point. "I, um, won't attend Johann in the fall."

The smile on her teacher's face diminished. "What? I was sure you'd be accepted. I ensured you'd met all criteria. There must be a mistake."

Victoria traced a whole note on the floor with her foot. "I turned it down," she mumbled.

"What? Speak up, so I can hear you."

After a deep breath, Victoria raised her head and looked her teacher straight in the eyes. "I told Professor Heinberg I couldn't study under him. Not after what he'd said." Not after what he'd done to Margaret.

A look of shock lingered on her instructor's face. Apparently neither she nor Professor Heinberg were accustomed to students thwarting their desires. She tapped her fingers on the desk as if to expel her frustrations on the immobile wood. At long last, she opened her mouth. "And what, may I ask, did he say that prompted such an egregious response?"

"Well, uh, first of all, he said my technique needs significant work—that I should have practiced more. Secondly, he didn't like my choice of repertoire. He considers compositions by black composers to be inferior and hated that I picked Bologne over Mozart."

Professor Chang's brow crinkled like an accordion. Was she angry with him? Or her?

"And your response?"

Victoria twisted her hands in her lap, head throbbing with anxiety. "I told him I couldn't study under someone who didn't share my values. Then I walked out."

The click of Professor Chang's fingers on the desk marked the painful seconds that ticked by. She pursed her lips and exhaled. "But you were accepted?"

"Yes."

Professor Chang covered her face with her palm, took a deep breath, then pierced Victoria with an icy glare. "I understand that Professor Heinberg's values can be, shall we say, *outdated*, but still, you shouldn't have responded in that fashion. I can't guarantee that I'll be able to undo the damage you've already inflicted. However, since you are my star pupil, I may be able to persuade Professor Heinberg to take you back. I'll tell him you were caught up in the stress of the moment and didn't know what to do."

Victoria raised her chin. "But I can't study under him."

"Of course you can. He's the premier violin expert in the country. You must reconsider. I'd hate to see you abandon your career." She fixed Victoria with a frigid stare.

Victoria shook her head. "I can't. He would destroy me, like he did Margaret."

Professor Chang's face blanched.

She'd stepped too far.

"That will be all for today. You may leave."

Victoria stepped outside her teacher's office. The silent treatment pained her worse than the usual verbal criticism. If only she'd applied to more places for graduate school. But dreams of New York had consumed and blinded her from other possibilities. What could she do now that her dream was shattered? Should she reconsider?

Something within her writhed at the thought. Deep inside, she knew that even if Professor Heinberg still offered her acceptance, she couldn't say yes. If she'd loathed the few minutes she'd spent with him, she'd never survive years under his study. She needed someone who understood and respected her musical preferences, and valued music from composers of a variety of ethnic backgrounds. Like Professor Chang. Would she ever find someone else like that?

The cacophony of instruments filled the hallway with a discordant ambiance, not unlike the storm that swirled inside her. A practice room door creaked open, and Jerry stepped out, which caused her heartbeat to quicken.

"Hello, Victoria." He didn't meet her gaze. "I didn't think you'd be back from New York already."

Too bad she couldn't hide to avoid the awkwardness of the situation. At their last meeting, he'd told her about his aunt's suicide. She should have listened to him sooner. "I returned yesterday."

He leaned against the door, arms folded against his chest. "How'd it go?"

"Not well."

"I am sorry." He grabbed her by the hand and pulled her into the practice room. "Tell me what happened."

She slumped onto the piano bench. "What do you want me to say, that you were right all along?"

A frown knit his brow. "What do you mean?"

"About Professor Heinberg. He was awful—didn't say anything positive throughout the entire audition. And he's racist."

Jerry's dark eyes flashed. "That pompous, arrogant jerk. Don't take a word of it to heart. I wish I could give him a piece of my mind." He pounded the piano bench with his fist. "I'm glad you didn't get accepted. I never wanted you to study under him, anyway."

"It's not exactly that…"

Jerry's face crinkled in confusion. "I thought you said—"

"I didn't say I wasn't accepted. I told you that he had nothing positive to say. But he *did* extend me an offer."

"What?" Jerry's eyes widened. "That makes no sense. So you'd go anyway, despite how awful he is?"

Victoria shook her head. "No. I told him I didn't want to study under him. Then I walked out."

Jerry's jaw dropped. "Bravo. That took guts."

"Thanks. But now your mom wants to contact him to see if he'll still accept me. She hopes I'll reconsider."

Jerry's eyes hardened. "Of course she does. Even after all these years, she still can't shake off his pernicious influence. You can't give in. Of all people, Mom should know better. But she never blamed him for her sister's death. She always accused herself, as though she could have prevented it. That's why she's such a driven teacher. She doesn't want anyone to end up like Aunt Margaret. Ironically, she thinks the way to prevent it is to demand perfection."

Victoria sighed.

Jerry scanned her face. "You won't agree to her demands, will you?"

"No, that much is clear. But I didn't apply anywhere else. What will I do, busk with Marie on the streets?"

Jerry chuckled. "Doesn't sound so bad. Maybe I'll join you. We'll be the best street musicians in this college town."

She laughed, then grew serious. "Until you go to medical school."

His smile subsided. "Yeah, I guess so."

Victoria sat next to him on the piano bench. "Have you heard back from any schools yet?"

He shrugged. "Not yet." He laced his fingers through Victoria's, softening her mood.

She squeezed his hand. "I'm sure you will."

"That's the problem. I almost hope I don't get accepted. Perhaps then Mom and Dad would let me continue to study music instead. Does that sound crazy?"

"Sounds like we both need to stand up to your mom."

Jerry slid his arms around her waist. "You're right. We need an acceptable alternative. I like the busking idea."

"We wouldn't make any money." Victoria laughed.

"But we'd be together." He held her gaze, then leaned toward her, meeting nose to nose. "And we wouldn't have to hide our relationship anymore." His soft lips brushed against hers. She wound her arms around his neck as he drew her closer to him.

"We've got to find a way to make our relationship work," she whispered.

Chapter 28

"I think I should sing closer to the front." Stella pointed her manicured hand toward the spotlight on the stage at Café Chocolat. "You guys can stand behind me." She gestured for Jerry, Matt, and Marie to move back. Victoria couldn't hold back a laugh at how her baby sister bossed everyone around.

Victoria's gaze turned to Jerry, dressed in jeans and a rock band T-shirt, who shrugged and took a step backward with his bass guitar. With a sweep of his arm he pushed his shaggy black hair from his eyes. His band-guy look still took her breath away every time. He caught her staring and grinned.

Heat rose to the tips of her ears.

"Don't be such a diva, Stella," Marie muttered as she kicked the cord of her electric red violin out of the way. "It's not all about you."

"It kind of is," Matt said. "She's the lead singer."

Stella flashed Matt a wide smile. "That's why I want this guy in my band."

"Lucky for me, the drummer hides in the back anyway." Eddie twirled his drumsticks. "Nice view." Marie cocked her head toward him, rolled her eyes, then faced forward.

"I agree. I don't want people to see me anyway," Louisa said from behind the piano. "Stella, I don't understand why I have to play in the first place."

"Because I need you," Stella exclaimed. "You and Eddie form the group's rhythm section. It would sound dumb without you."

"I guess I'd better get out my violin." Victoria slipped over to the wall behind the stage and pulled out her instrument.

"Wow." Jerry's unmistakable voice whispered next to her. Apparently he'd left his designated spot on stage. "You look—"

"Overkill?" Victoria ran her hands over the sequined material of the short, sparkling dress Stella had picked out for the evening.

187

"I'd say hot." Jerry inched closer.

"Watch it," Victoria whispered. Her skin prickled with the heat of his proximity—so close his breath warmed her neck. "We've got a full audience here tonight."

"I can't promise I'll concentrate very well with you next to me."

A smile tugged at the corners of her mouth. "How do you focus in orchestra?"

"At least there we've got Mr. Vatchev between us. And your dress is a little less ... flashy." He ran his fingers over the material.

She gave him a playful punch in the arm.

"Testing. One, two, three, testing." Matt's deep voice rang through the sound system.

"Time to start," Eddie yelled from behind his drum set.

The couple climbed on stage and took their places to the rear. Seconds later, Marie joined them, electric violin in hand, in time for Matt's intro. "Ladies and gents, thanks for joining us. Tonight, we've got a special guest singer. Let's give it up for Stella Pearson."

The audience raised their cups and cheered as Stella clasped the mic, her pink sparkles glistening in the spotlight.

"One, two, three, hit it!" Matt bellowed.

A blast of noise erupted all around Victoria. Matt's guitar wailed while Eddie's drums pounded in her ears. Jerry plunked out a bass line, his cool, nonchalant manner a total turn-on.

She squinted at the page in front of her. Several measures of rests.

Seconds later, Jerry's foot brushed against hers. As the pressure increased, she allowed his foot to move over her toes, around her heel, and up her ankle. Goosebumps shot up her leg. Of course, he'd choose a time like this, when she couldn't do anything about it, to play footsie.

He caught her gaze. Everything in her wished he'd close the gap between them and kiss her, shrouded behind the music stand. But now wasn't the time.

Perched on a stool behind her, Victoria couldn't see Stella's face, but hoped her pre-concert jitters had abated. Matt headbanged as he shredded the guitar, Jerry's head bobbed with the baseline, and Eddie, hidden behind the drums, pounded the rhythm. After a few bars, Stella's powerful soprano pierced the air—no hint of nerves. She kicked cords out of the way to strut back and forth at the front of the stage. A diva, but a talented one. She'd never truly appreciated her baby sister's knack for performance before. Maybe she'd be the one to move to New York someday. Victoria squeezed her eyes shut. The pain of her broken dream still stung.

At the end of the first chorus, Stella pointed to Marie for her instrumental solo. Cool and slick in her skinny jeans and tank top, Marie clutched the red electric violin under her chin and drew her bow across the strings. She started slow, but as the music grew in intensity, she picked up the tempo.

"Dueling violins!" One of the guys shouted from the front row.

Jerry turned to Victoria and cocked his head to the front.

"No," she whispered.

"Why not? Scared?"

Something leapt inside of her, calling her to the challenge.

Marie played an easy phrase, then waited for Victoria to answer.

Improvise. She responded with a few slow notes and grimaced. Marie flashed a you-can-do-better-than-that look, played another rift, and waited. This time, Victoria closed her eyes and let her auditory sense take over. Rapid notes burst from her instrument like an internal explosion.

Marie's face broke into a huge smile, and she played off Victoria's lead. The crowd clapped along as the girls dueled back and forth.

At the close of the chorus, everyone cheered. Victoria and Marie nodded, then stepped back to their places as a sweet melody crooned from the piano.

Seated at the keyboard in a pale green dress, eyes closed, Louisa's hands moved gracefully with the music. Her fingers danced over the keys like fairies in a field of daffodils. Out of place amidst the glitz and glamour of the stage, her angelic sound contained a hint of nostalgia Victoria couldn't put into words. An old soul for such a young person.

In a corner at the back, Adrienne lifted a coffee cup to her lips, wiping tears from her eyes. Happy tears? Or sad? Too bad she wasn't up here with them. Then they'd all be together.

All too soon, Louisa's interlude subsided, and the band recommenced its raucous motif. Stella twirled next to Matt, and the two sang together in perfect harmony for the finale. By now, everyone at the café had risen to their feet to dance along.

Victoria didn't need New York and Carnegie Hall. She raised her chin in satisfaction as she played the final bars. Here on this stage, in this town, with these friends and family, was exactly where she wanted to be.

###

Victoria beamed as she tucked her violin away. "That was amazing, everyone. Stella, your vocals blew me away. Gorgeous."

A wide grin spread across Stella's face. "Really? That means a lot from you."

"Yes, Stella. You were superb. All of you." Victoria swallowed as she glanced at the rest of the band. "I'm sorry if I haven't supported you guys enough in the past. I was so wrapped up in my own classical music world, I didn't bother to give the band a chance."

Marie met her gaze. "Thanks. Join us any time."

A sense of joy bubbled up inside Victoria. "Maybe we'd better start our busking group."

Marie laughed. "Thanks for filling in for Adrienne. I hope she feels better by the audition."

Victoria sighed. "Yes. It looks like she already left. I'd better check on her when I get back."

Once they reached home, Victoria traipsed upstairs to Adrienne's room as the strains of orchestral music filled the air. At least this song was in a major key. More upbeat than Beethoven's *Symphony No. 7* from a few weeks ago.

Victoria knocked a couple of times, then pushed the door open. Adrienne lay sprawled on her floral bedspread, a score in front of her. Victoria laid her hand on her sister's shoulder. "What are you listening to?"

Adrienne paused the music. "*Harolde en Italie,* my song for the concerto competition. The doctor said I can play a little again, but not to overdo it. If I can't physically practice much right now, I might as well run through the song in my head. I can't believe it's only a couple of weeks away."

Victoria's insides lurched. After the debacle in New York, the Belton Concerto Competition had slipped her mind. "Right." She ran her hand through her hair. "How's that going?"

"I think I've mastered it for the most part, although I've got to tweak a few things." She pointed to a couple of difficult passages in the score. "But overall, I feel like I've grasped the true essence of the work—the artist's passion for discovery. This piece makes me want to see the world, you know?" She lifted her gaze to Victoria. "I just hope my wrist will cooperate." She rubbed the brace wrapped around her injured joint.

Victoria lowered herself onto the bed. "It's still painful?"

Adrienne's hazel eyes clouded with emotion. "Yes."

"I'd take the pain away if it were possible. Trade places, even." Victoria wound her fingers around the slender ones of her sister's uninjured hand. "You still have a future in music."

"You do, too, Victoria," she said softly. "Don't give up. I'm sorry that I've been moody lately. I'm such a sea of emotions right now, I don't know which way's up."

"I get it. I'm the same way myself. After chasing the New York dream my whole life, I have no idea what I'll do now." Victoria sighed. "Marie suggested we form a street group."

A giggle escaped Adrienne's lips. "After the concert tonight, that's not a bad idea."

Victoria laughed. "Jerry agrees, too."

"I can picture it—all of us hanging out on Main Street. We'd bring a top hat for tips." Her face lit up with mischief. "Might be fun."

Victoria flopped backward on the bed. "Maybe we'll give it a try."

"After the competition, of course." Adrienne's features sobered.

"Right." Victoria bit her lip. Should she still compete? What was the point if she had no real plans after this year?"

"You okay?" Adrienne asked. "You're quiet."

"Yeah. I just have a lot on my mind right now."

"Me, too."

Victoria gave Adrienne a squeeze. "At least we have each other."

Chapter 29

"As you all know, Beethoven achieved legendary status as one of the most ingenious composers of all time." Mr. Vatchev pushed his glasses up higher on his nose as he paced back and forth in front of the class.

Jerry grew dizzy from the teacher's perpetual motion, not to mention the heat that permeated the space between the closely seated classmates around him. Especially Victoria.

"His brilliant compositions still baffle musicologists, performers, and audiences today." The maestro paused a moment, hands raised in dramatic effect. "His influence became so pervasive that many of his successors struggled with what to write after his death. How could anyone compete with Beethoven after he'd stretched the concept of the symphony to its limits with his legendary Ninth?

Jerry slid his hand under the desk and ran his fingers over Victoria's, which caused a tingling sensation. So hard to concentrate.

"The epic quality of 'Ode to Joy' left traditional composers little room for expansion. Music historians refer to this problem as 'The Beethoven Complex.'" Mr. Vatchev clicked his remote for the music to begin, the sound of "Joyful, Joyful" rent the air.

Jerry closed his eyes. What would it be like to experience this for the first time as a nineteenth-century listener? If this recording could fill this small classroom with such power, how much more impressive to hear it with a full orchestra?

By now, he'd completely intertwined his fingers in Victoria's and held them fast.

"So beautiful," she whispered as the last chords of the fourth movement died away.

"Like you." He squeezed her hand.

She blushed a gorgeous shade of pink.

Mr. Vatchev spread his arms wide, palms upward. "What next? After that, how many of you feel inspired to perform?"

No one raised a hand.

"We all face the Beethoven Complex as we struggle to create something new. At times we ask, 'What's the use? It's all been done before. Why should I write on this topic or perform this piece, when countless others already have?'"

"He has a point," a clarinetist whispered.

"The difference is," the professor continued, "you bring your own personal experience to the work, which no one else can contribute. Those who realize this key element and run with it become the next generation of artists."

Jerry fidgeted in his seat. Was he running away from his artistic calling by going to medical school? He wanted everyone to think him smart and talented. But deep down, what if he was just a coward?

Mr. Vatchev slid his fingers over his mustache. "Fortunately, the Romantic composers recovered from this complex and reached new heights of musical innovation. Imagine a world without Wagnerian operas, Tchaikovsky ballets, and Saint-Saëns concertos. Any one of you could be the next great composer, virtuoso, or teacher. But you must take the risk and try."

The maestro clicked out of his presentation and shut down the computer. "I look forward to hearing several of you perform your solos at the concerto competition."

Jerry straightened his jaw. Time to take the risk.

A half-hour later, he pulled into the parking lot at his apartment and trudged up the staircase. Dad would still be working at the hospital. Who knew if Mom would be home. But the sooner he got this conversation over the better. He took a deep breath and pushed open the door.

"Jerry, you're back." His mother held up a large envelope. "This came for you. From Yale. I think it's another acceptance packet to medical school."

Oh no. Not another acceptance. And to Yale, Dad's Alma Mater. That would make this conversation even more difficult.

Mom pulled out a packet off pre-packaged cookies. "I bought these to celebrate. Your Dad will be so proud."

Jerry pulled out a chair at the kitchen table and sat down. "Mom, we need to talk." He rubbed his forehead."

Her eyes narrowed. "Are you okay? Do you have a fever?" She moved to place a hand on his forehead."

"No, Mom, I don't have a fever. I'm fine. But we need to discuss something. I , uh…" By now his hands were sweating like a runner after a 5K. "I'm going to participate in the concerto competition."

She squinted at him for a moment, then reached for a cookie. "All right. I assume you already have a song in mind?"

"Yes, the Saint-Saëns *Cello Concerto No. 1.*"

"Good choice." She nibbled on her cookie. "Romantic concertos tend to win. Besides, you don't need to study much at this point now that you've been accepted to medical school."

"Mom, if I win, I don't want to go to medical school. I want to pursue music."

The cookie slipped between her fingers. "Jerry, you must be kidding. You've worked your whole collegiate career to prepare for medical school, been accepted into the top programs in the country. Besides, you haven't even applied to any music schools. What on earth is running through your head? You must be feeling under the weather. Please lie down until you recover."

He rose from the table. "No, Mom, I'm not sick. I understand what I have to lose. Believe me, I've played out the scenario over a hundred times in my brain, and it doesn't make sense. But I have to give music a try. If I win the concerto competition, with the scholarship I can stay at Belton for my master's degree while I prepare for orchestral auditions."

Her fingers clicked on the table. Silence. "And if you *don't* win?

His gaze met hers. "I'll go to medical school."

When Victoria reached the landing at the top of the music school stairs, the sounds of trumpets, clarinets, pianos, and vocals blasted her ears. She hadn't set foot here since her last lesson with Professor Chang. Her stomach lurched at the thought. What a disaster.

This morning, she'd willed herself to return to practice. She still wanted to graduate, even if she had no plans for afterward. Maybe she'd teach private lessons. She winced. Listening to beginners all day might be the death of her. That suited Mom or Marie. They possessed a knack with kids—the patience she lacked. Perhaps she'd manage better with older students?

Hungry, she padded down the studio hallway to grab a candy bar from the vending machine. As she passed the suite of studios, the cello professor waved to her as he entered his office.

Moments later, a boisterous cello caught her attention. She leaned against the wall outside the door, mesmerized by the magic of the music. *The Saint-Saëns Cello Concerto.* The notes, so pure and clear, raged with feeling and invigorated her entire body. The power behind the musical phrase made her feel she could conquer anything—even her uncertain future.

The cellist's technical prowess, combined with his gut-wrenching emotion, plucked a string inside her. Was it the influence of the composer, Saint-Saëns himself? Or the appeal of the performer? Either way, the musical muse swayed her, holding her captive in its magical, sonic web. Who was playing? The cello professor? She peaked through the window and her jaw dropped. Jerry.

She sank to the floor and leaned her head against the wall. So that's why he hadn't wanted to reveal his piece for the competition. The Saint-Saëns. He'd probably worried she might fly off the handle, mad that he'd chosen the same composer. Her heartbeat pounded. Frankly, she *was* mad that as his girlfriend he hadn't shared this important detail with her.

But as the cello music slowed, her heartbeat relaxed with it. The notes blended together in harmony, which sent a tingling sensation from her brain to her fingertips. The music transported her to the first kiss with Jerry in the practice room. The recollection of his chest pressed against her and the taste of his lips warmed her from the inside out.

Jerry deserved to win the competition. His innate talent combined with genuine kindness and a desire to help others made him the perfect candidate. Especially if he had to give up music for medical school next year.

Her jaw tightened at the thought. Why would his parents force him into a field where he didn't belong? Not that he didn't have the intellect for it. He'd make a brilliant doctor. But his passion lay elsewhere. Why couldn't Professor Chang open her eyes to the truth, rather than let the pain of her past hold back her own son?

Victoria released her breath. Maybe she shouldn't compete, after all. Besides, she hadn't practiced since the audition. Other students had been much more focused. Adrienne, for example. If anyone other than Jerry deserved to win, it was her sister. After Adrienne's injury, combined with her unwavering passion for the viola, she'd have a good chance. Thank goodness she could play again. She'd grown sullen and withdrawn over those weeks of recovery. Now a spark of her old self had returned. Winning the concerto competition might give her the lift she needed.

As the movement drew to a close, Victoria stood up, a renewed sense of determination pulsing through her veins. Adrienne and Jerry *needed* this competition. They had more at stake. She wouldn't compete.

Chapter 30

Victoria slid into the third church pew, flanked between Marie and Dad, with Stella on his other side. The church, filled with family and congregation members, as well as a few college students, boasted a larger audience than anticipated for a Monday performance. Because the concerto competition was only four days away, Adrienne wanted to perform a trial run for family and friends. She certainly knew how to draw a crowd.

To the left of the altar, Mom, the epitome of sophistication with her hair pinned in a French twist, spread her floral skirt over the piano bench as she played warm-up scales and arpeggios. Louisa pulled up an extra chair and took her seat as Mom's designated page-turner.

From the other side of the altar, a young woman dressed in white ran her fingers over the strings of a beautiful harp. The instrument resembled the stained glass window that portrayed the ancient Biblical patriarch David strumming a lyre.

When the harp music subsided, Mom began to play. A slow, haunting melody filled the church, similar to a somber hymn. Where was Adrienne? Wasn't this her viola solo? Fear rippled through Victoria's body. What if her sister couldn't play? She glanced at the program. *Harolde en Italie: Symphonie en quatre parties avec un alto principal, compositeur Hector Berlioz.* Of course Adrienne printed everything in French. At least Victoria made out the word symphony.

That's right, this wasn't an actual concerto. The word *alto* suggested a singer, but perhaps it meant viola in French since it played in the alto register?

One minute passed. No Adrienne. Two minutes. Still no Adrienne. Three minutes. By now the tension in Victoria's abdomen had twisted into an unbearable knot.

At three-and-a-half minutes, the door behind the lectern opened, and Adrienne strode to the center of the altar, framed by Mom and the harpist on either side. A yellow dress hung loosely over her figure, accentuating the blonde hair that fell in wisps around her temples. Her face radiated with a heavenly glow to match the Easter lilies that graced the front of the church.

She took a deep breath, nodded to the harpist, then drew her bow across the strings. A rich tone emanated from her instrument and cast a spell over the entire audience.

Victoria closed her eyes and allowed her imagination to run away with the music. As Adrienne played a pastoral melody accompanied by the harpist, images of their family farm floated before her eyes, the notes like raindrops falling on thirsty crops.

Moments later, the peaceful scene vanished as the viola expressed several plaintive cries, lost in a haunted melody. A pause, then Victoria's eyes flew open as a series of rapid notes thundered from the instrument. Adrienne stretched the fingers of her left hand to reach the double stop octaves and let out a sharp gasp.

With a quick motion, she lifted her pinky from the string, pursed her lips, and continued, pain etched across her face.

Jaw set, Adrienne finished the first movement. But before the commencement of the second, she stretched her wrist for several seconds.

Would she finish? Nausea washed over Victoria as she held her breath.

Mom shot Adrienne a concerned glance, but Adrienne waved for her to resume.

As she played the second and third movements, the pain in her eyes intensified. She winced every time her left hand reached for a difficult stretch.

At the opening of the last movement, Mom repeated the haunting melody, followed by Adrienne's entrance. The melody that soared from the viola held Victoria captive as everything else melted away. A hint of the old, vivacious Adrienne returned like a bird in spring after a long winter. The only thing that mattered was this moment—suspended in time as a prayer to heaven.

All too soon, the music took a dramatic turn— the peaceful serenity turned into a thing of the past. Adrienne's face clouded as Mom pounded through the battlefield of notes raging on the page. At least the accompanist shared the burden.

When the end drew near, the flurry of notes subsided. Adrienne raised her viola to her shoulder and drew her bow over the strings one final time. The notes poured from her like a last breath—a swan song.

Eyes closed, lips tight, she pulled through the final chord—finished.

###

Victoria released her breath as she joined the chorus of applause that swept the church. After a deep bow, Adrienne hurried offstage while the audience rose to their feet.

Eddie's mom, Mrs. Carter, clasped her hands to her chest. "Beautiful. Absolutely stunning."

"Yeah, she knocked it out of the park tonight." Eddie handed Victoria a bouquet of daisies. "I brought these for her. Hope they'll cheer her up. She seemed out of sorts after the coffee shop gig the other night."

"Thanks, Eddie." Victoria cradled the flowers. "I'm sure she'll appreciate them."

He frowned. "I worry she's pushed herself too hard. Gonna reinjure herself."

"Too late," Victoria whispered.

"What?" Eddie's eyes darkened.

"Didn't you see her wince every time she stretched her left hand tonight?"

He scratched his chin. "I just thought that was for dramatic effect."

Victoria shook her head. "No. She's in pain."

"Then go talk to her. She needs you most right now."

"You think so?"

"Yeah. You're her big sister. She looks up to you."

"Right." Victoria sighed. "I'll check on her." She meandered to the front of the church, found the side door, and tugged it open.

Backstage in the pastor's waiting room, Adrienne sat hunched over in a chair, her wrist clutched in her hand.

What should she do? Victoria moved closer to her and sat down. "You were phenomenal tonight."

Adrienne looked up, tears streaming from her eyes. "Thanks. But it doesn't matter now. I can't play Friday. It hurts too much."

"But you finished. That's what counts." Victoria laid a hand on her shoulder. "Besides, did you see the crowd? So many people came tonight to support you. Eddie even brought flowers." She handed her the bouquet.

"Awww, sweet Eddie." She held the daisies up to her nose and breathed in the fragrance.

"See, you're famous."

Adrienne brushed a tear from her eyes. "No. Besides, that makes it worse. Over the past several months, I've told everyone about the concerto competition. I asked them to support me by coming tonight. Music is my life. But now I'm like a bird who's lost her voice. Without it, I don't know who I am anymore."

By now, tears streamed down Victoria's cheeks as well. Her heart wrenched inside for her sister. "I wish I could wash away the pain. I'd take it for you if that were possible. But I can't." She clasped her sister's uninjured hand in hers. "We've got to trust that God holds us in his hands, even when we don't understand."

"It makes no sense." She sobbed as she buried her head in Victoria's lap. "There's no way I'll compete now."

Victoria stroked her hair. "That makes two of us."

Adrienne's head jerked up. "What? Why not you?"

"Why would I? Professor Chang is livid with me, I have no plans for next year, and besides, you and Jerry are more impressive soloists than me. I'm more of an orchestral musician, anyway."

"Of course you're a soloist." Adrienne jumped to her feet. "Perhaps you just have to dig deeper. Music is about self-expression, emotion—the art itself."

"I—" Victoria paused for several moments as the impact of Adrienne's words sunk in.

After all her own preparation for graduate school auditions, she hadn't considered the emotional impact of the music she played. In the midst of her obsession, she'd repeated difficult passages over and over like a factory worker in an assembly line, without thought to the art itself.

"You're right. That's why I wanted you to compete. You understand this stuff better than I do."

Adrienne shook her head. "I can't. Not after tonight. But you should."

But what about Jerry? "I'm not sure—"

"Please, Victoria." Adrienne clasped her hands to her chest, her hazel eyes pleading. "Do it for me. Be my voice."

How could Victoria use her violin to be her sister's voice? Was that possible? Either way, if Adrienne needed her to, she would try.

Three days before the competition, Jerry strode down the hallway to the practice room, the familiar cacophony of sound from each of the rooms music to his ears this time. How he'd miss this familiar place next year if he had to leave. No, he'd win this competition.

He turned the knob to an open practice room and stepped inside. The bare white walls, still lackluster, appeared more homey than usual. He opened his cello case and situated the end pin. The opening of the Saint-Saëns *Cello Concerto No. 1* filled the room with its powerful spirit. This was his ticket to freedom, to a life of music.

All of a sudden, the door flew open, and Franklin burst in. "I thought that was you. A little bombastic, don't you think?" He leaned against the door frame.

Jerry crossed his arms. "Franklin, I don't care a whit about your opinion."

"Watch what you say. You're looking at a future Johann Conservatory student." He straightened his collar.

"Congratulations. I got into Yale Medical School." Ugh. Why did he say that? He didn't need his medical school dilemma to spread throughout the school.

Franklin's jaw dropped.

Jerry cocked his head. "Surprised?"

"No. I figured you were going to graduate school for music. Are you caving to your dad?"

Jerry paused. What should he say? "Speaking of dads, I haven't seen yours at any of the orchestra concerts. Not a fan of classical music, huh? Thinks being a musician is too wussy for the son of a soccer coach?"

Franklin's eyebrows scrunched into a V. "How'd you know that?"

Jerry shrugged. "Mom told me. Apparently you use lessons as therapy sessions."

Fire blazed in Franklin's eyes. "Just wait, Jerry Chang. This won't be the end of it. I'll win that competition, move to New York, and put you and your snitch of a mother behind me." He nearly bumped into Victoria as he stormed out the door.

She stepped inside and set her violin case on the floor.

"We can't let that arrogant scumbag win this weekend." Jerry held up his fist again, jaw clenched. "I'll let him have a piece of this—"

"He's awful." Victoria sank onto the piano bench. "And I think you struck home with that last comment, even if it was a low blow. Did his dad really make fun of him for being a musician?"

"Yeah, that's what Mom told me."

"How awful. As much as I hate him, I do feel a little sorry for the guy. I can't imagine if my parents didn't support me."

"I can," Jerry grunted.

"I know." She snuggled next to him, which eased his pounding heart.

He leaned over and planted a kiss on her nose. "Do you think Adrienne will still compete after last night?"

She shook her head. "No. She says it's too painful. I know I told you I wasn't going to compete, but now she wants me to take her place."

His breath caught in his throat. "You've changed your mind?"

Her eyes bored into his. "Is that okay?"

He averted his gaze.

She slid her forefinger under his chin. "Jerry, I know you're playing the Saint-Saëns *Cello Concerto No. 1.*"

He stiffened. "You do?"

She nodded. "You could have told me. Maybe you thought I'd be mad, but I'm not."

"But I thought—"

She placed a forefinger over his lips. "Shhh. I'm proud of you. I'm just going to play for Adrienne's sake."

He slid his arms around her waist and pulled her to him. "If you win, you could stay here for graduate school."

"I hadn't even considered that." She pulled him in for a kiss. "Not a bad idea."

Chapter 31

On Friday afternoon, Victoria's fingers shook as she practiced in a warm-up room outside the symphony hall. This was it, the big day. She ran through scales, arpeggios, and the most difficult passages of her concerto. Over the past three days she'd practically lived in the practice rooms. She couldn't let Adrienne down. Not after all her sister had endured.

Mom poked her head inside. "How are you?"

"Nervous." Victoria wiped her free hand on her black dress. "I wish it were over."

Mom stepped inside, set down her music bag, and lowered herself onto the piano bench.

Victoria tipped her head at the bulging bag. "Are you the accompanist for everyone?"

"Almost. A few of the students hired another pianist, but I'm accompanying over half of them."

"Wow, you must be exhausted." Victoria sank into a nearby chair.

"Yes. I've rehearsed nonstop over the past several days." Mom performed a few hand stretches. "But I'll cheer for you, of course."

Victoria grinned. "I sure hope so. You're my mom, after all. Who's competed so far?"

"A clarinetist, two flutists, a trumpeter, and a couple of other violinists."

"How'd they do?"

"I'd say the clarinetist was the best so far."

"What about Franklin?" Victoria's stomach lurched.

"He hasn't played yet. Jerry's up next." Mom eyed Victoria, then rummaged in her bag. "He sounds good."

"Of course he does. He's the best musician at the school. I'd be insane to think I could beat him." Victoria glanced at the score in Mom's hands. *Cello Concerto No. 1* by Haydn. She frowned. "Who's playing that?"

"Jerry."

She shook her head. "No. He's playing the *Saint-Saëns Cello Concerto*."

"I thought so, too." Mom's eyes scanned the score. "I rehearsed it with him several times. But two days ago, he told me he'd changed his mind. Said it wasn't ready. I argued that it was, but he was adamant— insisted he wanted to perform his piece from last year."

Victoria's head spun. This didn't make sense. "But he'd never choose to compete with Haydn. He knows that a concerto from that time period isn't likely to win. Besides, he's a Romantic guy." Heat rose to her cheeks. Not just in regard to the time period.

Mom shrugged. "I'm just the accompanist."

"Why'd he switch songs the week of the concert? It's like he threw away his chance to win."

"Maybe he doesn't want to win."

"Of course he does. He told me this was his ticket out of medical school. His chance to pursue music. Why would he—"

"Victoria." Mom's eyes bore into hers.

"Oh." Victoria's heart almost stopped. "For me."

Mom nodded.

Victoria jumped up. "But he can't quit music. The way he played last week, he must've practiced the concerto for months. I heard him. He was incredible. Why would he give all that up for me?"

Mom reached for her hand. "Because he loves you."

Tears welled up in Victoria's eyes. "You think so?"

Mom smiled. "Yes."

Victoria swiped at the tears. "How am I supposed to compete now that I know what's on the line?"

The door clicked open, and Louisa entered. "Mom, it's time for Jerry's solo. Victoria, do you want to listen, or do you need more time to warm up?"

Victoria rose. "I'll listen." She had to change his mind.

###

Head held high, Jerry strode onto the stage, cello in hand. Time for the last performance of his musical career.

The curtain opened behind him, and Mrs. Pearson moved to the piano, followed by Victoria. She waved vigorously at him. Why did she look so concerned?

He ambled over to her and they stepped backstage. "Hey, what's up?"

"Jerry, you can't play Haydn. You have to play the Saint-Saëns."

"What?"

She cocked an eyebrow. "Don't play dumb with me. I know what you're up to."

He brushed a stray hair away from her face. "I have no idea what you're talking about."

"Don't give up your dream of playing music. Not for me."

Smart girl. What he wouldn't give to stay here with her. He swallowed. This was harder than he'd anticipated. "I'm not. Maybe I had a change in tune." He kissed her, then hurried back onstage before he lost his resolve.

Eyes closed, he played by memory, despite the fact that he'd planned to play another piece until two days ago. The Hadyn, so jubilant and radiant, exuded hope for the future—the future he wished they could enjoy together as a couple. Why did this have to be so hard?

Several minutes later, his fingers flew through the last couple of runs. As the observers in the hall applauded, he opened his eyes. His gaze moved to Victoria, who had given him a standing ovation.

Victoria wiped her eyes as Jerry took his place next to her. The fact that he'd revived his concerto from a year ago in two days, and still played it flawlessly, paid tribute to his genius. How she loved him.

All too soon, the curtain opened and Franklin sauntered onstage. He glanced at Victoria and Jerry and sneered. Victoria's insides churned. If he made one nasty comment about Jerry's performance…

With a powerful stroke, his bow bounded onto the strings for his thunderous entrance. The song he'd selected, the Khachaturian Violin

Concerto, even rivaled the Tchaikovsky Violin Concerto difficulty—more challenging than the Saint-Saëns. If he executed it well, he'd win.

She held her breath. He couldn't win. Adrienne would have surpassed him in musicality, and Jerry in both showmanship and technique if he'd selected a more difficult piece. But now it was up to her.

After he finished, Franklin grinned as he walked offstage. Like a contemporary Heifitz, he'd aced his song other than a lack of emotion.

Jerry leaned over, so close to Victoria his breath warmed her neck and whispered, "You got this. Knock 'em dead."

Heat spread from her neck to her cheeks.

"Thanks," she whispered back. "Two hard acts to follow."

"I have faith in you." He smiled.

She took her place onstage, clutching the Leclair violin as if to embrace a member of the family. What stories this instrument concealed she could only imagine, but the aroma of the antique wood invited her to create the next battle in its history.

The moment of truth had arrived. She turned to Mom poised at the piano, her ever-present, faithful accompanist. Mom understood this crazy, competitive music world, and yet she never let it get her down or go to her head.

Louisa sat next to Mom, her hands ready to turn pages to ensure a smooth performance. She'd had good practice at that with books. More than a page-turner, she was the family storyteller, the supportive sister who never sought the limelight for herself but served as the heartbeat of the family.

Victoria's gaze swept the audience and rested on Marie and Stella, Dad, and … Adrienne.

"I need you to be my voice." Adrienne's words echoed in her ears like church bells, a call to action. Time to let their voices sing, to share their story.

Victoria raised the violin to her shoulder and cradled it under her chin as Mom pounded the low rumble of a tremolo, Victoria's prompt to begin. She took a deep breath, then pulled her bow through the downbeat. Like an archer who hits the bullseye, she nailed her first big shift.

The angry motif that pulsed through the opening phrases resonated all too well. In the past, she'd given in to its powerful sway far too often. Memories of fights with Adrienne resurfaced and twisted a knife in her gut. The first movement, with all its dramatic flair, reflected her previous, angry self. Why had she allowed her temper to hold such power over her?

As her fingers ran along the strings in rapid succession, the notes cascaded over one another like droplets in a waterfall. Trills followed by ascending arpeggios marked the end of the first movement.

She cocked her head to one side, then the other. This brief pause allowed her to lose the rage of the first movement and refocus on the hope of the second.

The clenched muscles in her abdomen relaxed, and her thoughts took an amiable turn.

Like a magical time-turner, the peaceful music transported her to her first kiss with Jerry. Her mouth watered at the recollection. She'd melted in his arms, savoring the taste of his lips on hers.

Cheeks warm, she chanced a glance at him during her few measures of rests. Eyes closed, hands folded in his lap, he looked as serene as she felt. Perhaps he was thinking of that moment, too.

As the closing harmonics reverberated throughout the hall, she concluded her love song to him.

The first, bombastic chord of the final movement jolted her from her romantic reverie. In its place, new, painful images flashed before her eyes. The moment when she'd smashed Adrienne's instrument as a child and the Christmas program when her own violin crashed to the floor.

Worse, the picture of Adrienne clutching her injured wrist on the ice. The thought of Jerry's Aunt Margaret, who'd given up hope at the conservatory, then Victoria's own showdown with the horrible old professor. And lastly, the ever-present rivalry with Franklin, who even now threatened to win this competition. She shivered. Why this sudden torrent of nightmares?

Minutes later, the volatile energy shifted to a sweet interlude, a break in the storm.

Like the highs and lows of the music, maybe she'd needed to experience both the good and bad to appreciate what mattered most.

Although she'd lost her opportunity to move to New York, she'd gained something more valuable. She'd learned to value the support of family and friends, teachers, and loved ones. Music wasn't meant to pit one person against another but to bring people together in harmony.

As the music quickened, a joyful, triumphant tune burst from her violin as though to crush the painful ghosts from her past, once and for all.

Her bow moved faster and faster as she raced to the finish line. She pulled through the final chords—the battle over and she, victorious.

Applause filled Jerry's ears as Matt, Eddie, Marie, and Stella bounded to their feet around him.

"Bravo!" Marie yelled.

"You killed it," Eddie exclaimed.

A proud, papa-bear smile spread wide across Dr. Pearson's face.

Victoria bowed, then climbed down the stairs and moved to Adrienne, whose cheeks glistened with tears.

Adrienne held her hand over her heart and dipped her head. "Thank you."

Jerry slid in next to Victoria. Every ounce of his being wanted to kiss her.

"Thanks for your attendance today, everyone." Mr. Vatchev's thick, accented voice echoed from the podium throughout the room.

"After deliberation, the judges and I have made our final selections." He motioned for Jerry's mom and the other music faculty members to join him.

Once they'd taken their places up front, he continued. "The third-place winner of the bronze award is junior clarinetist Michael Hernandez."

Loud cheers burst from the wind section. They clapped their friend on the back as he climbed the stairs to accept his prize from the wind ensemble director.

Jerry held his breath. Down to the last two. Franklin had aced his concerto. What if he beat out Victoria?

"The second-place winner of the silver award and competition runner-up is senior cellist Jerry Chang."

He froze. How in the world had he won second place with his song from junior year? He hadn't even anticipated placing in the competition.

"Yay, Jerry!" Marie and Stella hollered. Victoria patted him on the back, nudging him toward the stage.

"And the winner, who will perform a solo with the Belton Symphony Orchestra for our final concert, is senior violinist Victoria Pearson."

Screams and applause erupted all around as Victoria's sisters and both parents enveloped her in a group hug. Jerry's chest burst with pride. She'd be able to continue here at Belton, with the support of her family.

"Lastly, we've amended our original offer. We promised to award a $20,000 scholarship to our first-place winner, along with a Graduate Teaching Position here at Belton if the candidate is interested in pursuing their graduate degree here. However, after a lengthy discussion with the music faculty about next year's increased enrollment, we have decided to extend the Graduate Teaching Position to both our first *and* second-place winners.

Had he heard correctly? Could he stay here next year with Victoria and continue to study music? Stunned, Jerry walked over to his mother, who held his silver medal. "Are you agreeing to this proposition?" he asked.

After a slight hesitation, she slid the medal around his neck. "Yes, your cello professor practically begged me to extend you the teaching position. He said he's never taught a more talented student, and he'd love to work with you as his assistant." She tipped her head toward him. "Of course, the choice is up to you."

Jerry's insides danced as though she'd handed him a million dollars. "Mom, this means the world to me." He pulled her in for a hug, the kind of hug he hadn't given her in a long time.

When she finally pulled away, tears glistened in her eyes. "I'm proud of you, son."

Tears streamed down Victoria's cheeks as she watched Jerry embrace his mother. After he moved away, she stepped up to her teacher.

"Well done, Victoria." For the first time in the past four years, Professor Chang smiled at her as she handed her the gold medal. "I want you to know how proud I am of all your hard work, and I'd be happy to work with you again next year. We would learn more repertoire, of course, to prepare you for upcoming auditions. I'd also train you how to teach violin at the collegiate level—give you a taste for the career of a college music professor. That is, if you're interested." She raised her eyebrows.

Exhilaration and a sense of relief washed over Victoria. She reached out to shake her teacher's hand. "I'd be honored."

When she rejoined her family, everyone started talking at once.

"You won!" Stella exclaimed.

"Best classical street-busker I've ever seen." Marie laughed.

A small hand touched Victoria's shoulder. "Great storytelling." Louisa's eyes shone with pride.

"Thanks." Victoria swallowed. So Louisa had noticed. "I tried my best to tell mine—ours, really." She turned to Adrienne, who pulled her close in a silent embrace.

"Don't I get a hug, too?" Jerry's deep voice made her jump. He extended his arms. "I *am* runner-up, you know."

Her desire for him ignited like fireworks. "You know what you did, Jerry Chang."

He flung his arms around her and, apparently oblivious to the crowd, kissed her—right there in front of everyone.

After a couple of moments, he drew back, and his dark, handsome eyes bore into hers. This time she initiated the kiss. His lips melted on hers as the heat of his chest warmed her from the inside out.

Eddie wolf-whistled and all the sisters cheered.

"It's about time." Marie punched her playfully on the arm. "I'm tired of watching you two play footsie at band practice."

"You knew?" Victoria's face grew hot.

"We all did." Eddie laughed.

Victoria's hands flew to her hips. "Since when?"

"Since our show at Café Chocolat." Eddie grinned. "You two haven't been able to keep your hands off each other. Believe me, I've taken notes." He winked at Marie.

"Well, good thing you're not moving to New York." Adrienne spoke for the first time. "Now you two can finally be together. We all can."

Chapter 32

"You look fabulous," Mom exclaimed as she pinned the last strand of Victoria's hair in an elaborate updo.

Victoria turned to face the mirror on the wall in the warm-up room backstage. Wow, Mom had twirled her hair into a stunning twist with ringlets cascading over her shoulder. Tiny sparkles glimmered in Victoria's hair from the spray Mom had liberally applied.

"Now for the makeup." Stella reached her manicured hand into Mom's cosmetic bag and pulled out several containers of eyeshadow, powder, blush, a tube of mascara, ruby red lipstick, and gloss.

Victoria frowned. "Do I need all of this?"

"Yes." Stella surveyed the selection of eye shadow. "I know all about stage makeup from my dance recitals. You'll look washed out under the spotlight without it." She picked out coffee brown and bright gold. "Here, these will go well with your red dress. Good thing I took you shopping. I can't believe you wanted to wear your boring black dress when you're the star of the show."

Victoria ran her fingers over the silky red fabric as she examined herself in the mirror. In her dress—V-necked, sparkly, and form-fitting— she looked like an older version of Stella. Or a younger version of Mom. In the past, she'd have protested the elaborate attire, but today, it fit the occasion. A sense of pride welled up in her chest. She straightened her shoulders.

"Thanks for choosing my dress, Stella. It's perfect."

Her fashion-conscious sister flashed a radiant smile. "You're welcome. Glad I could help. Now let's apply your lipstick."

"Not yet." Marie hurried over with a plate of sugar cookies in the shape of violins and music notes. She handed one to Victoria. "She's gotta eat before the solo. Don't want her to faint on stage."

Victoria took a bite. The sugary goodness melted in her mouth. "Marie, did you make these from scratch?"

"Of course. I figured we had to celebrate your big day with dessert."

"They're delicious. You should sell them at the reception."

"But there'd be none left for us," Stella protested as she popped a morsel into her mouth.

"How do you feel, Victoria?" Louisa asked, a hint of concern in her voice.

Victoria examined her. "I'm fine. But *you* don't sound so good."

"I'm nervous." Louisa bit her lip.

Victoria laughed. "You're nervous? I'm the one who has to perform."

Louisa wrung her hands. "I know. But I'm nervous for you. I saw a lot of people in the hall. Looks like Eddie and Matt invited their entire fraternity."

Marie rolled her eyes. "They would."

The door creaked open, and Professor Chang stepped inside, chic in a black lace gown. "Fifteen minutes until the concert."

Mom motioned to the girls. "Let's find our seats. I hope Dad saved enough. I have no idea how many of my brothers and sisters will show up."

"Half the town if Gigi had anything to do with it," Marie said.

Victoria hated to see them go. Her family—her support.

Professor Chang surveyed her for several long moments. "You look radiant, Victoria. Like the concert soloist you're meant to be." She lowered herself into the chair in front of the mirror. "Like my sister." A tear glistened in the corner of her eye. "You and your sisters remind me of us at your age." She brushed away the tear that spilled down her cheek.

The image of Margaret and Professor Chang from the picture resurfaced in Victoria's mind. The red violinists. She reached for her teacher's hand. "You must miss her."

Professor Chang nodded. "Yes. Not a day goes by that I don't think of her. I wish I could have saved her."

Victoria increased the pressure on her hand. "I'm sure you did everything possible. Some circumstances lie beyond our control."

To Victoria's surprise, Professor Chang looked up and smiled. "Like Jerry. He's determined to be a musician, even though I've warned him a thousand times against it." Her gaze dropped to her lap. "I suppose I wanted to spare him the grief I've experienced."

Victoria examined her professor who now confided in her more as a friend than a teacher. "Jerry has to create his own life, make his own decisions."

Professor Chang nodded. "He's made a good choice in his girlfriend. I couldn't have chosen better for him myself." She patted Victoria's arm. "Now, it's time for you to go backstage. The concert starts in a few minutes." She rose to leave and clicked the door shut.

Victoria sighed. Not that long ago, she'd watched her teacher perform as the soloist, but she'd passed the baton. Now it was Victoria's turn.

She gathered the Leclair family violin in her hands. In an inexplicable way, the instrument linked her to great violinists of the past—Great-Grandpa Leclair, his baroque ancestors, her musical mother, and Margaret. Thank goodness Victoria still had all her sisters with her.

As she stepped through the doorway, she bumped into someone.

"Sorry," she mumbled.

"Wow." Jerry's eyes moved from her updo to her peep-toed pumps. "I see you've exchanged the black dress for something more vibrant." He slid his hands around her waist.

"Stella chose it." She smiled.

"Your sister has good taste." He leaned in, lips parted.

"Watch it. I don't want you to break the violin."

He grabbed the instrument and bow and set them down on a table.

"I hope Franklin doesn't mess with it again like he did at the Fall Concert."

"Oh, don't worry, he won't." Jerry tightened his embrace. "He's practicing the Saint-Saëns orchestra part like a madman. Mr. Vatchev gave him a big lecture on how he ought to be better prepared as concertmaster if he wanted to deserve his spot at Johann Conservatory. Franklin's practiced like a maniac ever since."

"And what about you?" Victoria tickled his chin. "Have you practiced the cello part?"

He moved his hand to her back. His breath warmed her neck. "I might need to practice something else."

Her knees threatened to buckle as he pressed his lips to hers. Tingles rippled down her spine as he leaned into her. His strong arms moved over her back while he explored every part of her mouth. He tasted even better than Marie's cookies.

"Sorry to break up the makeout session, but the concert's about to start," a familiar voice rang out.

"Adrienne!" Victoria gasped as she and Jerry jumped apart. "I thought you were saving seats with Dad." She surveyed Adrienne's ensemble. Instead of a short, tight, dress, she wore Victoria's own black orchestra outfit.

Jerry eyed the two of them. "I'd better go warm up. My cello awaits." He grinned and sauntered off to take his place as principal.

Victoria turned back to Adrienne, who tugged at the sleeve of the gown.

"I'm here to play with you."

"But," Victoria said, "I thought the doctor told you to rest."

"He did," she muttered. "But he also gave me this." She held up her wrist, wrapped in a tight brace. "Said I could play for a few minutes at a time, if it isn't too painful."

Victoria frowned. "But the concert is over two hours long. That'll kill you."

Adrienne shook her head. "Mr. Vatchev agreed to let me play for one song if I sit in the back of the viola section." She sighed, then braced her shoulders. "I chose yours."

Tears threatened to spill down Victoria's cheeks. Keep it together. Stella would be furious if her mascara smeared.

"Two minutes," Mr. Vatchev announced.

Adrienne motioned toward the stage. "I'd better go. They'd never make it without the last chair violist." She gave a weak smile.

"Adrienne." Victoria lifted Adrienne's face to meet her gaze. "Listen to me. You'll find your voice again. I promise. But you might have to look for it in a different place."

She pulled Victoria in close. "Thanks," she whispered. "Love you, sis."

Victoria leaned her forehead against Adrienne's. "I love you, too."

###

The lights in the hall dimmed, and the audience fell silent. Franklin walked onstage to tune the orchestra, then took his seat as concertmaster. Next, Mr. Vatchev strode to his place in front of the orchestra and bowed.

Victoria peeked at the audience from behind the curtain. There, a few rows from the front, sat her entire family. Mom and Dad, Gigi and Papa, Marie, Louisa, Stella, Eddie, and Matt together, along with aunts, uncles, cousins, and friends. All there to cheer her on. Her heart glowed.

Mr. Vatchev flicked the tip of his baton at her. *This is it.* She took a deep breath, then crossed the threshold to the stage.

The red dress swished by her sides as her heels clicked across the front of the orchestra. She took her place next to the maestro. He raised his hands for the opening chords.

The lights shone so brightly she had to close her eyes. When she did, everything else faded away, and the music washed over her. Although vulnerability before such a large audience scared her, she had to release her inhibitions and share her story with the listeners. She lifted her bow and allowed the story to flow through her strings—a story with a long history, from the Baroque French violinists, to Great-Grandpa Leclair, to Professor Chang and Margaret, and lastly, to she and Adrienne. Victoria poured out her soul in tribute to everyone who'd come before her and made this moment possible.

As the concerto drew to a close, her heartbeat quickened. The spotlight-endured perspiration trickled down her temples. She moved her bow faster and faster until she reached the final chords. With one last breath, she pulled her bow across the strings for the final note with a dramatic flourish.

The audience burst into applause. Her entire family rose to their feet, followed by the rest of the hall, including Professor Chang.

Euphoria enveloped Victoria like a cloak as Mr. Vatchev shook her hand. She bowed, then extended an open palm toward the other members of the orchestra.

A moment later, she turned to Franklin and shook his hand.

He dipped his head in acknowledgement. "Well done."

"Thank you."

They held each other's gaze for a moment before he looked away.

Victoria spun around to find Adrienne at her side with a bouquet of flowers. She extended them to Victoria, who accepted them and drew her in for an embrace.

"Bravo." Tears flowed down Adrienne's cheeks.

Victoria beamed. "You, too." Her sister's accomplishment, her bravery to swallow her pride and sit last chair to accompany her struck a chord deep inside.

The audience continued to applaud. Time for another bow.

Adrienne turned to leave, but Victoria held her hand fast. "No, with me."

She raised Adrienne's hand in the air, and the two sisters took the final bow. Together.

Questions for Reflection

1. Were you familiar with the composers mentioned in the story? Who was your favorite?
2. The Pearson sisters and band bros play a variety of musical genres. Which is your preferred style? Why?
3. Which character did you like best? What drew you to that person?
4. The seasons play a fun role in the stories. Which season is your favorite? How do you like to celebrate?
5. Had you heard of a concerto before, where the musician performs a solo with the orchestra? Whose solo did you like best? Why?
6. At her audition in New York, Victoria stands up for her values, even though it takes sacrifice. When have you stood up for what you believed was right? Was it worth the cost?
7. Victoria chose to play a composition written by the eighteenth-century composer Joseph de Bologne. How can we increase awareness for minority composers?
8. Although Jerry is passionate about music, his parents encourage him to pursue a different career. Is your family supportive of your career choice? If not, how can you help them better understand your decision? Do you believe Victoria's large family helped or hurt the pursuit of her musical dream? Do you identify more with Jerry or Victoria in relation to your family?
9. One of the characters in the story dealt with a significant mental health crisis. Unfortunately, this is often a widespread challenge for the music community. How can we help our fellow musicians who struggle in this area? What resources are available to people who face these challenges?
10. Faith plays an important role in the Pearson family. Do you adhere to a certain faith/philosophy? If so, does it affect your approach to music?

French Glossary

Tap into Gigi and Adrienne's love of French!

I developed a passion of French from my father, who spent a semester of college studying in Paris. His mother, my paternal grandmother, is of French descent. I am so grateful that they shared their enthusiasm for the language, culture, and travel with me.

Look forward to more French in the next story when the Pearson family goes to France!

(In order of appearance)

- chocolat: chocolate
- voilà: here
- magnifique: magnificent
- Bonjour: Hello
- Je suis…: I am…
- haute couture: high fashion
- chérie: my dear
- quelle horreur: how horrible
- tarte aux fruits: fruit tart
- Grandpère: Grandfather
- Maman: Mom
- merci: thanks
- avec plaisir: with pleasure
- mon amour: my love

About the Author

Ashley Rescot is a professional violinist, educator, writer, and Fulbright Scholar. An aficionado of music, pedagogy, family, faith, and language, she writes about her life as a musician. With degrees in both music and literature, she hopes her stories will inspire the next generation of musicians, encourage music professionals, and educate others about the exciting world of music.

www.rescotcreative.com

Other Works by Ashley Rescot

Meet other Belton University music students in *The Chronicles of Music Majors*. Follow these students through a collection of eight short stories as they learn to navigate the world of music, discover friendship, fortitude, and love in a variety of ways.

Order a copy form fine bookstores everywhere.
ISBN 978-1-7366044-0-3 paperback
ISBN 978-1-7366044-1-0 eBook

If you enjoyed this story, the author would greatly appreciate if you could leave a review on your book retailer's website. This helps others discover the series and allows her to continue writing music fiction.

Come join my free music fiction book club online! You can sign-up on my website at www.rescotcreative.com (or scan the QR code below). You can also access additional resources created for this series, as well as information about other books by Ashley Rescot, on her website.

The Strings of Sisterhood: A Change in Tune

ISBN 978-1-7366044-5-8 paperback
ISBN 978-1-7366044-4-1 eBook
ISBN 978-1-7366044-6-5 audiobook